Spinechilling Tales
for the dead of night

Spinechilling Tales
for the dead of night

Illustrated by John James
Cover illustration by Oliver Frey

Hamlyn
London · New York · Sydney · Toronto

Falcon Fiction Club

Titles in this series you will enjoy

Amazing Stories from the world of crime
0 600 38870 0

Animal Stories from around the world
0 600 36678 2

Exciting Stories of fantasy and the future
0 600 36677 4

Haunting Stories of ghosts and ghouls
0 600 36676 6

Romantic Stories of young love
0 600 38869 7

Spine-Chilling Tales for the dead of night
0 600 38965 0

Star Struck Stories of stage and screen
0 600 38964 2

Thrilling Stories of mystery and adventure
0 600 36679 0

Published 1984 by
The Hamlyn Publishing Group Limited
London · New York · Sydney · Toronto
Astronaut House, Feltham, Middlesex, England

ISBN 0 600 38965 0

Printed in Yugoslavia

Contents

BLIZZARD
by John Agee

High above the snowy wastes the stars sparkled coldly, like tiny glittering diamonds on a purple velvet robe. To the north, a river of fire surged across the horizon. One moment it seemed to overflow its banks in a spectacular display of light that covered half the sky. The next moment it receded, forming a narrow stream of light. Every snow crystal was a frozen gemstone from which the flaming lights were thrown back in glittering sparks of red and blue, yellow and green.

It was an awe-inspiring sight, a sharp reminder of the strangeness and mystery of the natural world in an age that believed most problems were solved, most secrets probed. Perhaps one day the aurora borealis would be explained away in dry, matter-of-fact terms; but surely even then, the wonder of its sheer, breathtaking spectacle would remain.

To those who careered across the hard-packed snow that freezing night in 1894, the wonder and the spectacle of the Northern Lights were ignored, thrust aside. For terror clawed at their hearts with a more chilling grip than the icy air lashing them in their mad race.

Three sleds whirred over the ice, their runners hurling up a dense white spray on each side. Eighteen dogs, six to a sled, raced along, muzzles dipped, their hard pads pounding at the trail. Six men, two to a sled, ran beside or crouched upon each sled, stark fear burning in their eyes. Their features, without exception, were shaped into masks of hopeless horror.

The three dog teams hit a smooth hillock and streamed over it, gaining more speed as they hurtled downwards. Branner, a lightweight, was humped on the pile of furs roped to the rear sled, gripping the stock of his Sharp's repeater and glancing over his shoulder. Beside the sled on his right, the burly old Swede, Gustafsson, clung on to the tail-rope and pounded along. His face under his fur hat was brick-red, his breath gushed out in great clouds of foggy white. Behind, the trail was still clear. But the sound that had first alerted them to their danger so short a time ago, the sound that had sent them racing off along the trail, was now louder on the clear air. It was the blood-chilling howl of a wolf-pack in full cry.

The dogs raced up another short rise and down again, none of the runners springing on to the sleds to rest because the slope was too short. They hurtled past a ragged plantation of balsam firs and bare larches, dipped down towards and across a small frozen lake. Then up a longer slope, the dogs slowing perceptibly as they neared the top. Then over, almost neck and neck, and down. The slope ahead was a long one, leading down to a wide valley. A few scattered trees could be seen by the wildly flickering lights in the northern sky, but no cover of any kind. Branner groaned.

As the dogs cascaded over the top and raced down the long, gentle slope, Gustafsson shouted and leapt for the sled. He grabbed for the bottom of the gee-pole to steady himself and knelt on the rear-board, his massive body bent forward towards Branner.

'They get near,' he yelled, 'you pick 'em off! Don't miss, boy. They stop to eat their dead!'

At the top of the slope, a black wave seemed to boil over the crest, staining the pure whiteness of the snow. In the flickering light of the aurora, it was impossible to count them, but at a rough guess there seemed to be over a hundred. Their individual cries merged into one nerve-shattering yelp of triumph that echoed horribly around the valley.

Branner did not even take aim. He simply fired into that dark hurtling mass. Four of the pack leaders sprang into the air, thudded to the ground, and disappeared beneath the pack. There was a quiver rather than a pause, a ripple in that heaving mass of bodies. Then they swept on, leaving behind them four picked skeletons, white almost as the snow upon which they lay.

Branner gazed in horror at the sight, feeling despair clutch at his heart. Other shots rang out. More wolves rolled over in the snow. But the main body of the pack, the rear of which was still streaming over the crest of the hill, merely seemed to shiver slightly before dashing onwards towards the sleds.

Branner glanced to the front. The slope was ending, and ahead lay a flat area before the next hill. Mackendrick and Costigan in the lead sled had already reached the bottom, and their dogs were speeding along. But they soon had to slow down on the flat and Mackendrick, gripping the tail-rope, leapt from the sled and began running alongside. The second sled, manned by Teal and Heller, shot on to the flat, and Heller did the same, casting horrified glances backwards as he clung to his rope.

The men sent shot after shot into the pack, but the dead wolves seemed only to serve as a sop to the rest. They stripped the carcasses while still running, and sped on in hot and dreadful pursuit.

'We got no hope!' screamed Gustafsson as he also leapt from the sled and began to pound alongside the hurtling vehicle. 'They'll catch us on the next slope!'

Branner knew the big Swede was right. The wolves were constantly gaining on them, and their own dogs, strong and swift as they were, could not keep up this punishing pace for much longer. He half-turned and grabbed for the whip. He cracked it again and again above the dogs' heads and mushed them on in a voice high-pitched with desperation. The courageous animals now seemed almost to be flying along the trail.

As the dog teams pelted along the flat, the wolf-pack gained rapidly. Branner was just about to spring off the sled to join Gustafsson in running when disaster struck.

The second sled suddenly bucked into the air at an angle, hurling Teal off and breaking Heller's hold on the rope. Heller, screaming with terror, blundered straight into Teal's flying body, and both men crashed to the snow. The dogs careered on, and with their load lightened, passed Mackendrick's sled at full tilt.

'Stop!' howled Branner, clawing at the gee-pole. But Gustafsson smashed his hand away.

'No! Mush on! Mush on! Or we all die!'

Branner watched aghast, almost mesmerised, as the raving pack slewed to one side and engulfed the two yelling men. Then he pulled his eyes away and shook his mittened fist at the firs beneath him. He knew in his heart that the big Swede had been right. Nothing they could have done would have saved their companions, and horrible as their fate was, it had given the others a chance.

Even now they were approaching the next slope, a long one. The aurora flamed blood-red above them, lighting up the snow on every side in splashes of deep crimson. As the lights receded, the crimson patches turned to black shadow, with only the light of the stars reflecting back from the frozen ice.

Branner sprang off the sled as the dogs began their hard climb. Soon his breath was coming in long, racking bursts as he sprinted up the trail, clutching at one of the ropes. Up ahead he saw that Mackendrick and Costigan had topped the rise and stopped, and for a moment he thought that some new danger had revealed itself on the other side of the hill.

Branner watched aghast as the raving pack slewed to one side and engulfed the two men.

Then, glancing back, he saw that the wolves were still milling around the kill, too busy for the moment to take up the chase again. At last his sled reached the crest and Branner applied the gee-pole, bringing both sled and dogs to a skidding halt.

Mackendrick pointed to what lay beyond. Branner saw that his face was screwed up into an expression of bitterness and frustration.

'We hit the wrong trail!' snapped the big man. 'Should've gone more to the west. Look!'

A gentle slope lay before them, ending at the edge of a wide, ice-free lake that stretched away as far as the eye could see on both sides. Far beyond the lake, a spangle of lights glittered in the darkness.

'Medicine Bend!' muttered Gustafsson. 'Great God, this is bad. I know where we are. That is the Little Tecumah Lake, and across it is Medicine Bend. To the left the lake narrows, and there is an underwater causeway. Walkable, it is, but impossible to find! Not in the heat of the chase with those grey devils snapping at our heels! The old trappers found it, the men who knew Hudson's Bay like their own hands. Charlie Burns, Peter the Trailer, Bear Hudson, Yuerba Carlsen, they all knew the way.' He laughed harshly. 'But where are they now, my friends? Hey? *Where*?'

Branner gazed at the Swede. Gustafsson had been trapping in this part of Canada for thirty years or more. He was an old man now, over sixty, and yet he seemed to have the strength and vigour of a man half his years.

'They would help us if they could,' he growled. 'Peter the Trailer . . . yes . . . if he could . . . if . . .'

Suddenly he clutched at his chest, his face working jerkily, hoarse whistling sounds erupting from his mouth. He staggered, then gave a coughing groan and tottered sideways, like an old tree crashing to the ground.

Mackendrick sprang forward, bent low over the bulky

figure and slapped at his exposed face. He gazed up at Branner. 'His heart, I guess. He ain't gone yet, but he's close.' He stared at the younger man. 'It'll lighten your load, boy.'

Branner stooped down and managed to push his hand inside the Swede's furs. The heartbeat was weak, irregular. It was ironic that only seconds before he'd been thinking about how young Gustafsson seemed. It was the running, of course. The old man's heart had been under an immense strain. For a second, Branner felt guilty. Then he realised that was foolish. This was the Wild. There were rules for survival, rules that had to be followed to the letter. He was the lightest and had to be sled-man. Had Gustafsson been sled-man, it was possible – no, certain – that the dogs would have tired long before, and he, Gustafsson and their dog team would have met with the same fate as Teal and Heller. By the rules, what Mackendrick was hinting at made perfect sense. To leave Gustafsson here would be the logical move. No one would blame him in the slightest. Nevertheless . . .

Abruptly, Branner shook his head. 'No. Help me strap him to the sled.'

'Your decision, boy.' Mackendrick shrugged. 'Pity there ain't no friendly Injuns around. They'd know how to get across the lake for sure.'

They finished tying the old man to the sled, and Branner went to the huskies, patting and caressing them. It was another rule he'd learned from the Swede: look after your dogs and they'll look after you. They wagged their tails, their heads up and inclined to one side, tongues lolloping out to lick his face.

'Let's go, Cost!' barked Mackendrick, and then stiffened.

The Northern Lights had faded to a dull glow on the horizon, only barely lighting the grim scene. Above, the stars were winking out as though someone were crushing them one by one. The air was filled with a low moaning sound from the north-west, which rose gradually until it was like the wail of a lost soul. Then suddenly, a sharp, stinging wind, icy cold.

'Oh my Lord,' whispered Mackendrick, his face white and strained. 'Blizzard!'

He jumped for his sled, on which Costigan was already hunched, screaming '*Mush, boys, mush*!' The sled hurtled off down the long slope. Branner followed, cracking his whip and yelling to his own dogs. Even as they did this, the last star blinked out and a howling fury of white smashed into them.

Almost instantly, the whole face of the night was blotted out by that terrible sweep of snow. Only moments before, the sharp, crisp cold had been bearable. Now, almost in the space of a single heartbeat, the cold had become savage. Flying snow and ice particles curtained everything from view.

Branner, eyes narrowed and head bent to escape the furious blast that came shrieking at him, scrambled on to the sled and let the dogs carry him. The wind tore at him, and he had to cling on to the ropes that held the furs down with both hands, keeping the rifle underneath him. The sled careered on down the slope at a speed that seemed like flying. They swooped down on to the flat, and Branner tugged at the gee-pole as Mackendrick's sled loomed out of the furious whiteness. Head low, Mackendrick staggered towards him through the whirling wall of snow.

'We'll go left! The wolves'll be holing up somewhere!'

'We can't go on much longer, Mackendrick. We need to hole up, too. We used up everything running from those devils. Our food went three days ago. We'll never make it round the lake to Medicine Bend!'

'The lake narrows!' shouted Mackendrick. 'The Swede said so.'

'But it extends for quite a distance. I remember Gustafsson talking about it months ago. There's that causeway that'd bring us close enough to the town for us to be safe, but we don't know where it is.'

'And we'd die looking for it in this blizzard!' snapped Mackendrick.

To one side Branner saw Costigan looming up out of the murk. Then he narrowed his eyes in shock as he realised it wasn't Costigan at all, but a tall figure dressed in lynx furs, a dark-faced man with a long scar running down his right cheek. Mackendrick swung round with a grunt.

'Thank the Lord! Injuns!'

The man was alone, however. He came up close, gripped Branner by the arm, and peered down at him with dark, fathomless eyes.

'Follow me. I take your dogs. The big man takes his dogs and holds on to you. The other man brings up in the rear.'

Branner glanced at Mackendrick, who nodded. Anything to escape from the desperate situation they were in, and the Indian seemed to know what he was doing. The Indian took the front harness of Branner's dogs and led off, Branner holding his sled's handles. Mackendrick, clutching at Branner's belt, led his own dogs. Costigan stumbled after.

They were now at the water's edge, and suddenly Branner grunted with shock as the Indian suddenly turned and plunged in. But he was only up to his ankles.

'Do not let go!' he shouted.

Branner had no intention of letting go. He gritted his teeth and plunged in after the Indian, who was pulling the dogs along at a swift rate. Beneath him Branner could feel solid rock. Yet, when he looked down, it seemed that he was actually walking upon the water.

The journey was a nightmare. The wind buffeted them and tugged at their clothes and sleds. It needed all of Branner's strength to keep himself on an even keel, especially when the blizzard eased for a few seconds, and he could suddenly see nothing but the sullen waters of the lake, whipped up into choppy waves. It was a terrifying sight, bleak and eerie and nightmarish. Yet, beneath his boots, there was solid rock on which the sleds' runners scraped and lurched.

Then, all at once, their journey was over and the dogs were scrambling, yipping with excitement, on to the far bank. Branner heaved the sled up the slight incline, tugging at Mackendrick, and found himself on firm ground once more. He knew that they were safe. It was only a short trek to Medicine Bend, and the trail was an easy incline all the way. The dogs would make it, and so would they. He bent down to see how Gustafsson was, and saw with a start that the old man's eyes were open.

'We made it, Gus!' he shouted above the noise of the wind, and then looked up as Mackendrick blundered towards them.

'The Injun! He's gone! Just vanished!'

Gustafsson opened his mouth, and Branner bent over to hear.

'Indian . . .?'

'Yeah, must be one of the tribes from up Hochuppay way. Guy with a scar. He brought us across the lake.'

The Swede's eyes widened.

'Big man? Scar down his right cheek?'

'Yeah. Looked like a bear-claw did it. Wearing lynx.'

'Peter the Trailer! By God, he came back!'

Branner frowned down at the old man.

'You mentioned him before. He been away, Gus?'

Gustafsson nodded, a serious expression on his craggy face.

'Long way away, boy. He died in the Great Blizzard of '79 . . .'

Around them the wind rose to a deafening howl. Then, as though suddenly aware that it had been cheated of its prey, it died to a little whimper . . .

DEATH CHASE

M.S. Goodall

FIREBALL MARK TWO was the finest motorbike ever built by the Yatshibushi Company of Japan. It had a 1400cc Tornado Vee-Twin engine, aerodynamic fairings, microfine fuel injection, built-in radar scan and drogue-assisted emergency brakes. Top speed was a cool 346 km (215 miles) an hour. As the advertising blurb said, it was a 'mean fast machine for the mean fast pace of the twenty-first century'. An engineering thoroughbred.

In a weatherproof viewing pod above the company's sprawling test circuit on the outskirts of Tokyo, Fireball's designer Shinzo Takura watched with quiet pride as one of his machines came hurtling out of a rain squall and accelerated down the long straight ribbon of track below the pod. Fireball's rider seemed to crouch a fraction lower over the gleaming black bulk of the fuel tank, his short, pointed nose piercing the wind, his smooth, curved head spattered with raindrops and his bulging yellow eyes flashing rhythmically, brightly, every two and a half seconds precisely.

Fireball's rider wore no protective clothing at all, because Fireball's rider was a robot.

'I'd better slow him down,' said Takura as the bike roared towards the end of the straight, where one of the test track's sharp, sloping left-hand bends was just visible through the mist and rain.

'No!' As Takura's fingers hovered over the impulse switches which controlled every movement made by

Fireball's robo-rider, his hand was knocked away sharply by the colleague who stood close beside him in the viewing pod. This man was older than Takura, round-shouldered, sharp-featured, his heavily slitted black eyes darting almost poisonously from side to side. He was Toshio Wanamoto, creator and builder of the robo-rider. 'I'm not slowing down today. I want more speed. *Full power.*'

'But they'll crash,' said Takura helplessly.

'If they do, it'll prove conclusively that Fireball Mark Two has a design fault,' said Wanamoto. 'That's why we're here, isn't it? To give your machine the ultimate test ride.'

'But the track's too wet. Any bike could crash in conditions like this.'

'Not with my *robo-rider* in control,' said Wanamoto triumphantly. 'That robot is the finest walking computer ever built. No given situation is beyond its capabilities. Weather conditions? They mean nothing to a well-programmed droid. That's why I persuaded Yatshibushi to let me build the robo-rider. With the element of human failure removed, any motorbike can be tested to an infinite degree of perfection. As I have just said, if Fireball crashes out there today, it will be caused by some fault in your design, and not my robot's riding performance. So here goes . . .'

With the brief flash of his protruding teeth, Wanamoto jabbed at the impulse switch marked 'speed'. Instantly, there was a distant howl of engine response from the rain-soaked track. Fireball was winding up to full power! Dimly, through binoculars, Takura saw robo-rider heel sharply to the left and then to the right as both machines, wedded in perfect harmony, raced through a slalom on the far side of the circuit at an incredible 298 km/h (185 mph). The built-in radar scan had cut in now. Takura knew that its invisible sensors would be probing the track ahead, slicing through wind, rain and flying spray to project a perfect road image on to a tiny screen sunk into a binnacle between the bike's handlebars. This image would show every twist and curve of the track ahead, every tarmac chipping that was out of place. It was a gigantic step forward in road safety, and one that was now being tested to the last point.

As Fireball and the robot completed a lap, Toshio Wanamoto danced excitedly round the viewing pod. Then he pointed, and when he spoke, his voice was little more than a high-pitched scream. '*Here they come*!'

It was full power plus ten. Even Takura couldn't believe his eyes as the product of ten years' work came rocketing out of the gloom like an earthbound missile. By all the laws of mechanical engineering, Fireball should have been aquaplaning out of control over the water-soaked track. Yet unbelievably it roared on, held steady, straight and true in the iron grip of the yellow-eyed robo-rider.

Then it happened. A short distance past the viewing pod, there was a subdued flash from somewhere deep inside the bike's streamlined casing. Robo-rider's metallic tones echoed eerily from the control panel's voice projector. 'Malfunction! Malfunction! Malfunction!'

Wanamoto hit the emergency impulse switch and raced to the window. Fireball was veering two degrees off the centre of the track, the faintest of wobbles in the wheels shaking the massive frame from stem to stern. Robo-rider tried to correct, but at that speed there was no hope. In the next second, the bike flipped sideways, there was a curling puff of black smoke, and then an arc of fiery sparks as it bounced once and slid in a ruined heap of metal into the driving rain.

Wanamoto turned to Takura with a restrained, almost smug expression on his face. 'That proves it,' he said crisply. 'Your Fireball Mark Two has a design fault.'

The younger man nodded. 'It's possible,' he said, 'and the loss of one machine isn't all that important. But aren't you even interested in what has happened to your *robot*?'

Wanamoto smirked again. 'Unlike your motorbikes,' he said with relish, 'my robo-rider is indestructible.'

And so it proved. Two hours later, when salvage crews deposited the Fireball wreckage in Wanamoto's workshop, Takura saw that the robot was standing almost untouched in a corner of the room, yellow eyes still blinking with their monotonous two and a half second pulse rate. Wanamoto followed the designer's look and gave a brief explanation.

'When your machine malfunctioned, I hit the robot's emergency impulse switch. He ejected himself backwards off the bike. Built-in shock absorbers ensured a soft landing and the smallest amount of damage.'

'It strikes me that your robot is a very clever chap,' said Takura sarcastically.

'He is more than that,' said Wanamoto with a dreamy, almost worshipful look in his eyes. 'Twenty-five years of my life have gone into building him. Even in this age of high technology, robo-rider stands head and shoulders above other work-droids of the same design and type. And I'll show you why.' Stepping forward, Wanamoto stabbed at a guidance nodule on the robot's side. Instantly, the light in the bulging yellow eyes intensified.

'Tell me,' said Wanamoto sharply, 'what your primary function is.'

'To dismantle . . . adapt . . . improve.'

'Again. Say it louder.'

'*Dismantle . . . adapt . . . improve.*' The robot's metal voice reproduction system echoed tinnily round the room and, in spite of himself, Takura shivered. Just for a second, the inhuman tones had sounded almost angry. Then Wanamoto spoke again. 'Good, that is correct. Then proceed at once to the wreckage of the Fireball Mark Two. Commence your primary function. Say what that is just one more time.'

'Dismantle . . . adapt . . . improve,' droned the robot, and lurched stiffly towards the heap of twisted metal.

Takura watched, fascinated, as robo-rider began his task. Fingers of colossal strength, yet as delicate as a brain surgeon's, swiftly probed, dissected and stripped the shattered components of the bike. 'You see?' whispered Wanamoto with a tremulous excitement in his voice. 'Now you know why I consider my creation to be no less than a work of genius. Robo-rider is no ordinary droid, but one that can analyse faults in a manner that is actually ahead of human intelligence. With his "dismantle, adapt, improve" programming, he will find out what is wrong within a matter of minutes. Then he will immediately go ahead to build something better, as he is doing at this very moment to the Fireball Mark Two.'

Sure enough, the fault was traced to a weak component in the electrical system, and within half an hour, robo-rider had adapted it, improved it and then produced an entirely new part. Takura was more than a little impressed, but it didn't have to make him actually *like* the robot. There was something about those flashing yellow eyes that reminded him of a medieval gargoyle; a force of evil and deep-seated power. As the weeks went by and the work of making Fireball Mark Two perfect went on, Takura, Wanamoto and robo-rider seemed to be forced into closer and closer contact. The test rides continued, more design faults were located and corrected by the uncanny 'dismantle, adapt and improve' method of the company droid.

More than once in those passing weeks, Takura lifted his head from the drawing board and caught the robot staring at him. If not at him, then at the totally absorbed figure of Toshio Wanamoto. Takura knew it was impossible, but a subtle change seemed to have come over robo-rider's metallic face. The bulging yellow eyes continued to flash, but now they seemed to be less vacant, less inhuman than they had once been. They seemed, thought Takura, groping for the right word, to have the faint suggestion of *expression* in them. As though . . . as though the robot had actually begun to . . .

'Rubbish!' said Takura angrily and out loud. 'A robot is a robot is a robot. Droids like him can't think; they just do what they're told. Admittedly, he does it better than any other automaton I've seen, but he's still just metal and wires.'

Then came the day when something went very wrong. Very wrong indeed.

Toshio Wanamoto had been on holiday for a week. Left alone with robo-rider and two young apprentice designers, Takura had continued to make good progress with the work in hand. One evening he was bench testing a more powerful version of the Fireball engine when his two apprentices dashed into the workshop. They looked pale, uneasy and shaken. 'It's robo-rider,' said one. 'He won't do what he's told.'

'What do you mean?' Takura shut down the power and reached for his jacket. 'That droid always does what he's told.'

'Not this time. He's just standing in a corner of the lab and staring hard at any human who goes near him. His eyes have stopped flashing too, but the yellow light is still on. And a lot brighter. So bright it almost dazzles you.'

'It can only be an electronic fault,' said Takura with a conviction he certainly didn't feel. 'You two stay here and I'll check it out.'

It was quiet in Wanamoto's lab. As the apprentices had said, robo-rider stood in a corner, his glaring yellow eyes fixed unblinkingly on Takura as he came quietly into the room and closed the door. 'Robo-rider,' said the designer sharply and angrily. 'What is your primary function?'

The robot didn't reply. There wasn't even a hum from his main micro-circuits.

'I'll ask you again,' said the designer, louder this time. '*What is your primary function*?'

Silence.

With a scowl of anger, Takura stepped boldly up to the robot and jabbed his finger fiercely on the side-mounted guidance nodule. 'I ask for the third and last time . . . *what is your primary function*?'

Robo-rider stirred, his head swivelling sideways, his yellow eyes staring fixedly into Takura's. 'Dismantle . . . adapt . . . improve,' the metallic tones said almost grudgingly.

'That's better! And who *gave* you that function? Who built you and programmed you?'

'Wanamoto . . . Toshio Wanamoto . . .'

'Very good,' said Takura with satisfaction. 'That's all I wanted to hear. Now readjust your circuits and get back to work. Do what Wanamoto wants, as always. Create, build, obey your primary function. *Dismantle, adapt, improve*!'

Suddenly the robot's massive frame gave a violent lurch. His right arm swung up and across in a mighty, swinging arc. The steel fist caught Takura full on the side of the head, sending him reeling across the floor to crash into a boxed pile of motor-bike components. 'Wanamoto! *Toshio . . . Wanamoto*!' Robo-rider's voice reproduction system boomed the name out with the clarity and force of an amplifier on full power. In two strides he was across the room, and his flexi-steel body smashed through the closed wooden door as though it were made of tissue paper. Another few strides and the robot was pounding towards the factory parking area, where a long line of gleaming Fireball Mark Twos were waiting for final adjustments and delivery.

Even as he dragged his bruised body off the floor, Takura

heard the deep, growling note of an engine start up, then the high, revving howl of power as robo-rider rode the machine at and through the main factory gates. His surge of speed left several security men gasping in disbelief. And even as he rode, the robot's booming voice drifted eerily back on the air. 'Wanamoto . . . Toshio . . . Wanamoto . . . Toshio . . . Wanamoto . . .'

Minutes later, Takura was on the 'phone. Wanamoto had gone on holiday alone, for two weeks' fishing to a private lake not far from Tokyo. In common with many other Yatshibushi employees, Wanamoto owned and rode a Fireball Mark Two, and he had ridden it to his lonely holiday chalet on the edge of the lake. When the droid inventer answered the designer's call, his voice was disbelieving and more than a little sharp.

'What do you mean robo-rider has gone on the rampage?' he demanded harshly. 'That droid of mine simply obeys orders. Didn't you remind him of his primary function?'

On the other end of the line, Takura wiped blood and sweat from his face and tightened his grip on the receiver. 'Of course I reminded him, but it didn't work. You'd better listen and listen good, Wanamoto. Your robot's gone rogue. Don't ask me how or why, but suddenly we're not dealing with a work-droid any more. We're dealing with a micro-man that can think.'

'Rubbish,' said Wanamoto roughly. 'Where is he now?'

'Exact location unknown,' said Takura, 'but he's astride a Fireball Two and moving like forked lightning. And he kept repeating your name . . . over and over. My hunch is that whatever has gone wrong in his main circuitry is somehow related to you. I think he's riding down to the lake to be with you! It sounds crazy, but when he took off from the factory, I had the impression that all he wanted was his own inventor.'

'It's possible,' said Wanamoto slowly. 'Some malfunctioning quirk might have set off an impulse in the droid to make him return to the only person who could help. And he'll know where I am, because my planned holiday arrangements were all part of his work-programming schedule so that he would carry on under your guidance while I was away, and so on.' The robo-rider's creator stood up. 'Thanks for 'phoning, Takura. Just leave this with me now; I can handle it.'

'I hope so,' said Takura. 'For your own sake.'

Wanamoto slammed the receiver down and reached for his crash helmet and leather riding gear. If robo-rider was on his way to the lake, it would be best to meet him halfway, perhaps by the main turnpike turn-off at the end of the lakeside road. There he would be able to slow the robot down, check his performance print-outs and discover exactly what was wrong.

The inventor was getting on in years, but he was an excellent rider. On half throttle he powered his blood-red Fireball over the rutted lakeside track and headed for the black ribbon of the highway slip-road beyond. It was a gentle upward curve which merged finally with the arrow-straight lanes of the motorway itself.

Wanamoto stopped at the junction and looked to his left. That was when he saw it. A gleaming blur of metal that was coming towards him at close on the bike's full speed. It was robo-rider! Pulling out, Wanamoto accelerated and took a parallel course, hoping to flash an impulse signal to the robot from a hand-operated miniaturised control nodule mounted on his bike. But the signal that went out was repulsed. Wanamoto frowned. Something was wrong, all right. The droid was taking not the slightest notice of his commands.

With the slightest twist of his glinting steel fingers, robo-rider changed direction on the motorway and powered his howling machine straight at the slower-moving Fireball of his inventor. With desperate urgency, Wanamoto braked hard,

His Droid was not only uncontrollable, but was out to ride him off the road.

broke the back end of his bike away from the oncoming robot, and accelerated across the tarmac a split second before the collison that would surely have taken place.

Up ahead, robo-rider skidded to a halt, turned and came back. That was when Toshio Wanamoto realised the truth. His droid was not only uncontrollable, but was out to ride him off the road. All at once it was a chase. A death chase! But why? The inventor had no time to ponder on the question. To survive he had to ride as he had never ridden before.

Heeling left, he roared down the slip-road again and took to the lakeside track. He couldn't beat robo-rider for speed, but perhaps he might be able to shake him off amongst the trees. Jink, skid, double back, twist this way and that, use cover and try and get from the expressionless hulk astride the leaping machine too close behind.

Wanamoto tried every trick in the book . . . to no avail. Tiring fast, sweat blurring his vision, he failed to see a jagged tree root rising out of the muddy track directly in front of him. His front wheel rammed in hard, and the heavy bike pitched him sideways. He landed in a sprawling heap in a patch of ferns.

It was there that robo-rider found him. With brightly shining eyes glaring yellow, the robot sat down on a fallen log and pulled Wanamoto firmly across his knees. It was only in the brief micro-second before he died that the inventor knew what was going to happen. As those massive steel fingers tightened and bent to twist his head off, Toshio Wanamoto realised that his robo-rider had discovered a new primary function.

Dismantle, adapt, improve . . . *and build a better human being.*

FIGHT FOR LIFE

by Angus Allan

HIS NAME WAS ANDY COULSON, and nothing in his scant eighteen years of life had prepared him for such abject terror. The stamping fury of the artillery barrage had torn his nerves to shreds, and now, with the heavy serge of his battledress rasping against his sweating skin, and the weight of the man he was carrying turning his flight into a leaden-booted stumble, he heard his own babbled prayers for deliverance. He was afraid and desperate.

It was the spring of 1940, and the relentless advance of the Germany army had thrust the British Expeditionary Force back towards Dunkirk, in northern France. Andy's outfit, a flanking platoon of an infantry battalion, had been decimated. He, and the badly wounded Lieutenant Thomas Hardacre, the man draped like a sack across his shoulders, were the only survivors.

Never before had Andy Coulson felt so alone and so utterly helpless. He could hardly believe that, mere months previously, he had been a junior clerk in a clothing factory: a meek, unambitious lad content to say 'yes' and 'no' to whatever his seniors decreed, to write up his ledgers in a neat, careful hand. Oh yes, he had volunteered for the army at the very outbreak of war, but he had been stung into doing it by the taunts of his colleagues. 'It's men they want,' one of them had said. 'Maybe they'll post you to the Boy Scouts.' His training hadn't been as bad as he'd imagined. He had kept himself to himself, obeying his orders as dutifully as he had done in civvy street.

Now, Andy tasted the salty perspiration on his lips as he footed open the door of the deserted, ivy-grown Picardy farmhouse at the dip of the sunken lane. Once, one could have imagined, it had been a gentle spot. The farmer and his family would be quietly going about their tasks, with the swifts and swallows wheeling in the blue skies above. But not now. Now it was no more than a structure of stout wooden beams and sturdy stones, set squarely in the teeth of the enemy's line of advance, all trace of civilians and soaring birds long gone.

Sobbing for breath, Andy laid Lieutenant Hardacre in one corner of the empty living room and stared down at the officer's pallid face. Was it only six hours since Hardacre himself, then unharmed and stalwart, had given Andy his field promotion to corporal, on the tragic death of the platoon's other NCOs? 'Me! A corporal!' Andy started at the sudden sound of his own voice, and screwed his eyes shut against the pressure of his white knuckles. He found himself laughing, with that sort of laughter born of stress and strain. 'Me! A nothing! A total nonentity! Did he honestly think that *I* could take charge . . .?'

Ashamed of his own hysterics, he slapped himself across the face, hard. It didn't help. Although the barrage had long since lifted, he could still hear the whining evil of mortar shells as they spun in to destroy his comrades, could still see the awful moment when Hardacre fell, struck by shrapnel. For one second, he saw himself as a hero, heaving the lieutenant up across his back despite the weight of his Bren gun and the load of its magazines in his webbing pouches. Then he sagged, dismally. 'Me. A hero. That's rich. I'd have left him and run, if I'd had time to think. I'm scared out of my wits, he's unconscious, and I've nobody to turn to. I might just as well sit here and wait until the Jerries come, so's I can surrender.'

It was at that moment that Andy heard, or fancied he heard, the voice. Guttural, foreign-accented, yet quite distinct, it said: 'Nonsense. Perhaps you underestimate yourself? Your promotion cannot have been a thoughtless act. That one, at least, had faith in you. Did the officer see something in you, something that you yourself have never recognised?'

'Who the devil . . .?' Andy took a pace forward, his eyes searching the shadows of the ancient room. But nothing stirred. 'Oh, blazes. That's all I need,' he muttered. 'I'm hearing things now. I must be cracking up.' He made the effort to collect his wits, and knelt by Hardacre, following exactly the routines of his training to make field dressings and do what he could for his superior's wounds. He splashed lukewarm liquid from his water bottle on the officer's face, willing him to regain consciousness, but to no avail. 'Please, sir! *Please* come round! I don't know what to do!'

Something at the edge of his vision made him whirl. For a split second he fancied he saw a fleeting form – a short, squat man with a two-horned hat on his head. But it was surely his imagination . . . as much his imagination as that voice, which again seemed to come from nowhere . . . perhaps from within his own overwrought mind.

'He will live,' it said. 'Your duty is to return with him to your battalion so that you may both continue to fight against the invaders who overrun this unhappy country . . .'

Andy frowned. One part of his brain told him that he was indeed going mad. The other listened to the halting words, delivered as though from someone not perfectly acquainted with the English language . . .

'They come,' continued the voice. 'A scouting patrol for their advance. They are not sure of this farmhouse. It would be well to make them think that it is more strongly held than it is, and thus to delay them.'

'What *is* this? Who *are* you?' Andy wrenched open the door of a cupboard and blanched. For the merest millisecond, he saw a face – gaunt, hooked of nose, with lank hair escaping beneath the hat. Then he realised that it was no more than the image of cobwebs among hanging harness. And yet, a strange calm began to steal over him. 'It's all within me,' he breathed, aloud. 'And it makes sense . . .'

'Corporal Coulson?' This voice was for real, and it came from Lieutenant Hardacre. With a cry of relief, Andy fell to his knees beside him. 'How do you feel, sir . . .?'

'Terrible. What's the position, young 'un?' The man's voice was scarcely more than a rattling croak. Andy didn't even register that it was ridiculous for the lieutenant to call him 'young 'un', as Hardacre was no more than a year older than himself. He replied, grimly: 'Scouting patrol's approaching, sir.' Then, without consciously meaning to say the words: 'I can use the Bren to keep 'em off. Maybe fix up a couple of tripwires to set off a grenade or two. If they fall back, it could give us enough time to get clear.'

'Good boy, Andy,' whispered Hardacre. 'I knew I could trust you.' His head sank back as he relapsed into unconsciousness.

Andy stood up. 'What did I say? That surely wasn't me talking . . .' But as if in a trance, he unclipped grenades from his belt and, as though something guided him where to find it, took a reel of farm twine from a cupboard beneath the stairway. He kept swivelling his head, for he was sure that someone was beside him all the while, an unseen presence that became more and more definite. It was still with him as he slipped cautiously into the open, and, the coast apparently clear, made his way up the rising lane away from the house. The weed-grown track gave plenty of opportunity for concealing triplines, and he rigged them with an ease that astonished his unpractised hands. Surely it was more than just instinct that was guiding him. The ghostly shape. Some sort of guardian angel? He was imagining things, of that he had no doubt. Hunger, that was it. Hunger and fear. They were behind it all. Light-headed now, he actually conversed with the strange entity he started to call 'pal'. Pal. The word amused him, and he sniggered uncontrollably.

'See? I rig the grenades here, and here,' he babbled. 'Now, if any Jerries come this way, they'll think there's blokes on their flanks. And back in the house, when the grenades go off, I'll open up with a full magazine and send 'em scuttling.'

'Excellent,' said the voice. 'Corporal, you are doing well. But you must be careful. Your ruse will only hold them off for a short while. You will need to make a truly rapid retreat with your officer. You will require transport.'

'Transport!' Andy sat on his hunkers and laughed out loud. 'There's none of that round here! Maybe you think I should creep forward and nick a Jerry tank . . .?'

'My dear fellow, you must use your wits,' came the reply. 'The owner of the farm took his family away in their lorry. But his old motorcycle still remains in the shed . . .'

'Now you're kidding me, pal,' said Andy, reproachfully.

'You disbelieve me? Go and look for yourself . . .'

Again as though guided by some spectral hand, Andy slipped back to the farm and the outhouses behind. He used his bayonet to break a cheap padlock on one of the doors. To his astonishment he came upon not just a motorbike, but a motorbike and sidecar combination. 'How on earth could I have *known* this . . .?'

It was in bad repair. The tank was full, but the starter didn't respond to his kick. Good thing that he had owned a bike in civvy street. Not a similar model, but Andy didn't care about that. His whole attention on the machine, he grabbed the tools that lay on a bench in the shed and set to work. Tinkering with that engine was exactly to his liking, and although he seemed to be conscious of 'pal' actually watching him, he was engrossed enough in his work to accept the phantom without question. 'She'll do,' he said at last. 'I do believe she'll do.' He saw that petrol was flowing, and rapidly and skilfully unscrewed the plugs to clean them. Satisfied now, he sat back and slapped the machine on the saddle. 'Now to try her out . . .'

'It would be better not to,' interrupted pal's voice. 'The enemy draws near, Corporal . . .'

Andy turned. His heart jumped, for now he was sure that he could see him: a short, beckoning figure silhouetted in the sunshine of the doorway. A youngish man in a cutaway coat, its buttons gleaming. A strong, stern face, dark and swarthy. The bicorne hat perched squarely above the flowing black hair. Yet it was no more than a fleeting impression, for in a trice it had gone. 'Pal . . .?' Andy stumbled to the door and peered out, his hands on the jamb. There was nothing. Nobody.

The corporal ran back into the main building. He was surprised to realise that all his previous feelings of inadequacy were gone. He felt calm. In control. Almost confident.

Lieutenant Hardacre was in one of his all-too-brief periods of consciousness. 'Corporal . . .? What's going on . . .?'

Andy hunched the Bren gun up on to a table top, thrusting the entire bulk of it against a window commanding a direct view up the lane. He slapped a magazine into the top-feed and hauled back the cocking-handle. 'Enemy patrol's coming any minute, sir. But I'll have you out of this, see if I don't.'

Eye glued to the sights, Andy watched for the first sight of the German troops. Hardacre said: 'I could order you to make a dash for it and save yourself, Corporal. It's me for the hospital, and frankly, it doesn't seem to make much difference whether it's back home, or in a Jerry prison camp.'

'Don't talk like that, sir. Pal says we've got to get back to Blighty so's we can fight again.'

'Pal . . .?' Lieutenant Hardacre raised himself on one elbow, fighting the pain of his wounds. 'Someone else has joined us . . .?'

'Not one of our chaps, sir,' said Andy. Then he flushed. 'Sorry, sir. I – I can't explain it. Some sort of a make-believe character, maybe. Think I've been going a little loopy.' But he added: 'Still, he did show me where to find the motorbike.'

'The – *what* . . .?'

'Motorbike and sidecar, sir. It'll run, I'm sure of it. It's a British hospital for you, if everything goes to plan . . .'

Just before his senses fled once more, Hardacre lay back with a long, shuddering sigh. But there was a smile on his face. 'You've got . . . my every . . . confidence,' he faltered. The sun, already well on its way to the horizon, dipped away and left the lane in dusky shadows before Andy caught his first glimpse of the opposition. Suddenly, the gentle brush-work of the weeds on the lane's horizon was broken by the bobbing curve of a coal-scuttle helmet, and then the entire head and shoulders of the 'point' – the leading man of the German reconnaissance patrol – rose into view. Andy waited. Now the man breasted the rise and stood for a moment, his Schmeisser machine-pistol held warily before him as he took in the aspect of the silent farmstead. He turned and beckoned before he walked on, and his strung-out companions began to follow him . . .

'Point' tripped the twine of Andy's first grenade, and all six men of the patrol fell flat as the explosion sent fragments of steel whanging past them. Almost at once, there came the blossoming flash of the second bomb, and in the same moment, the staccato bark of the Bren as Andy squeezed the trigger. Taken by surprise, the Germans hugged dirt. Twigs

Andy waited. The man turned and beckoned before he walked on, and his strung-out companions began to follow him.

and leaves pattered amongst them as the nickel-clad bullets cut close across the hedgerows.

They fired back, naturally, but their aim was wild and startled. Like a man possessed, Andy darted from side to side, loosing off random shots from the lieutenant's pistol in between firing the Bren gun in brief bursts. He was yelling, too, his voice cracking and breaking with excitement, and nobody could have blamed the enemy for imagining the house to contain, not one almost mad defender, but perhaps an entire section.

The Germans retired, without losses and in perfect order. Their sergeant said that it would be prudent to wait until daybreak, in the meantime calling up a mortar squad to bombard the house.

In the gathering darkness, Andy Coulson, keyed up to a point of exhilaration he'd never known, saw them go and roared a triumphant battle-cry. There was no point in taking the Bren, so he field-stripped the weapon and threw the working parts down the lane into the dank undergrowth. No sense in giving the Jerries a buckshee gun . . .

Gently, Andy picked up the lieutenant and eased him into the motorcycle's rusty sidecar. Then he kicked the starter. On his second attempt, he heard the joyous response of the stubborn engine.

He also heard the voice. It said: 'Corporal, I salute you. There lies within all people something which they may never suspect.' And again fleetingly, Andy saw that figure in the buttoned coat, its arm raised to take off the two-horned hat and wave it in farewell . . .

To say that Andy's journey on his borrowed motorcycle was easy would be absurd. He drove through the night. Twice he came under fire from German advance units, but he survived. Though he never again caught the voice of 'pal' nor saw the ghostly figure, he and his officer won through. And they were amongst those who were successfully lifted from the dread beaches at Dunkirk to return to the shores of Britain. It is of no importance to this story to trace either of their subsequent careers, except to say that both finished the war in one piece – Hardacre a captain, and Andy a sergeant major whose entire character had undergone a startling change in that lonely Picardy farmhouse. Never again was Andy Coulson to doubt his own ability.

What does concern us is what happened at the farmhouse on the morning after the corporal's against-the-odds escape.

It took a fighting patrol under the command of Feldwebel Hans Warth a cautious hour after dawn to encircle the place. They were not, of course, opposed. But they were still very wary as they booted their way into the place to find the useless Bren amongst its litter of spent ammunition.

'It looks like there was nobody here but one man,' said Gefreiter Johann Koltz.

'One man and a wounded companion,' said the Feldwebel, mystified, as he peered at the blood from Lieutenant Hardacre, which had stained the floor. '*Teufel*! I think we were well and truly fooled!'

They were not bothered, those victorious Germans, for at that time they were certain of final victory. Yet they were all interested when, just by chance, one of their squad uncovered an inscribed plaque, half hidden by the ivy on the farmhouse wall. 'Come and look at this,' he yelled.

The plaque read: 'In this building, while serving as a corporal in the Army of the Revolution, the Emperor Napoleon Bonaparte single-handedly held off a company of Royalist infantry. 1791. Vive l'Empereur!'

'I wonder,' mused Feldwebel Warth, 'if history has somehow repeated itself. . .' His men only laughed, but from within the confines of the old building, there came a chuckle.

A RICH INHERITANCE

by Hilary Lloyd-Williams

AFTER SO MANY HOURS, Barry hardly noticed the sound made by the four Rolls Royce engines as the Boeing 747 Jumbo jet thundered southwards. Below, he could see the dark red soil of India and the tiny specks that were ships, starting or completing their journey across the Indian Ocean.

It was a dream come true!

When, six months before, Barry Tayler had entered the competition which promised the winner a trip to Australia, he never really thought he would win. In fact, he had forgotten all about it until the registered letter arrived at the children's home, where he had been brought up.

The housemaster had summoned Barry to his study. Barry went in nervously, thinking he had done something wrong. But when he saw the expression on Mr Hardcastle's face, he knew it was good news!

He had won first prize – a trip for two in Australia for three weeks!

Barry's parents had been killed in a car crash just after he was born. He had no relatives and there was no one to care for him. The Children's Home was the only answer. He had been there for nine years. They had not always been happy years but it was the only life he knew.

Winning the prize was the biggest thing in his life! Arrangements were made. Barry had to get a passport. He was allowed to purchase special clothes and it was agreed that George Hardcastle, his housemaster, would accompany him.

As he gazed out of the aircraft's window, Barry thought back to the events of the past few weeks. Everything had gone so quickly. Saying goodbye to his friends. Heathrow Airport. Take-off. Flying across Europe. The re-fuelling stop in India.

He looked down at the blue waters of the Pacific. George Hardcastle was alongside him.

'Feeling happy, Barry?'

Happy? That was the understatement of the year!

Meal times seemed to come round very quickly aboard the Jumbo. Barry was just about to start his latest meal when Mr Hardcastle pointed out of the window. It was their first view of Australia!

Then a strange thing happened.

As he saw the Australian coastline for the first time, a cold, eerie chill seemed to take over his whole body. Barry shivered, despite the warm atmosphere inside the aircraft.

'Is something wrong?' His housemaster looked worried.

'N-no . . . it's all right,' said Barry. 'I just had a very odd feeling come over me. I . . . I can't explain it!'

'Perhaps you're eating too much!'

Barry smiled. 'Perhaps you're right!'

For Barry, it was a magic moment when the big jet's wheels touched down on Australian soil. They landed in Perth and left the 'plane to meet the full force of the Australian summer.

'No more shivers?' asked Mr Hardcastle.

'No more shivers . . . not in this heat,' Barry grinned. 'I've never felt the sun as hot as this!'

Their first night in Australia was spent at a luxurious hotel on the outskirts of Perth. As he lay in bed that night, Barry could still hardly believe his luck. He had never known such a comfortable bed!

Even though the room was air-conditioned, he decided to leave the windows open, so he could hear the sounds of

Australia. A gentle breeze sent the bedroom curtains swaying gently. Barry watched them for a while, then his eyelids felt heavy and he fell asleep.

He wasn't sure just how long he had been asleep, but suddenly the room felt much, much colder. He shivered and pulled the blankets more closely around him. But it didn't help.

It was the same feeling. The feeling he had had on the aircraft when he first saw Australia.

He was frightened!

For a moment he thought it was the curtains moving, as they had been when he dropped off to sleep. But it wasn't the curtains. It was a strange white mist drifting into the room. A ghostly, glowing mist that seemed to radiate the cold which was filling the room.

The mist came together into a shape. It swirled around until Barry, wide-eyed with fear, could see that it resembled an old man. The figure floated silently at the foot of the bed. It didn't say anything. It just stared, with unblinking eyes. Staring at Barry with an intensity that gripped the boy with a cold terror.

Finally he could stand it no longer. He grabbed the blankets and pulled them over his head!

For almost an hour he lay there, hardly daring to breathe. From the other side of the blankets there was no sound. Then, just as suddenly as before, the temperature began to change. This time it was getting warmer.

Barry risked a look over the top of the blankets. The figure had gone!

Had it all been a dream? Barry wasn't sure . . . but he quickly got out of bed and closed the window, just to be certain that nothing could get it again. He got back into bed.

A combination of jet-lag, fear and excitement sent him to sleep. He was not disturbed again. Not until Mr Hardcastle came in, to announce that breakfast was in half an hour and afterwards they were going to sample an Australian beach and some swimming.

At breakfast, Barry was unusually quiet. 'Are you sure you're all right?' asked the housemaster. 'No more shivers?'

'I'm okay. But tell me . . . do you believe in ghosts?'

'Ghosts? Of course not. Why do you ask?'

'It . . . it doesn't matter. It's not important. Let's go swimming and forget all about shivers, ghosts and everything!'

Barry had never known sea water so warm and so clear. He swam for almost half an hour and then went back across the golden sand to join Mr Hardcastle.

'Remember to use plenty of suntan lotion!' warned the housemaster.

Barry plastered himself with lotion and lay in the sun, thinking how wonderful everything was. This was just how he imagined Australia to be!

Soon, despite the lotion, he was beginning to get red. It was time for another swim. This time, he went a little further out, revelling in the clear water and the large waves which were so popular with surf-riders. As each wave came in, Barry tried to dive in the centre of it, then swim strongly through the water, remaining submerged for a considerable time.

As soon as he dived into a particularly large wave, he knew something was wrong. The water was unusually cold. And then he saw it. The same ghostly figure as he had seen in the hotel room. This time it was floating just above the water, among the spray of the giant waves.

In panic, Barry glanced back at the beach. It was almost deserted and George Hardcastle was asleep, under a giant beach umbrella. Barry shivered, his heart racing. Fear almost made him turn and swim frantically back to the beach. But suddenly he stopped.

This was his holiday. His once-in-a-lifetime trip and no one, not even a ghost, was going to spoil it. The figure was still there, as silent as before.

'What do you want with me?' yelled Barry, turning to face the ghostly shape. 'Can't you say anything? Why don't you just leave me alone!'

Barry gulped as he trod water, waiting to see if there was any reaction to what he had said. Maybe you shouldn't yell at a ghost. It might just turn nasty!

But nothing happened. The misty figure stayed there for another minute, then began to fade away. At the same time, the water temperature increased and everything returned to normal.

The boy swam back to the shore. No one else had seen anything. He decided it was best not to tell Mr Hardcastle. His housemaster would probably think he was mad, and it might ruin the rest of the holiday. So Barry kept quiet. Perhaps, next time, Mr Hardcastle would see the ghost for himself!

The following day, a trip had been arranged into the Australian outback. George Hardcastle hired a car and, along with a guide, he and Barry motored out of the town and drove for hours until they were going along a rough, winding road that led into the foothills.

Everything was tinder dry. The ground was dusty and there were only occasional clumps of dry bushes and bare trees. The guide, a local Australian girl, was trying to make the journey as interesting as possible, but for the first time on the trip, Barry was feeling bored. He wanted something to happen.

It soon did!

Ahead of them, through the dust, Barry suddenly spotted a familiar figure. It was the ghost! The old man was standing at the side of the road, about a hundred metres ahead of them.

At last! Now all three of them would see it! Barry pointed up ahead.

'Look there!' he yelled. 'See that old man – he's a ghost. I keep seeing him, ever since I came to Australia!'

The girl and Mr Hardcastle looked at each other. 'There's no one there,' said the housemaster. 'Stop playing tricks!'

'It's not a trick. See . . . we're just passing him. He's right alongside of the car. You MUST be able to see him!'

'I think he's been in the Aussie sun too long,' said the guide, as Mr Hardcastle drove on. Suddenly Barry realised the truth. He was the only one who could see the ghost! He looked back, through the car's rear window. The old man was still standing there.

Then it happened!

There was a sudden loud noise, like a gun going off, and the car swerved violently across the road. George Hardcastle fought to control the car, braking hard to bring it under control.

'What a place to get a puncture!' he exclaimed, as he got out of the car to look at the rear wheel with its flat tyre. 'Lucky we've got a spare. Shouldn't take me long to change the wheel.'

Barry got out of the car and saw that the ghostly figure was still there, about fifty metres back down the road. 'I'm just going for a little walk,' he said.

'Don't wander too far,' Mr Hardcastle warned. 'We shan't be many minutes.'

Trying to act casually, Barry walked towards the old man. When he was about twenty metres away, the man started to move. The figure wasn't walking . . . it was floating across the ground, away from the road.

Barry hesitated. He was not sure if he should follow. His mind was made up for him when the old man stopped and beckoned him to follow. Barry checked that Mr Hardcastle and the girl were not looking and moved off the road. When he felt the others couldn't hear, he called to the figure. 'Look, this is crazy. Just what do you want with me? Cut out the fun and games and TELL me!' He was surprised at his own bravery. If anyone had told him, a week before, that he would be shouting at an Australian ghost, he wouldn't have believed them. It was like a nightmare. But one thing was certain: this was no dream!

The ghost was floating towards a clump of bushes, half-way up the side of a small hillside. Once again, it stopped and looked back at Barry and indicated that he should follow.

His heart thumping madly, Barry walked on, convinced that at last he was getting near to the solution to the mystery. The old man seemed to move through the bushes as if the branches were not there. Barry reached the spot and pushed the branches aside. Then he gasped. The bushes had been hiding the entrance to a small cave. Cobwebs almost covered the entrance and over the years even the sparse vegetation had managed to almost block the hole in the hillside. What was inside?

For a while, Barry could not see anything. The dark of the cave contrasted with the bright sunshine outside and it took him a few minutes to get used to the dark. Further on, inside the cave, the ghost figure was standing alongside some old pieces of furniture. Barry could just make out an old cupboard and a chair, and near them a shovel, a pickaxe and an old miner's helmet.

Barry moved forward, and for once the ghost did not back away. Barry was almost up to it when he saw that there was a smile on the old man's face for the first time. Then, slowly, the figure began to fade, turning into swirling mist and then vanishing completely.

Barry was alone in the cave. He looked around and could tell that the cave had not been used for many many years. It

He saw that there was a smile on the old man's face for the first time. Then, slowly, the figure began to fade . . .

was obviously an old gold working, he figured, looking at the equipment that littered the floor. He pushed thick cobwebs aside so he could look at things more clearly.

Suddenly he froze as a hand clamped on to his shoulder!

Barry screamed, whirling round to see . . . Mr Hardcastle! 'What the heck are you doing?' the housemaster shouted, angrily. 'It's lucky we saw you go up here, or we wouldn't have known where you were. We told you not to wander too far!'

'I . . . I'm sorry,' Barry explained. 'But there WAS a figure by the side of the road . . . and he led me up here, to this cave.'

George Hardcastle produced a powerful torch. 'Let's just see what sort of place you've found.' The torch's beam swung round the small cave.

'Here's an old photo!' The Australian guide had followed them into the cave and she was examining a faded photograph that had been on the cupboard. The three of them looked at it. It showed an old miner posed alongside a pile of ore and holding a pickaxe, with which he was indicating something in his hand.

'It's him!' Barry shouted, suddenly very excited. 'It's the old man I've been seeing ever since I got here. It's the ghost!'

'There's something very odd going on,' the housemaster said wearily. The girl had continued to look at the photograph. 'Look what's in his hand . . . I think it's gold! He must have struck it rich!'

Mr Hardcastle blew the dust off an old book that had been alongside the photograph. 'Seems to be some sort of diary. Let's take a look at the date . . .' But before he could even check the year, he read something which made him gasp with amazement.

'The . . . the name on the front of the diary. I . . . I don't believe it. The diary belonged to someone called Jim Tayler!'

'But that's my surname,' said Barry, reaching for the book.

'And that's not all,' the housemaster went on. 'Look at the spelling of Tayler. Most people spell the name with an "o" at the end . . . but you both spell it with an "e"!'

'Do you think we were related?'

'You know something . . . I'm sure of it!' The housemaster scratched his head. 'I can hardly believe this myself. But I think that old man you saw WAS some relative of yours. That he appeared to you to give you some sort of message. Perhaps to bring you here!'

'But why?'

Their guide had taken the torch and was shining it on the walls of the cave. 'I think I've found the answer,' she said. 'Just look at the walls . . . see what's shining out of them. It's GOLD!'

For a moment, there was a stunned silence.

'Then . . . then the ghost wanted me to have it!' Barry spoke in an awed whisper. 'It . . . it's sort of my inheritance. THAT'S why the ghost brought me here!'

There seemed to be pieces of gold everywhere and they had soon collected a large amount of rock, containing lots of the precious metal. 'We'll take this back into town with us and get it looked at,' Mr Hardcastle said as they left the cave. 'Whatever happens, we must remember this exact location. That cave's been lost for a hundred years. We don't want to lose it again!'

The girl and George Hardcastle carried out the chunks of rock. Strangely, Barry was more interested in the photograph and the diary. 'They just seem to be more important at the moment,' he said.

Just how important was soon to be revealed!

'Fool's gold . . . that's all it is!'

Barry, Mr Hardcastle and their Australian guide were in the office of a local mining company. The man they had shown the 'gold' to was roaring with laughter. 'This may look like gold,' he said. 'But it's worthless. In the old days, lots of miners would find this stuff and convince themselves they were rich, but it's only pyrite, a worthless metal!'

So there was no inheritance for Barry, after all.

'I'm sorry lad!' George Hardcastle put his hand on Barry's shoulder. 'It must be a terrible disappointment to you.'

Barry sniffed. 'Not really. What you've never had, you never miss!'

'And I'm sorry about this as well!' Mr Hardcastle took a folded newspaper out of his pocket. 'I was so convinced you had made a rich find, I gave the story to the local newspaper. Take a look . . . they've printed a big story about you, complete with photograph!'

The boy read the details under the headline, 'British Boy Strikes It Rich!' It was strange. The fool's gold had really fooled him . . . but he couldn't imagine how it could fool a ghost!

Barry was still trying to work out that problem when he fell asleep that night. He had an undisturbed night. There was no ghostly visitor.

In the morning, he found himself a national celebrity! The local newspaper story had been taken up by television and radio stations and there was much sympathy for the visitor from Britain.

Barry was soon giving interviews to journalists about the ghostly figure he had seen. For a couple of days, the story continued to make headlines and get lots of radio and television coverage. But then other stories took over and it seemed that everyone had forgotten about him.

But not quite!

Two days later, a beaming Mr Hardcastle announced that Barry had two visitors. A smiling, middle-aged couple entered the room. Barry was surprised to see there were tears in the woman's eyes. She suddenly rushed forward and put her arms around the startled boy, sobbing uncontrollably.

For a few moments, Barry was completely bewildered, but then George Hardcastle told him the amazing story.

It seemed that the couple were Barry's aunt and uncle! They had emigrated to Australia many years before and the woman had lost touch with her sister, who was, in fact, Barry's mother! They had not even known of his parents' death and that he had been left alone, with no relations to care for him.

'We . . . we've no children of our own,' said the man. 'We would like you to come and live with us, here in Australia. We could adopt you . . .'

'You mean I'd have a proper family at last?'

'Of course you would. We would care for you, as if you were our own son!'

Suddenly, everyone was hugging everyone else!

'To think we would never have known anything about you if we hadn't read that story in the papers!'

Then everything became clear to Barry. The old miner had wanted him to have riches. But not gold. He wanted Barry to have a family, to be with the relatives the ghost knew were in Australia!

The woman smiled.

'To think we owe all this to Great Uncle Jim! If he could see us now, he'd be so happy!'

Barry glanced up towards the door and gasped. There, in the doorway, was the glowing figure of the old miner. There was a smile on the old man's face.

Ghosts don't normally wink . . . but this one did!

DOOR TO THE BEYOND

by Angus Allan

IT LAY LIKE A CROUCHING BEAST crosswise on the muddied road that ran dead straight through the glistening flatness of the fens. A mouldering mansion stark against the cold autumn sky. The house's twin gothic turrets, in silhouette, looked like horns thrusting up from the dismal, weeping laurels and yews that surrounded it.

Centuries old, Sighsmere Grange knew little of the modern world. It heard only the booming of the bittern, the croak and rustle of the nameless marsh-creatures who came by night. It was shunned by people, for its reputation as a haunted house of terrifying evil had grown upon it over the years like some ghastly, tangible canker, and few were those who cared to approach it, even by daylight.

Such tales, however, bothered Martin Mason not one whit. A first-year student in medical college, for whom his professors grimly prophesied nothing but failure and disgrace, Martin Mason was, by his own confession, a cynic. He believed, he said, in nothing. Nothing, that was, beyond the pursuit of his own pleasures – if necessary, at the expense of those around him. He lived, he confessed, 'for the moment'. His parents had given him up. Abroad anyway, they had washed their hands of him, only continuing to see to it that his fees – and his debts – were paid.

Like all wastrels, Martin had drawn to him a group of toadies; companions who, though they secretly loathed him, were happy to share in his thoughtless extravagance, so long as he footed the bill. He fondly imagined that they were 'true friends' . . .

He was expensively, if casually, dressed, and now he stood with one hand languidly on his hip, scornfully running his eye over Sighsmere Grange. 'Well, ghosts! Here I am!' His voice was echoed by a chorus of sycophantic laughter from C.D. Corkwell, known as 'Seedy', Timothy Winch and Corcoran 'Corky' Musgrave, the last of whom had brought them from Cambridge in the hired car.

'Talk, Martin! Just talk!' simpered Musgrave. '*I* can see the sweat on your brow, dear fellow!'

'Sweat, my auntie,' snorted Martin. 'You fellows made a bet, and I'm going to win it, never you fear.'

'Oh, *we* don't have to fear,' said Seedy. 'It's *you* who've got to spend the night in the Black Room.'

'Seedy, old scout, I *said* there were no such things as phantoms, and I meant it,' replied Martin. 'I shall take my sleeping bag, bung it down in the Black Room, and snore the hours away while you dopes get headaches trying to kip in the car. Come morning, I shall walk out all merry and bright, and collect my winnings. *And* I shall tell 'em all at college what a stupid bunch of twits you are, to waste your bunce making such a crackpot wager.'

Timothy shrugged his shoulders, huffily. 'You're too ruddy confident, by half. Just remember the story. There's supposed to have been a horrible murder and suicide committed in that room, and the horror's still there, living on.'

'Bosh. Tommy-rot. If ghosts really existed,' sneered Martin, 'we wouldn't be able to move for 'em. There's been enough dark deeds done to make every square inch of this country haunted. Anyone care to come and take a look inside with me?'

They declined, and it was alone that Martin crunched the weedy gravel to the forbidding oaken door of Sighsmere

Grange. Once it had been padlocked, but the lock and its chain had long since rusted, and although it didn't impede his entrance, the door groaned in protest as he thrust it open. He snapped on his torch and let the beam play around the deep dust of the creaking floor, the ancient, frowning portraits on the walls, the toppling suits of rusted armour flanking the carved balustrades of the web-hung staircase.

'Bosh,' he said again. But it was cold in here. Colder than the night outside.

He knew where the Black Room was, and decisively, he strode up the stairs, his footfalls curiously muffled by the thick grime. Oddly, he felt the urge to whistle, but dismissed the idea, and let out a short bark of laughter. 'Ghosts!' he snapped. 'Utter nonsense.'

The Black Room lay at the end of an echoing corridor at the rear of the house. It was a strangely shaped room, octagonal, with alcoves on every wall except the one that housed the blackened lattice window. Martin Mason's torch showed him a candelabra in each alcove, and not a stick of furniture save a tottering four-poster bed, its hangings in spidery threads. He flung his sleeping bag down on it, and dug for a box of matches in his pocket. Smirking to himself, he lit each candle, momentarily irritated that he felt happier in the wan flicker of their light. He looked at his watch. It read eleven forty-five p.m. 'About eight hours to dawn,' he said. Was it his imagination, or did his voice sound somewhat strained and high-pitched . . .?

He was about to crawl, fully clothed, into his sleeping bag, when, unaccountably, the candles in the farthest candelabra went out. His tongue clucking with impatience, he went across and re-lit them. He felt no draught, and checked the windows. They were long sealed with accumulated dust. Had he closed the door properly? He ran his hand up and down. No, nothing. And yet, in rapid succession, another two pairs

Oddly, he felt the urge to whistle, but dismissed the idea, and let out a short bark of laughter. 'Ghosts!' he snapped. 'Utter nonsense.'

of candles guttered and extinguished themselves.

Martin was conscious of himself beginning to shout, as though in defiance. 'This is absurd! You can't scare me!' He struck two matches, broke both, and by the time he got the candles re-lit, two more had gone out. Now he was running round the room. He barked his shins painfully against the bed. And for the first time, he had to accept a rising and uncontrollable feeling of terror as the last of his matches failed to stem the surging darkness. With a hoarse cry, he dived for his torch – but it wasn't there! He stood shaking, inky blackness all around him, and he could hear, quite clearly, the pounding of his own heart!

The door. It must be this way. He took a few cautious paces, arms outstretched. He would search the house, find some more matches, maybe. Five, six, seven paces. Surely he must reach the wall soon? The room couldn't have been this big!

All at once, a strange, greenish light flooded the place, and Martin Mason froze. He blinked his eyes. Rubbed at them. But it was true. His entire surroundings had dramatically changed shape and form! Gone was the bed, gone was the lattice window. He was in a long, tall corridor, so tall that its ceiling was lost in mist. And at the far end was a single wooden door, its surface studded with iron nails. He tried to speak, but nothing would come, and as he took three faltering steps forward, the door opened itself. A strangled cry forced itself out of Martin's throat as he beheld the robed figure, the head hidden by a cowl, one gnarled hand raised and beckoning.

'This way!' The voice was no more than a whisper, but Martin obeyed it. His backbone was like a column of ice, his eyes stood out from their sockets in abject fear, and his every limb shook as though with the plague. But there was no denying the spectral summons.

'Who . . . what *are* you . . .?'

'That is the very question you will have to ask yourself,' said the spectre. 'This night, you have chosen to intrude upon the realm of the unknown. Be it on your own head, my rash friend. Will you accompany me through the door to the beyond . . .?'

With all his heart, Martin wanted to turn and run. But to where? From a Black Room that no longer seemed to exist? Frozen by the chill of his phantom guide, he forced himself to pass through the iron-studded door . . .

Instantly, it seemed, he was in a public house. It was familiar. He was in The Crown and Compasses, haunt of students from his own college. And there at the bar were Seedy, Timothy and Corky, in the company of a vague, shadowy figure that defied recognition. And yet it seemed to be somebody he knew, somebody who had had far too much to drink, and was slumped on the bar-stool, spilling beer from a glass.

'Behold,' said the spectre. 'You see him, don't you?'

'It's . . . it's as if I can see *through* him,' said Martin. 'As though, like a doctor, I can analyse everything that's happening to him. His brain is that of a wretch. His heart, his liver . . . no good . . .'

The spectre snapped its bony fingers, and at once, the scene changed. Now they were in the plush, glittering surroundings of a casino. It was not in England. Seedy was there, but neither Timothy nor Corky were with him – only that indefinable figure, now hunched over the roulette table, as if in despair. Martin heard the croupier exclaim: 'The black wins!' but the rest of his gabble was lost in the buzz of conversation as Seedy shook his head and turned to the girls. There were two of them, glamorous butterflies both, by his side. 'He's lost again. He can't go on like this . . .'

Martin tried to clutch at his friend. 'Seedy! This is me,

Martin! Where is this? What's going on . . .?' But his fingers found nothing solid.

'You cannot affect what you see,' intoned the spectre. 'There is no use in trying. Come. There is much yet for you to witness . . .'

His mind whirling, Martin seemed to be flying through space. He could feel the phantom's clutch, hard upon his arm.

It was a courtroom. The unrecognisable figure, who Martin knew instinctively was the same person, stood with bowed head in the dock. A stern-faced judge was giving sentence. All around were stony, accusing faces. 'The jury has found you guilty,' droned the judge. 'It is my painful duty to sentence you to twenty years' imprisonment for your callous crimes . . .'

'It's me, isn't it?' Martin Mason turned to his ghostly companion, searching the dark void beneath the cowl. There was no reply, but the cowl dipped a fraction, as if the head within had made a nod. Martin shuddered as the figure in the scene was led by two uniformed policemen from the dock.

'Do . . . do I survive . . .?'

Once more, the phantom gestured, and Martin saw himself in the stark confines of a prison cell. Now that he had accepted that he was being shown the future, he recognised himself at once. But old. So old, beyond his years. He was hunched at the foot of his bunk, sneered at by the three other inmates of his room. They mocked him for his education, his weakness in bringing himself to ruin by throwing away his chances. 'We started out with nothing,' said one of them. 'But you . . . You're a waster, Mason.'

Tears stung Martin's eyes. 'Surely, surely this won't come to pass?' He groped for the spectre's arm. 'Tell me I can change it!' But there seemed to be no hope for him. Abruptly, Martin saw himself being released from the jail, a battered, shabby man with furtive eye, and not a soul to meet him or give him aid. 'He – I – look *broken* . . .'

Images whirled round like a kaleidoscope from that moment on. Martin glimpsed himself in a mean, worthless job. Saw himself stealing. Knew what it was to be on the run. Briefly, he met up with a woman, and even married her.

'I shall desert her, of course,' said Martin bitterly to the ghost.

'Her, and the child,' intoned his guide. 'But there is worse. You must steel yourself, Martin Mason . . .'

It was in London, on the Thames embankment just beyond Charing Cross, and Big Ben was striking two o'clock on a misty winter morning. Totally down and out, the figure of Martin Mason appeared from the shadows, in his hands a bloodstained knife. The spectre said: 'Yes, you have committed murder. For a crust of bread owned by one of those luckless castaways like yourself. But now, you are overcome with remorse as, in a moment of lucidity, your past flashes before you . . .'

'Like my future is flashing before me now . . .?'

'Exactly. Watch, hapless man . . .'

Martin did as he was bid, and to his heart-wrenching horror, saw his image hurl the knife into the dark waters of the river, then scramble feebly up on to the parapet before, with a choking cry, he flung himself into the swirling embrace of the Thames . . .

The drifting eddies told him nothing as, the phantom at his side, Martin rushed to the stone and peered over. He had gone to his doom, and that was certain. The over-indulged cynic, fooling his way through medical college, had reaped the reward of his utterly wasted life . . .

A wan light was filtering through the lattice window of the Black Room. The autumn sun did its best to penetrate the grime, and it was enough to rouse the sprawled figure on the floor, the empty box of matches just out of his grasp. Martin Mason groaned and rolled over, feeling the bump on his head where he had collided with the corner of the fourposter bed. Groggily, he pulled himself to his feet, and snatched at the crumpled sleeping bag on the frame. Memory, and the realisation of a dream that had been a nightmare, flooded back to him. He laughed, but it was a painful croak.

'A dream! Just a *dream*! It – it was *horrible* . . .'

He looked around him. The candles were still there. The door in its appointed place. He ran his hand over his chin, prickly with a night's stubble. 'Did it, though. Got through the night. Won the bet . . .'

He rolled up the bag, tucked it under his arm, and retrieved his torch. He nodded, casually, to the room as he left. 'Okay, ghost, you tried. Funny what a fellow's imagination will do, if it's left to run riot.'

He *was* whistling now, as he strode down the stairs and out of Sighsmere Grange into the open. He crunched down the gravel and chuckled at the sight of Seedy, Timothy and Corky painfully stretching themselves after their uncomfortable sojourn in the car.

'Bet's won, you lot! Fork out!'

Timothy said: 'Cocky devil. Didn't *anything* happen?'

'Nightmare, that's all. Do I have to take the money out of your wallets?'

They paid up, grudgingly. Soon afterwards, Corky, who was roaming round the laurels and yews skirting the Grange's garden, came upon an old broken monument that had once supported some sort of statue. 'Hey! Come and look at this!'

'Is it a tombstone?'

'Hardly. This isn't a churchyard. But there's writing on it. Here, clean off that lichen a bit . . .'

It said: 'To the unworthy memory of a failure. Though

well-born and rich, he spurned his chances and wasted his life. He drank, he gambled, and fell to the depths from which no man can ever rise. At the end, he sank to murder, and took his own life in London's river, anno Domini 1783, on the 9th September. May God have mercy upon his soul.'

'The 9th September! Hey, that's today,' said Seedy.

'There's got to be a name somewhere,' said Timothy, kneeling to thrust away the clinging vegetation. 'Yes, here it is . . .'

Corky shoved him aside. 'Give me a look. It's pretty worn. Ah! Antram. Simon Antram. Must be the bloke the legend of Sighsmere Grange is all about!'

As if to show Martin that they were as cynical as he, Timothy, Seedy and Corky grabbed at the stone, and, all of them laughing, overturned it, kicking it and dancing round it in capering idiocy. 'Pity it's so heavy,' cackled Corky. 'Or we could have taken it back to college as a sort of trophy!'

Martin Mason remained silent. He had felt a shiver run down his spine as his so-called friends fooled round, and had seen once more the image of the phantom of his dream. Without consciously knowing he'd done it, he'd worked out that the name of the unfortunate wastrel on the memorial, Simon Antram, was a perfect anagram of Martin Mason!

The realisation was to change his life . . .

ANCIENT LIGHTS

by Christopher Bendel

THE DAY HAD NOT STARTED OUT at all well for Sydney Arthur Lamprey.

While parking his gleaming Rolls Royce in the specially reserved slot outside Mega-Maison Mansion, the steel-and-glass skyscraper headquarters of his vast building and real estate business situated in the classier part of London's East End, he had accidentally run into an electric milk-float. The milk-float was badly damaged and most of the milk ended up in the gutter. The Rolls only suffered a minor bump on the front wing.

The fact that it was his fault entirely, and that a queue of people waiting for a bus down the road had all witnessed the accident, meant that Lamprey could not simply tell the milkman to push off or get a thick ear, but instead had to give the man his name, address, phone number, details of his insurance company, and other relevant information. Being a secretive man by nature, he disliked giving such details of his life intensely.

As he was doing so, an articulated truck, travelling fast, piled into the rear of the Rolls, which was stuck out into the road. The results were devastating. This time it was the other driver's fault, but that was hardly the point.

Seething, Lamprey strode into the foyer of Mega-Maison Mansion and summoned a minion to deal with the matter, which was fast getting to be serious. By now the police had been called, crash-barriers had been erected, danger-lights switched on, and east-bound traffic was already being diverted off through a maze of side streets.

Normally, it took Lamprey precisely three minutes and forty-six seconds to get to his office from the time his car entered the car park, to the moment when he actually stepped out of the lift into the executive suite on the twentieth floor. Today it took something like half-an-hour. It would have been slightly less but for the fact that, on hurrying to the lift on the ground floor, he had tripped over a stoneware urn containing a large rubber plant, fallen against a wall, slid off it, and cannoned into a secretary carrying half-a-dozen box-files, one of which was thrust as far as it would go into his open mouth, badly grazing his upper gums.

Lionel Sliggers, Lamprey's confidential secretary, general factotum, and whipping-boy, sensed that his employer was not in the sweetest of tempers the moment Lamprey entered the vast executive office that was the nerve-centre of his empire.

He sensed this because Lamprey's face was crimson, there was blood on his lower lip, his jacket was scuffed and dusty, and he slammed the door with such violence that the wall actually shivered as a large portrait of Lamprey, painted in oils and in a heavy gilt frame, slid sideways, then crashed to the pine-panel flooring, its glass shattering.

Pop-eyed, Lamprey halted in mid-stride, turned slowly and stared at the mess. Then he walked back to the door, opened it, took hold of a part of the frame and heaved at it. The wall shook.

Lamprey turned on his secretary.

'Who built this flamin' place?' he snapped.

Even thinking as fast as he was paid to do, Sliggers could not come up with an answer that might pour oil on clearly troubled waters.

'Uh . . . you did, sir.'

'*I* did?!' screamed Lamprey.

'That's to say, *we* did . . . one of our companies . . . *your* companies . . . one of the companies owned by you . . . or rather, owned by SAL Holdings . . . that is . . .'

Lamprey slammed the door again and strode past the babbling Sliggers to his huge desk. He sat down in the leather-backed swivel chair with a thud and jabbed a forefinger towards his minion.

'Find out which firm, sack the staff, and put the company into liquidation, lock, stock and barrel!' he snarled.

Sliggers gaped at him.

'But . . . but you can't do that, sir!' he bleated.

Lamprey shot him a look of such poison that, if bottled, it would have made a useful rat killer.

'I . . .' he said through his teeth 'can . . . do . . . *anything!*'

Sliggers was stumbling towards the door when Lamprey's bellow stopped him in his tracks.

'WHAT'S THIS?!'

Lamprey was holding a sheet of paper by forefinger and thumb as though it were infected with the plague. Sliggers' heart sank.

'It's, uh . . . old Mr Farquaharson. He's, uh . . . refused your offer.'

From bright red, Sydney Arthur Lamprey's face shifted into a deep puce. For a moment, Sliggers thought his employer was about to have a fit.

'He's what?' whispered Lamprey.

'He's . . . turned down your offer . . . for the, uh . . . Bell Street place . . .'

Lamprey stared at him unbelievingly, as though Sliggers had suddenly arrived from another planet.

'But I offered him a cool quarter of a million quid for the crummy dump . . .'

'He, uh . . . says he wouldn't sell even for, uh . . . five

million . . .' Sliggers muttered miserably.

Lamprey erupted out of his chair.

'Get the Rolls!' he howled. 'No! That's smashed to blazes! Get the Rover, the Bentley, *anything*! I'm gonna sort the perisher out myself! With *bare hands*, if necessary!'

Sydney Arthur Lamprey sat back amongst the cushions in the rear of his Mercedes and simmered as one of his chauffeurs piloted the car smoothly through the city-bound traffic.

Three years before, Lamprey had bought up one of the last remaining bomb-sites in the City of London. It was half a street that had been blitzed during the War; but, as was sometimes the case, due to the bizarre effects of the mammoth bomb-blast, one single building had been spared. It was a corner shop on the northern boundary of the site, inhabited by an antiquarian bookseller called Farquaharson. He had a sinister reputation in the area.

Farquaharson's family had owned the building for generations, some said for over 300 years, and for the past eighteen months Lamprey had been trying to winkle him out. But the shop owner had proved obstinate.

This was now getting to be expensive for Lamprey, whose original idea had been to build a multi-storey car park combined with a supermarket warehouse and two office blocks. That could not be achieved, however, until Farquaharson's modest three up, three down had gone the way of the rest of the houses on the street. As it was, the site remained in the same state of rubble-strewn, weed-choked ruin as it had for the past forty years.

Nor could Lamprey build around the old house. Apart from the fact that doing this would spoil the look of the thing as envisaged by his tame architect, who had come up with as ravishing a site plan and scaled-down model as Lamprey had

'I'm not selling,' he said without looking up. His voice was like the rustle of dry leaves.

ever paid out £2500 for, a further complication had arisen when Farquaharson had pointed out that his home was protected by the time-hallowed Law of Ancient Lights.

What this meant, in essence, was that if a house or dwelling place was so protected, no one could erect a building next to it that was higher by even so much as a brick.

Lamprey's lawyers had checked this out. Their report made gloomy reading. Antiquated as it was, the law still held. It had stood the test of time. It was, in short, entirely legal.

In front, the chauffeur half turned his head.

'We're here, Mr Lamprey.'

'I can see that, you idiot!' snapped Lamprey.

He was out of the car even before it had rolled to a stop, and started to stride across the dusty pavement. To his left lay the site, an unlovely expanse of waste ground that, in his hands, could be transformed into a gold mine. He clenched his teeth.

In front of him was Farquaharson's house, the ground floor frontage having two bow windows stuffed with old books. Near to the roof, to one side, was a cracked and weather-beaten wooden board with the words 'Ancient Lights' on it, painted in faded characters. Lamprey winced.

He banged open the shop door and glared at the old man behind the counter. Mr Farquaharson was slowly turning the old and crackling pages of a massive leather-bound tome that took up most of the counter space.

'I'm not selling,' he said without looking up. His voice was like the rustle of dry leaves.

Farquaharson was not merely old, he was ancient. He was certainly in his eighties, possibly in his nineties. There were times when Lamprey got the strong impression that the man was as old as the house he was living in.

Suddenly, Farquaharson banged the hefty tome shut with a thump that shook the counter.

'A notable rarity,' he said with satisfaction. 'A book I have been seeking for . . .' he cackled softly '. . . a very long time indeed. Turville's *Discourse on the Arte and Theorie of Practickal Magick.* The pirated edition, of course, printed in Leipzig in 1693. Nevertheless, still worth a great deal. And not only money . . .'

Strange things were said about Mr Farquaharson. It was suggested that he had the gift of the Evil Eye. It was hinted that he was no stranger to ancient and forbidden rituals. It was whispered that magic, to him, was no mere Music Hall act.

Sydney Arthur Lamprey banged his fist down on the counter. All that was rubbish! This was the twentieth century, for Heaven's sake!

'Now look, you doddering old fossil . . .!'

Mr Farquaharson did look. He gazed at Lamprey with eyes that were dark and piercing.

'I'm not selling,' he said crisply. 'What I suggest, Mr Lamprey, is that you turn the site into a *pleasance*, a city garden full of trees and roses and flowering shrubs, with seats and benches and areas of lawn. There's too much concrete round here as it is.'

'You must be out of your mind!' yapped Lamprey. 'I'll get you out . . .!'

'You can't. I'm not selling,' repeated Farquaharson. 'And you can't build round me, either. I have the Right of Ancient Lights, and as your lawyers will by now have informed you, no building can be erected next to mine that is higher by an inch, or so placed that its shadow cuts off my sunlight.'

'Ancient Lights!' barked Lamprey. 'Before you poked your nose in, I'd never even heard of these blasted Ancient Lights!'

Mr Farquaharson formed a steeple with his long, skinny fingers and gazed up at the cobwebby ceiling.

'I dare swear, Mr Lamprey,' he said, almost as though he

were a judge passing sentence, 'that the time will come when they will force themselves even more vividly upon your consciousness. And sooner than you may imagine . . .'

Sydney Arthur Lamprey stared at a view that was as bleak as his thoughts. Spring had not yet arrived fully in Suffolk, and the mud flats were bare and grey. The North Sea was even greyer as it rolled and whispered half a mile away.

It being Friday, and Lamprey being in no mood to return to the office, he had booted his chauffeur out of the car and driven straight down to his weekend cottage on the coast south of Aldeburgh.

It was a lonely spot, especially as the light grew steely in the falling dusk and the mournful cries of duck and wild fowl were the only sounds to be heard. But at times, like now, it suited him precisely because of this.

He stumped along the top of a high-sided channel that carried a mill-race of a stream hurtling towards the open sea. Above, in the vast acreage of sky, now darkening swiftly, wheeled flocks of spidery dunlin, curlews, teal, and red shanks giving out their harsh, distinctive alarm calls. To Lamprey, they were just damned birds, making a devil of a row.

For some unaccountable reason, the old man's parting words had unsettled him. It was almost as though they had been a warning.

He shrugged irritably. There was no way of getting Farquaharson out, other than by putting a bomb under him. And violence was not to be resorted to for the very simple reason that he would be the prime suspect if anything untoward should happen to the old codger.

As he thought this, he became aware of a group of small flashing stars to his left, bright pinpoints of light that pulsed and flared in the gloom. He turned to look, narrowing his eyes.

There they were again, possibly 100 metres away, hovering in the air. Fireflies of some kind, he thought.

He began to move towards them curiously, but instantly they, too, began to move, shooting swiftly away from him at an angle. He started to run – and immediately sank into the mud up to his ankles.

He cursed and sloshed onwards, following the lights, which had now assumed a wedge-shaped formation, rather like a flying V. They flashed and sparkled like jewels caught by the sun, although that was hardly a fitting simile in this gathering darkness.

He tripped on a grass tussock and fell, splashing on hands and knees in the ooze. The glittering stars wheeled and swooped around his head.

Lamprey tried to grab at them, but they were always just out of reach. He shouted in frustration. The tiny lights hurtled off, then stopped in mid-air, a hazy cloud of twinkling stars just a few yards away. He scrambled to his feet, by now boiling with rage. He lunged at the lights, and then gave a startled cry as his feet met . . . not solid ground, but empty air.

Somehow, he'd come round in a circle and had fallen into the gully that carried one of the many rushing streams towards the sea. The water was icy cold – the shock of it was numbing. The current seemed to grip him like a vice; seemed, indeed, actually to be pulling him *downwards*, as well as along. His screams were cut off as he gagged on water and went under. Then he was struggling upwards, gulping for air, and trying to yell as loud as he could.

Just as his struggles were becoming feebler and despair was making him grow passive, something clutched at his arm. It heaved at him and tugged him cross-current and up out of the water, on to the slime of the bank.

Sydney Arthur Lamprey felt like a landed fish.

There were lights above him, but not those devilish fireflies that had almost lured him to his doom. There were torches, farm lamps held by roughly dressed, stocky men in waders and oilskins. Wild fowlers!

'You'll be all right, mister,' grunted one. 'Soaking's all you've had. Good fire and a hot rum'll put you on your feet again.'

'The . . . the lights . . .' gasped Lamprey.

One of the men pulled him to his feet, chuckling darkly.

'The pixies have been after him, lads, them ole ancient lights!'

Heart thudding, Lamprey gaped at him.

'What did you say?' he whispered hoarsely.

'What us round here do call the ancient lights, mister. 'Orrible bad for the revenue men in the old days were the ancient lights. Sent 'em every which-away when our lads were a-landing baccy an' silks an' brandy from the Dutchies an' Frenchies. Been quite a few whose last sight on earth were them ole ancient lights . . .'

Half-an-hour later, safe and snug and warm in his cottage with blankets round him and a glass in one hand, Sydney Arthur Lamprey was on the telephone.

'You *deaf*, Sliggers?' he was bawling. 'I said *cancel* the Bell Street scheme – and get Levison to draw up plans for a city garden! Shrubs, trees, benches, bit of grass! . . . Yes, of course I'm all right, you drivelling oaf! And tell him I want those plans on Monday – *without fail!*'

THE EAGLE

by June Williams

He had been working far too hard and for too long without a break in a tough job, and finally it had happened. A nervous breakdown. Or, at least, the beginning of one. 'It's nothing serious,' his doctor had told him. 'But it will be, if you carry on the way you have been. What you must do is to take a holiday. A long one – away from it all.' He had not wanted to do this, but his company had insisted. 'You're a valuable man,' his Managing Director had said. 'And we shall miss you while you are away. But better to have you away for a month or so, than forever.'

'Perhaps just for a few days,' he had murmured.

'No, Peter. You must go away for at least two months.' The tone had been gentle enough, but there had been a look in those hard blue eyes that had told him that to argue any further would have been unwise. A paternalistic arm around his shoulder had guided him to the door. 'Now go away and rest.'

That same evening he had begun to look for a cottage that he could rent on a short let. He found it almost at once, advertised in one of the national newspapers. 'For rent – a delightful cottage in Cumbria,' the advertisement had said, 'set in idyllic surroundings. An ideal rustic retreat for someone who wishes to escape from the stresses of modern day living.'

Which is how Peter Stannard came to arrive at Eagle Cottage one late afternoon.

Paying off the taxi driver who had brought him from the tiny country station some twenty minutes' drive away, Stannard watched him leave before turning to take a good look at the cottage. For a few moments, he wondered if he had been brought to the wrong address. The garden was a wilderness, with a few over-blown roses struggling to exist amongst a tangle of weeds and waist-high grass. Beyond it stood the cottage, presenting to the world a depressing vista of flaking paintwork, grimy windows and walls covered with dusty ivy. The advertisement had been misleading, to say the least of it.

It's not important, he told himself. You are here to rest. To read a great deal and to take quiet country walks, with the occasional visit to the local pub to exchange a few words with the natives. Nothing else matters as long as the house is reasonably clean and comfortable and has hot and cold water. He pushed at the gate which unwillingly gave way to his hand.

Using the key the agent had sent him, he opened the front door and stepped inside. Apart from a faint smell of damp, the interior of the house was more re-assuring. The furniture was of the sort one normally finds in rented property, cheap and cheerful and not too comfortable looking. But it was new, as were the carpets. The recessed bookshelves, he noted with approval, were full of books. When a closer inspection revealed that most of them were text books dealing with the rearing and habits of eagles, he was not greatly disappointed. One of the two suitcases he had left in the hallway was crammed with books.

The books on the shelves, however, had answered one question for him – the reason why the house had been called Eagle Cottage. Obviously its owner was something of an authority on eagles, and had, indeed, probably owned one.

Upstairs there were three bedrooms, one of them looking

across an uninterrupted view of green fields, with mountains in the far distance as a backcloth. It was this one he chose for his bedroom.

Going downstairs again, he found the groceries he had ordered waiting for him in an outhouse. As he unpacked them slowly in the kitchen, he became conscious for the first time of how quiet the house was. Normally surrounded by the constant clatter of a telex machine in the day, and the sound of traffic going by his flat at night, he found the silence slightly unnerving. Whistling loudly, he put the groceries away and then went off to unpack his bags. He put his clothes away, after which he stacked his books in a neat pile beside the most comfortable-looking chair in the lounge. What do I do now? he asked himself. A brisk walk to work up an appetite, he decided. Then a quick fry-up of bacon and eggs before settling down with a book for the evening.

He did not enjoy his walk. Perhaps it was because, like a few people who live and work in big cities, he had always found something rather sinister about the countryside. As he wandered down a country lane, pestered by flies all the way, large black crows silently circled the sky above him, while the undergrowth around him rustled constantly with the sound of unseen creatures. To say that he fled back to the house would be an exaggeration, but his pace was certainly a hurried one as he made his way back to the cottage. Once there, he closed the door on himself with something like relief.

In the evening, with a scratch meal out of the way, he prepared to settle down and read. Turning on the portable radio he had brought with him, and finding some background music, he debated whether to start on Tolstoy's *War and Peace*, a massive work which he had been waiting to read for years, or to indulge himself with a thriller. In the end, he began browsing through one of the books on the shelves, a slender volume titled *A Handbook on the Golden Eagle – The King of Birds*. 'His Majesty, the Golden Eagle,' it began, 'is capable of carrying off hares and foxes, and has even been known to kill a deer calf. Its terrible beak will make short work of a lamb. Obviously, therefore, any human approaching it, should treat it with extreme caution.'

Stannard read a few more paragraphs and then put it aside, deciding that the subject was of no particular interest to him. Reaching for *War and Peace*, he read until eleven o'clock, went to his bedroom, and slept soundly.

The next three days and nights passed uneventfully. He tried, without much success, to bring some sort of order to the front garden, paid a visit to the nearby market town, and did some shopping at the local store, but otherwise kept himself very much to himself.

On the fourth night, the eagle arrived.

He was in a deep sleep when he was awakened by the sound of something tapping sharply against his bedroom window. Still only half awake, he lay there in the darkness, trying to identify the sound. He was unable to do so until the insistent tapping was joined by another sound, which he recognised immediately as the flapping of a bird's wings. Assuming that it had come down the chimney and was now trying to get out of the room, he sat up and switched on the bedside light, only to shrink back into his pillows with a gasp of horror. From the other side of the window pane, a pair of glowing yellow orbs regarded him balefully. In the same instant, he had an eerily fleeting impression of a pair of outstretched wings – and then whatever it was outside was gone.

Allowing his racing heart to quieten, he finally ventured from his bed and went over to the window. He could see nothing at first, and then it appeared, silhouetted against a full moon as it circled slowly in a series of descending arcs before disappearing into the darkness beyond the edge of the moon.

Still a little shaken by the experience, he made his way back to bed and turned off the light. Although he knew very little about birds, he knew enough to recognise that what he had seen was an eagle of some sort.

The next morning, when he awoke and recalled the visitation he had received in the night, the whole business seemed so unlikely that he could hardly believe that it had happened. Eagles, he knew, shunned human beings. So what would it be doing here? He toyed with the possibility that it had belonged to the owner of the house, and was merely returning home. This idea he dismissed immediately. Once it had escaped or had been set free, it would never have returned. He found the whole business most disturbing, and something he could well do without in his state of mind. He was consoled, however, by the thought that it was most unlikely that the eagle would ever return again.

In this, he was very much mistaken.

The eagle came back again the next night in the early hours. This time it did not fly away as soon as he switched on the light. Instead, it remained perched on the window sill, its wings half outstretched, regarding him with mesmerising, unblinking eyes. For what seemed for ever, but must have been no more than a minute or so, they stared at each other across the room. Then abruptly the bird took off and disappeared into the night.

Needless to say, Stannard did not sleep very well for the rest of that night.

The next day at noon, he took himself for the first time to the local inn. He had decided to go there for two reasons. Firstly, his self-imposed solitude was beginning to get on his nerves, and secondly, he hoped he might meet someone who knew something about the eagle. If he learned that it was in

The eagle came back the next night in the early hours. It remained perched on the window-sill, regarding him with mesmerizing, unblinking eyes.

the habit of visiting other people in the area, he would at least know that he was not being singled out for its unwelcome attentions. If the truth were known, that second visit had frightened him. There had been an expression in the eagle's eyes which he had recognised as being one of sheer hatred.

He found the inn easily enough. It was a few miles down the road, a rather tumbledown building with a small sign that made it obvious it catered for the locals rather than passing motorists. He lifted the latch of the single door leading into the inn and found himself in a large tap room, where a dozen or so of the locals were drinking and talking amongst themselves. Conscious that everyone was watching him, he made his way to the counter, where his presence was acknowledged by a curt nod from the landlord. Ordering himself a pint of beer, he watched the landlord pulling it from the tap. 'My name is Peter Stannard,' he said. 'I'm the new tenant at Eagle Cottage.'

The landlord nodded. 'We heard that someone had taken it. How are you finding it up there?'

'Quiet, but it suits me well enough.' Deciding that it was too soon to bring up the subject of the eagle, he took his beer and sipped at it for a few moments. Then he asked casually: 'I suppose you know the owner?'

'I did,' the landlord said shortly. 'Not that he ever put a foot in this place.'

I'm not surprised, Stannard thought to himself, looking around at the smoke-stained walls without a single picture. 'You mean he was something of a recluse?'

'It wasn't that.' The landlord put Stannard's money in the till. 'He didn't come here because he knew that he wouldn't be welcome.'

'Why was that, if I may ask?'

'It's not for me to speak ill of the dead,' the landlord said. He drifted off to serve a customer at the other end of the bar and afterwards stayed there, making it quite clear that he had no wish to continue the conversation. Stannard had no intention of being shut up so easily.

'May I ask you something?' he called out.

The landlord reluctantly returned. 'Yes?'

'I've been visited by an eagle twice,' he announced. 'I wondered if you had seen it around yourself.'

The landlord stared at him. Behind them, the tap room had become silent. 'No,' he said finally. 'It wouldn't be natural for one to come down here.'

'Natural or not,' Stannard said. 'I've seen it.' He changed the subject abruptly. 'Tell me about the owner of the cottage. Why did he give it that name? I see there are a lot of books around the house on the subject of eagles. Did he own one himself?'

'Yes,' the landlord admitted. 'He caught it up in the mountains and brought it home. A golden eagle.'

Aware that everyone in the tap room was now listening to their conversation, Stannard said: 'You mentioned something about the owner not being too popular around these parts. Was it because of the eagle?'

The landlord nodded. 'That's right. It was because of the eagle. He kept it in a large cage. He was bent on taming it, you see. When he found he couldn't, he started ill treating it–so much so that it came to hate all humans. I had to deliver some crates of beer to the cottage, and I tell you that bird scared the living daylights out of me.' He wiped the counter with a cloth. 'If ever a man asked for trouble, he did, treating that bird like that.'

'What happened to him?'

'He was killed,' the landlord said. 'The eagle eventually turned on him and tore him to pieces.'

Stannard looked at him, stunned. 'What happened to the eagle?'

'It flew away when they found the body.' The landlord gave him a faintly apologetic smile. 'I didn't really want to tell you all this, you living at the cottage, and all that . . .'

'It's all right,' Stannard said. It was, of course, far from being all right. Listening to the landlord, he had felt his stomach beginning to tighten with fear. But he persisted. 'Who owns the house now?'

'It was unoccupied for years,' the landlord said. 'It was inherited by a married daughter, but she could never bring herself to visit the place after what had happened there. She died quite recently and it went to a nephew who decided to rent it out. You're the first tenant he's had.'

'That eagle I've seen around the place,' Stannard said slowly. 'It must be the one that escaped.'

'Impossible,' the landlord said, fixing him with a steady gaze. 'All that happened donkey's years ago. That eagle would be dead now!'

When he left the inn, Stannard had already made up his mind what he was going to do, which was to pack his bags and return to London by the next train. Later, when he had calmed down a little, he allowed logic to prevail. What we have here, he told himself, is not some ill-used eagle coming back to the scene of torture with murder still in its heart, but merely an eagle that probably had flown down from the mountains for no other reason than a search for food. It was both annoying and somewhat disturbing, but he should not flee from it. Indeed, why should he lose the two months' rent he had paid in advance? He would stick it out for a while.

The night brought only uninterrupted sleep. When this happened for several more nights in succession, Stannard was convinced that he had seen the last of the eagle. When a month had passed, he had almost forgotten the whole affair. That was, until he had the nightmare that coincided with the return of a full moon.

In his dream, he awoke to find the eagle in his room, sensed rather than actually seen, which made the horror of it even worse. Flinging himself from his bed, he ran blindly around the room, cannoning into furniture at every turn, pursued all the while by the sound of beating wings. Then he was lying on the floor with the eagle perched on him, its foul breath filling his nostrils with the stench of carrion flesh. He screamed endlessly, but no sound came. Then the eagle took a firmer hold on him and its beak began to rise and fall. It was then the terrible pain began . . .

At that point, he mercifully awoke. He switched on the light and sat there, wiping the perspiration from his face. Then he went down and made himself a cup of tea. Sitting at the kitchen table, nursing his cup in his hands, he said half aloud: 'You can't stay here. You must go home as soon as possible.' Not because the nightmare had given him any sense of impending danger, but rather because it had brought home to him that the eagle had been preying on his mind far more than he had realised. I'll go tomorrow, he told himself.

But the next day was a Sunday when no trains ran, and he had to content himself with pottering around the cottage and finishing off *War and Peace*. When it was time to go to bed, he took one of the sleeping tablets the doctor had given him, and had no trouble in going off to sleep.

As expected, he slept heavily. But the tablet was still not sufficient to prevent him from being awakened by a faint breeze on his face. Realising that he had unintentionally left the window open, he rose to shut it – only to fall back with a low scream of terror as he became aware that the whole of the open window was filled with a pair of outstretched wings. Rooted to where he stood, he watched the eagle as it launched itself from the sill and flew towards him.

The rest of what was about to happen, he knew from his nightmare . . .

DEVIL'S ISLAND

by John Sanders

As the gaunt, black-coated figure came round the corner of the harbour wall, his three-cornered felt hat pulled low over his face to mask his eyes, young Harry Meadows felt an involuntary chill of fear stab his heart.

Harry was fifteen now, and by the standards of Key Point Cove, where he had lived all his life, he was a man. But he still felt that life-long chill of fear when, each day, he saw the black coat and the shaded, lean yellow face that topped the striding figure of terrible Captain Kerr.

The young lad would tell you that it was what you *couldn't* see that made Kerr seem so sinister. No one ever saw his eyes. Under their shadow, a long, shining scar ran from the corner of his mouth to his right ear. Popular legend said that Kerr had fought with the great Nelson in the Battle of Copenhagen, and had been cut on the face with a Frenchman's sabre.

Parson Meagan was the only one to scoff at that. The only battles Kerr had ever fought, declared the parson, were under the Jolly Roger. The only men Kerr had ever killed were innocent English seamen. The parson was the only man at Key Point Cove who ever spoke out against Kerr. Everyone else was silent. Truth to tell, everyone else was secretly as much in fear of Kerr as Harry was. Most of the fisher-folk at Key Point agreed that the man was wholly evil. As the parson said, he was the Devil in person.

When Kerr came down the harbour wall every morning,

seven days a week, anxious mothers called their children and disappeared with them into their cottages. The fishermen stopped their chatter and leaned over their net-mending, and even the gulls seemed to stop squawking.

Through this unearthly silence, Captain Kerr strode like a messenger of Satan. He looked with interest upon the catch of each fisherman, seeming to make mental notes of each one's value. No one spoke to him, and he spoke to no one. But as regularly as clockwork, each time he passed by old Don Savage, that crazy old seadog-turned-fisherman looked up from his net-mending with his wild eyes, spat into the water, and seemed to incline his head in a hidden bow.

Was it mockery? Or was it respect from an old rogue for an evil blackguard? Dan Savage wasn't telling, for he was a deaf-mute.

Only when Captain Kerr had disappeared like a phantom round the far corner of the harbour wall did the bustle and noise return to Key Point Cove, and the sun seemed to shine again.

Captain Kerr did not live in the village. Each morning, after the last fishing boat had come back from its night's work, he sailed over from Stark Island, where he lived alone. That in itself, the wiser fishermen whispered, was a feat of seamanship. For the fishermen kept clear of the tide race between the headland and Stark Island which, for no reason, could change and whirl like a creature in torment and swallow up a boat in an instant.

Stark Island, guarded by rough rocks and treacherous currents, was fit for no one to live on – except a man like Captain Kerr.

Strangely, Harry had probably sailed closer to Stark Island than anyone else in the village. For despite his youth, Harry had inherited all his family's feel for the winds and the tides. He sailed his father's cutter like a veteran while old

Matt Meadows slept off his night's work. He knew each crag, each point, each rock along the Key Point coast, and his memory for what was where in all the seasons surprised and delighted the fishermen. That included even those who had sailed with the great Lord Nelson against the French, and even Jud Wright, who had once been a Solent pilot.

Now, as Harry watched the thin, haunting figure of Captain Kerr coming down the harbour wall, he felt more than a chill of fear. He felt a great surging tide of hate welling within him.

That morning Harry's father had told him that he was now old enough to take his place in the family boat and earn his living. 'You can start with us tomorrow night, laddie,' old Matt said, with just a touch of fatherly pride in his voice.

Harry's face brightened. He had known this moment was close. 'And do I get a share of the boat, father?'

Matt Meadows turned to his son in astonishment. 'A share of the boat?' His brow knitted in bewilderment. 'A share of the boat? Ah, I suppose you picked up that idea in the schoolroom?' The old man thought for a moment, then sat down heavily.

'There's something else you're old enough to know, laddie,' he said at last. 'Captain Kerr owns this village. He owns every man in it, bar the parson. He owns the cottages, the boats, the fishermen and all the fish we catch. He gives us back just enough to live on. No one has a share of anything. Captain Kerr has it all.'

It was then, for the first time in his life, that Harry Meadows understood the evil presence of Captain Kerr at Key Point Cove, his daily visits to the village and the shadow he cast over it. Furious and frustrated, he stormed from the cottage down to the harbour, just in time to see the evil figure coming round the harbour wall . . .

Harry stood there mute and trembling, rage ebbing and flowing in him with all the force of a spring tide. There was nothing he could do. If he were to argue with Kerr, his father would surely suffer and nothing would be gained by it. The Captain bore down upon him with all the importance of a three-master making for port. He drew level, sniffed sideways and scornfully at a catch, and passed on.

The next night was Harry's first in the ranks of the professional fishermen.

A strange boat was an unusual sight in Key Point Cove, for it wasn't the sort of place that brought visitors. So when, a week later, the day dawned on the pretty sight of a new schooner at anchor under the lee of the headland, a buzz of interest went round the fishing village.

The schooner's crew, three swarthy men, could be clearly seen from the harbour wall, furling the sails and lowering a boat. A knot of fishermen unloading their night's work eyed them as they came ashore. When the fishermen thought that the three strangers might be settled in the Harbour Tavern, they reminded each other of their raging thirst and began to drift in that direction, too.

Strangers! Now that was something to talk about in Key Point Cove . . .

The three men eyed the local fishermen across their ale pots and sized up the situation. After a long silence the tallest of them, a thin, cadaverous fellow, addressed the gathering of locals:

'We're looking for someone who knows the waters hereabouts better than any other man.'

'Why, that'll be Matt Meadows' lad, young Harry,' Jem Shipley said at once.

The fishermen looked round at Harry, standing at the back of them and trying to look unconcerned.

'Come forward, then, young Harry!' barked the tall stranger.

Harry stood his ground. There was nothing at all he liked about the man. Something in his bearing, his great height, his arrogant manner, reminded him vaguely of the hated Captain Kerr.

'What is it you want?' he growled back.

The tall man cackled, and his two companions cackled after him in unison.

'We want a pilot to Stark Island, boy, and we'll pay you well!'

A ripple of excitement spread round the tavern bar. Stark Island! No one went there – no one except Captain Kerr. What business could these three seafarers have with the dreaded captain?

Harry didn't know, but he was in no mind to help them. He had taken an instant dislike to all three. For the first time in his life he felt on the side of Captain Kerr or, at least, against these three strangers.

'I've no wish to sail to Stark Island,' he said sullenly.

The tall man sneered. 'And you've no wish to make yourself rich, I'll be bound,' he said. 'Well, then, who's next? Who's good enough in these waters to pilot our schooner to Stark Island and earn a handsome bounty for doing it?'

'Jud Wright! Aye, Jud Wright!' chanted the fishermen. Self-consciously, the former Solent pilot shuffled forward. His eyes glinted as the tall man swung a bag of gold from his pocket to the top of the bar counter.

'Jud Wright!' exclaimed the tall man, leaning forward with an evil leer. 'You've got yourself a job. We'll sail on the noon tide tomorrow.'

All that day Harry warily watched the anchored schooner as he worked on his nets. He was filled with unexplained disquiet. A dozen times he asked himself, should he have taken the job? His family could well do with the money. But there was something unpleasant about the tall man and his

'We want a pilot to Stark Island, boy, and we'll pay you well!'
A ripple of excitement spread round the tavern bar.

two companions, something that suggested evil . . .

That night the wind came up and the lowering clouds scuppered up the sea, making heavy work for the fishermen. By dawn, when they turned the helm wearily for Key Point Cove, the sky was made of lead, the sea churned angrily, and the men had to shout to make themselves heard above the whine of the wind in the wire rigging.

'There's a storm coming up from the south-west!' cried Harry's father. Harry looked at the scowling sky and thought grimly of the three strangers and the task that awaited their pilot.

That morning the storm came up and beat the waves against the harbour wall. The fishermen at their net-mending were forced to decamp to the shelter of a nearby gun turret. At midday, Harry watched Wright prepare his boat, embark his three passengers, and row like a bobbing cork to the anchored schooner. He watched the four men climb gingerly aboard and raise a single sail – sufficient canvas to send the schooner into the wind like a bullet.

Harry pursed his lips. He looked up at the ugly sky and back at the thudding waves. He had a feeling that Wright's chances of making Stark Island in that rising sea were very slim indeed. With no further thought, Harry ran to his father's cutter. He slipped the painter and hoisted the mainsail. It was a day for three reefs but he took in only one; he had to risk as much canvas as she could carry. The cutter beat out of the harbour and rode like a cork close to the wind. In a trice, Harry was drenched to the skin with spray.

Eyes narrowed against the stinging salt, he took the helm firmly, luffing before the squalls, paying away as the wind dropped to gather its breath, nosing his way forward, holding it steady as the boat was lifted in the air and shaken like a rat by a dog. Clear of the harbour and in the open, tossing sea, he searched for the schooner. But already Wright and his three companions were beyond vision, screened by the curtain of salt spray.

The cutter lifted, then scudded into a pit of foam, almost flattened by a squall. Harry decided to run for the northern end of the island, the only place where a landing was possible. There he might stand off in the hope of seeing the schooner.

The wind dropped suddenly and it began to rain, flattening the waves. Harry paid away until the wind was just aft of the beam; then he slackened off the mainsail and settled down to a long, steady reach. The rain became a blanket of fine mist and Harry began to feel nervous. He knew that the island he could not see would soon be upon him.

Cautiously he crawled forward to the bows, trying to listen for the breaking of waves or the roaring of the race which would indicate that Stark Island was near. Then, over his shoulder, he saw a thin, grey outline forming through a gap in the mist at the port quarter. He knew the shape at once. It was the island, and he was close to its northern point. If the weather had not cleared for that one brief instant, he would have missed it altogether.

The rain stopped, but the mist stayed in great banks. Anxiously, Harry peered into it as he brought the cutter round on a new course. There was not as much as a speck that resembled Jud Wright's schooner.

Bearing down on the island, he decided to abandon his plan to drop anchor and stand off. If the schooner was anywhere, it must be anchored at some unseen cove beyond the rocks. Ahead of him through the mist curtain he could occasionally see a break in the rocks. Was there an anchorage within? It was impossible to tell, impossible to know whether the break led on to a cove or merely to an inlet. He could see the waves crashing on to the rocks, and then he was close enough to hear them, close enough to have to decide at once either to drop sail and anchor, or go on into the break and risk crashing on to the jagged teeth . . .

Suddenly the cutter was in broken water. The noise of the waves and the swirling sea was instantly deafening. Blinded by spray, Harry felt his heart pumping madly. He knew he was trying to run into a lee anchorage, almost certainly trying the impossible.

What happened next was a series of events that were telescoped into a second or two. Harry looked up and saw a hole in the mist. Through the hole the silent, stock-still figure of Captain Kerr could be seen, standing on the rocks like some legendary sea phantom. Harry cried out in shock. Then the sea took over. The jib filled violently and flew across to starboard with a crack like a pistol shot, knocking him against the shrouds. The mainsail followed the jib, tore through the weather runner and beat in tatters against the sea. The mast, strained too far, came crashing down, bringing all the rigging with it. The cockpit filled like a bottle, and the cutter turned without a struggle on its side, into the sea.

Carried beneath it, Harry felt the weight of water engulf him and began swimming desperately upwards towards the light. As his head broke the surface of the yellow water, the wreck was all about him. He was aware of a noosed rope lying between two spars and instinctively he grabbed it, dropping the noose over his head until it reached his waist. The rope, guided by an unseen hand, tightened and pulled Harry like a drowned rat across the shallows on to the rocks, out of the swirling sea. As he staggered up the narrow beach, he could see the end of the rope a few yards ahead of him. The hands of Captain Kerr held it.

Harry tried to hold back, but the rope, pulled with incredible strength, drew him onwards. He could now see the evil, yellow face of the hated captain, the vivid scar from ear to mouth, the shadow across the unseen eyes. Then all his strength was spent and he fell unconscious on a patch of sand.

Harry's eyes flickered. He was aware at once of half a dozen images. He was on a bed in a dark room. His drenched clothes were gone. There was a curtainless window and, beyond it, a night of stars. He lay still, scarcely breathing, wondering if he was injured, considering how much time must have passed.

Cautiously he raised himself from the bed. The pale outline of a table was visible in the darkness on his right side, and he could see a candle and some tinder on it. He struck the tinder and the candlelight illuminated the room, throwing long shadows into its corners. He peered into the gloom. Then, drawn by a pile of what seemed to be rough blankets in the far corner, swung his legs off the bed and carried the candlelight to investigate.

What Harry saw then struck a chill of fear right to the depths of his bones. Protruding from the blankets was a human leg, then another, then two white veined hands, all grotesquely deformed. Shaking, he flung off the wraps, and stepped back with a strangled cry of horror.

On the floor before him lay the bodies of four men. One glance was enough to tell him they were Jud Wright and his three companions from the schooner.

Harry fell back in disbelief at the ghoulish sight and, panic-stricken, reached for the door. It was locked, and held fast. Instinctively he turned towards the window, but it was heavily barred. There was no escape. Desperately he looked for some weapon, some means to break out of the bedroom prison. Then he heard it – a steady footfall coming down the corridor outside. Slowly he backed on to the wall farthest from the door . . .

The footfall stopped outside and Harry heard a creak and a bolt drawn back. Then the handle of the door was turning to open. In the next moment, the sinister figure of Captain

Kerr stood framed in the dark, open rectangle. In one hand Kerr held a pistol, cocked and ready to fire. In the other, he held a spade.

Harry stared at the black figure, nerves screaming, waiting. Suddenly Kerr motioned with the spade towards the four corpses. 'Bring them out one by one and follow me,' he said. 'You will dig their graves and bury them.'

With a start, Harry realised that this was the first time he had ever heard Captain Kerr speak.

Harry Meadows thought that the next two hours would never end. Laboriously, with an occasional prod from Kerr's pistol, he dragged the corpses out into the night, one after the other, and dug one large grave for them all in the soft, sandy soil. There was Jud Wright, grinning toothlessly and horribly in death; the tall man's two companions, staring sightlessly up at the night sky; then the tall, cadaverous man, with his vague resemblance to Captain Kerr, who only the day before had offered Harry a bag of gold to make the fatal trip to Stark Island.

'You've done yourself a good night's work of killing here, Captain Kerr!' Harry muttered angrily. 'But the hangman will get you for it.' The captain stiffened and waved his pistol. 'I didn't kill them,' he said. 'They came from the mainland to search me out and kill *me*, as I always knew they would one day. The storm caught them. They must have missed the island. It's easy to miss when the rain comes down like that. And they must have run aground on the northern rocks. They were drowned. Their bodies were washed up on this beach only two hours ago.'

A wave of relief tinged with unease came over Harry Meadows. He paused over his gruesome task, leaned on the spade and looked questioningly at Captain Kerr. 'Why should they want to kill you?' he asked.

'For the same reason that you do,' replied the Captain.

'I don't want to kill you. I came here because these three men asked Jud Wright to pilot their schooner here, and I knew they wouldn't make it in that storm. I came here to help them out of trouble, specially Jud.'

'I see.' Slowly Captain Kerr lowered his pistol. 'Then perhaps there has been some misunderstanding as far as you are concerned.' For a brief moment Kerr looked up from under his cocked hat, and for the first time, Harry saw his eyes. 'If you wish me no harm, then I'm sorry to have suspected you and treated you harshly.'

'I shouldn't worry about that too much,' Harry said. He felt much more relieved than he sounded. He looked down at the half-dug grave and his brow furrowed. 'You still haven't explained why these three men should want to kill you.'

For answer Kerr stabbed his foot at the sprawling corpse of the tall man, and when he spoke, his voice was heavy with emotion. 'This one was my brother,' he said. 'We sailed together against the French in the days of the great Lord Nelson. We had a crew of brave men, I can tell you. One of them was Dan Savage, the deaf-mute who's a fisherman today at Key Point Cove. I took a French warship as a prize in the Battle of Copenhagen, and it turned out to be carrying a hoard of gold. The government gave me half the money, and that made me passing rich. After that, my brother never stopped tormenting me, following me everywhere with his ceaseless demands. All my life he has been the rock around my neck, always seeking more and more money, everything I had, threatening, always threatening. I had to get more and more money from the village fishermen just to pay his never-ending debts. Finally, I refused to pay him any more. I knew he would come for revenge. And now he is dead. I have paid his last debt. Now the fishermen can have their boats and cottages back. Now the future is theirs.'

Harry looked in astonishment at the tortured Captain.

Could it really be that this terrible man was really human, that the fates had been cruel to him? Could it be that all the hatred he had earned from the fishing families at Key Point Cove was horribly unjust? And that the reason for it all was his own brother, now lying dead at his feet?

Harry Meadows pushed the spade into the sandy soil and, stepping forward, he did something he never in his life dreamed he would do. He put his hand gently on Captain Kerr's arm.

'I'm sorry, Captain,' he said. 'I'm sorry.'

SEA MIST

by Angus Allan

'NOW, RODDY, YOU KNOW THE RULES. You can look at it, but you can't sail it until tomorrow. Tomorrow's your birthday, not today.'

'Aww, but Mum! There's just the right sort of breeze, and it's only a few hours!' Roddy Lane, touching fourteen, tore his eyes away from the spanking new dinghy with its red and blue paint, its mast already stepped, its glistening white painter just begging to be untied, and looked pleadingly at Winnie, her florid country face mirroring his own pleasure. 'Please, Mum! *Please*!'

'No son. And that's final. Besides, the forecast says there's mist on the way, despite the sun burning our backs off, so there.'

'Dad . .?' Roddy turned hopefully towards Geordie Lane, the quiet man who'd lived on the banks of Sandway Creek all his life, who'd taught Roddy every single thing he knew about handling a boat, fishing, digging for bait and a hundred more skills besides. 'Come on, Dad! You come, too.'

'No, boy,' said Geordie, giving his old, slow smile. 'Launch day's tomorrow, like your ma says. The best things in life always wait for you, as you'll find out. And they're the better for that waiting, believe you me.'

Roddy laughed. He wasn't the sort to worry about a refusal. 'I *do* believe you, Dad,' he said. Involuntarily, he threw himself at the man, hugged him, and then did the same for Winnie. 'Thanks a million for the boat! It's a cracker!' He threw up a creditable naval salute. 'Captain Roddy Lane acknowledges command of this vessel,' he said, importantly. 'A fine, sea-worthy ship, which I now name *Curlew*!'

'Straighten your fingers out, young man,' barked Geordie, grinning. He'd been a Chief Petty Officer in Her Majesty's Navy, and wasn't about to forget it. 'Call that a salute? Bah! Twenty lashes an' ten days without rum!'

'*Curlew*,' said Roddy again, after he'd reassembled his fingers to Geordie's satisfaction. 'We'll have some adventures, you and I. We'll ply the coast. We'll sail the seven seas! Maybe, I'll get Mum to make a skull and crossbones, and we'll pirate our way from the Tyne to the Humber, preying on merchantmen.'

'You daft ha'porth,' said Winnie. 'Come back and have your tea, do. Pirates! I've never heard the like!'

In the small coastal house where he'd been brought up, well outside the limits of the nearest village, Roddy tucked into bread and jam, strong tea (he called it 'seafaring' tea) and Winnie's unequalled scones. A solitary boy, used to biking to the distant school, he was full of imagination, and counted his friends as the estuary birds, the very banks, bars and rocks that made up his environment. Always the loner, he could happily spend his time dreaming daydreams and imagining himself in a thousand-and-one unlikely situations. He was eating his third scone, imagining it was his last, scooped from his pack as a prisoner of Turkish corsairs, when Winnie's voice broke his vision.

'There's something else about tomorrow, Roddy. A secret we were not to tell you until you're fourteen.'

'Now then, Winnie,' said Geordie, cautioningly. 'Watch your tongue. No sense in worrying the lad.'

'Aye. Maybe I shouldn't have said that,' she said, nervously.

'What, Mum? What?' Roddy was all ears. 'A secret? Hey,

is it good?'

'There's a secret, for sure,' said Geordie, looking uncomfortable. 'Your mam shouldn't have said. Aye, and another present, too. But what's written has to be right, and there's an end to it, until tomorrow.'

'I don't know what you're talking about, Dad.'

'Nay. Neither you will. But come dawn, it'll all be explained. Eat your scones.'

After tea, Roddy went down again to *Curlew*. He was dying to paint the name on her stern, but the sun was already dipping in the West behind him, and with a whole weekend ahead of him, he knew there would be plenty of time. He ran his fingers over the smooth transom, shipped and unshipped the rudder. The sails were there, stowed in their bag under the thwart, and he could picture the new kedge anchor, down in the waters of the creek, holding her head-to-painter as securely as any vast merchantman in Newcastle Dock. 'Aye,' he breathed. 'We'll have *rare* times . . .'

It was the Lanes' habit to turn in early. Roddy lay awake in his bed for a long time, imagining himself at the tiller, hauling on the sheet, listening to the slap of the water under *Curlew's* bow. When he drifted off into sleep, it was with a contented smile on his face.

But the clock said no more than five when he awoke, and the summer sun was already streaming through the window. He studied the ceiling. It was, to him, a map of the world, with all the tracks of the great explorers upon it. The light-fitting was India, and over there, by the cobweb in the corner, that was the North West Passage. For twenty minutes he traced imaginary voyages, and then he got up. 'I'm fourteen now,' he said to himself as he pulled on his jeans and shrugged into a T-shirt. 'I'll make 'em a cuppa when I get back.'

Grabbing up the yellow bulk of a lifejacket from his

cupboard, he softly let himself out of the house and stole down to the bank of the creek. And there she was! *Curlew.* Waiting for him. Beckoning.

Deftly, the sun in his eyes, Roddy cast off the painter and stepped inboard. Hand over hand, he pulled the dinghy forward until the anchor tripped, then heaved it in, coiling the brand-new rope expertly into the cuddy. The fractional tide began to carry him out towards the river estuary and the open sea beyond.

'Up you go,' said Roddy, as, having taken the mainsail from its bag and bent it to gaff, mast and boom, he swung down the halliards and braced them taut. The sail was red and bright, and the registry number stood out bravely. He wished not only that the boat's name was on the transom, but that he'd got a burgee – a flag – to fly from the masthead. 'That'll come later,' he chuckled.

The boom swung as he moved forward and clipped on the jib. And now *Curlew* was a going concern – 11 feet of worthy craft that responded beautifully to his touch on the tiller, his pull on the sheets. The wind on his cheek, he sent her scudding out beyond the river, and was instantly lost in a daydream of valour that took in Horatio Nelson, Captain Hornblower, Henry Morgan and every seafarer who roved the deep from Viking days to those of the Falklands.

And then he lost sight of land.

'That's funny! I can't be that far out!' Roddy swivelled his head and saw nothing but a faint haze behind him. He altered course, aware that the sun was not quite so strong as it had been, that the golden orb was diminishing. 'It's what Mum said. Mist's on the way. Trust it to be late, and not in the night . . .'

Roddy wasn't worried. Not at first. He'd sailed in misty weather before. And as long as he kept his wits about him . . .

And yet it came down thicker, and thicker. 'I'm sure I'm

heading back inshore,' said the boy, aloud. 'I changed course clean about, and the wind's on my other cheek.' A fickle wind, perhaps? Swinging around all points, and dying to a mere whisper of nothing . . .?

The sail flapped once. Twice. Then was still, hanging limply. Mist had turned to fog, and *Curlew* was in the charge of a current, refusing to respond to the tiller, no matter which way Roddy thrust it.

'This is no good,' he said. 'I dunno which way I'm going. Could be getting carried out to sea, and there's shipping lanes out there . . .'

There was no sound save the chuckle of the water under *Curlew's* stern. It was cold. The mist was fog now. All at once, Roddy heard the boom of a coaster's siren, far, it seemed, on his port bow. Or was it to his stern? The dinghy seemed to be turning . . .

He knew there was no sense at all in panic. And no sense in sitting there, doing nothing. He dropped the sail and bundled it into the bottom of the boat, relinquishing the useless tiller to go for'ard and take in the jib. There were oars, but how could he use them? When he didn't know in which direction to row . . .?

'WHA-OOOOOO-OOOOOO'. The siren was closer now. Roddy felt the first chill of real fear as he pictured himself crushed to fragments beneath the bows of an iron ship. And now that very ship loomed out of the fog, towering above him! He yelled with fright, thrusting out his arms as if to keep it off – but a swirl of the current took him barely clear, and although he fell prostrate on top of the stowed sail, *Curlew* was spared destruction by mere inches! Yawing wildly, she swung away on the coaster's bow-wave, the tip of her mast writing desperate scribbles into the fog above! And nobody on the bridge of the coaster even guessed that the dinghy was there!

'Help!' yelled Roddy. '*Help!*' He knew the shout was hopeless.

'Why didn't I wait? Why didn't I do what I was told, and let Dad come out with me?' Roddy slammed the tiller to and fro in his frustration. It could only be a matter of time . . .

Distantly, he heard the tolling knell of the Longships Bell Buoy that marked the lanes of the big ships, the North Sea freighters that plied up and down the British coast. From Norway, Germany, Russia. Ships that could swamp the tiny vessel, even with their wakes. Was it possible that *Curlew* could have been carried so far from home?

And then he saw it. The little boat, scarcely bigger than his own, under full sail, emerging from the mist towards him. For a moment, he wondered how it could be sailing at all, with such a lack of wind. But his attention was caught by the man in the stern, a gaunt-faced, bearded man, wearing oilskins. His gleaming eyes fixed on the boy. 'Hoist your mainsail!' The man's voice was deep and commanding. Bewildered, Roddy did as he was told. 'There's wind enough for us,' said the man. 'We'll go back gunwale to gunwale.' He drew alongside, and Roddy saw him take up a curious, old-fashioned compass, brassbound and heavy. 'Steer with me!'

'I . . . I don't remember you from these parts,' said Roddy. 'Were you caught in it, too? Maybe on holiday? I'm glad you've got that compass! I'm completely lost!'

The man said nothing, but the piercing blue eyes seemed to bore into Roddy's, intently. 'That's an old boat you've got,' said Roddy, feeling a strange prickling down his spine.

It was an old boat. Clinker-built, unpainted, with tarred ropework so much heavier than the nylon tackle of *Curlew*. Roddy couldn't take his eyes of it, as it creamed through the water alongside him. He was aware, though, of their speed. Impossible, since he could still feel no wind. 'But – but the sail's billowing out . . .'

And then he saw it. The little boat, scarcely bigger than his own, under full sail, emerging from the mist before him.

'Mister – who *are* you . . .?' Roddy hugged the responsive tiller and stared at the man, who merely pointed ahead and kept glancing down at the curious brass compass, which Roddy noticed had a conspicuous dent in one side of it . . .

'Home. *Home!*' The man at last spoke, and vaguely, it seemed, the fog ahead began to thin.

Roddy saw, looming in front of him, the familiar marker buoy of the river entrance channel, signalling danger from the treacherous Landway Bank that nobody would ever go near. Automatically, he swung down on the tiller and veered away from the peril, aware that the other did not follow suit!

'Hey! The *buoy!*' He half stood up as the other dinghy passed the buoy on the wrong side, vanished in a bank of mist, and disappeared. Just before he lost sight of it, he saw the man's hand rise in salute . . . still holding the brass compass, which gleamed in the light, though there *was* no light . . .

Abruptly, *Curlew's* sail flapped and was still. Drifting, she spun in a current, and before he knew it, Roddy felt her ground on the familiar shore of the creek. Dimly, he could see his home through the murk.

He sprang out, hauled her up to safety, and double-tied the painter around its hitch. As he slung the kedge into the mud, he was aware of Winnie and Geordie running down towards him . . .

'Oh, you fool, Roddy! Whatever made you take her out now . . .?'

'I'm sorry, Mam! I know I shouldn't have. But I reckoned I *was* fourteen!'

'You soppy nothing,' said Winnie, hugging him. 'We've been so worried!'

'Not half as worried as I was, Mam! If it hadn't been for a bloke in a funny old boat, I'd still be out there. I reckon he might have gone aground on Landway Bank . . .'

'I'll phone the coastguard, just in case,' said Geordie.

'Meanwhile, you come inside and get something hot down you . . .'

A mug of cocoa in his hands, Roddy re-lived the worries of *Curlew's* first voyage for his parents. And then . . .

'You'll remember we had a secret to tell you, lad. We know it's going to be difficult for you to understand, but we're not your parents at all.'

Roddy looked from one to the other in amazement. 'Not my parents? What do you mean?'

'Your real name's Roddy Jenkins. Your mother died when you were born, and your father when you were scarcely one year old . . .'

'Well – who *was* he . . .?' Roddy was unaware that his cocoa was slopping out of his mug on to the table.

Geordie said: 'He was my best friend: A master mariner. One of the greatest you'd ever have wished to have seen. Served with me aboard *Tiger* for four years. But he was a bit of a lad, and when the war ended, he spent his time fooling about in small boats. He'd go out in all sorts of bad weather, despite what anyone told him . . .'

Roddy leaned forward. 'Go on,' he said.

'Well, there was one day, he took out a dinghy. Fog came down. Nobody ever saw him again.'

Winnie laid a hand on Roddy's arm. 'He'd asked us,' she said, 'if anything ever happened to him, to look after you, and bring you up like our own . . .'

'Oh, you did, Mam, you did!' said Roddy. Tears were pricking his eyes. 'You're my parents . . . you *are*!'

Winnie and Geordie, themselves in tears as well, came close to the boy. In his hands, Geordie held something tied up in oilcloth, which he started to unwrap. 'Your Dad's name was Freddie,' he said. 'And this was the only one of his possessions that he left behind him. Winnie and me decided that your fourteenth birthday was the time to tell you the truth, and give you this keepsake of your *real* old man . . .'

Geordie held it out. And Roddy's eyes fell upon a curious, old-fashioned compass, brass-bound, with a conspicuous dent in one side.

'Don't phone the coastguard, Dad,' he said. 'There won't be any wreck on the Landway Bank. I've *seen* Freddie Jenkins . . . this morning . . .'

Roddy Lane never chose to call himself Jenkins. In future life, he was often to return to the edge of that creek on the river estuary, overlooking the North Sea. His career took him to the ownership of a prosperous shipping company, and like all business magnates, there were many times that he felt himself in deep trouble. Yet when in need of help, he shunned the accountants and advisers around him, and went to look out over the Landway Bank. And, as long as Roddy had the battered compass in his hands, the ghost of his father never refused him. His company, by the way, is called Jenkins Worldwide – and nobody but Roddy Lane knows why . . .

A HEAD FOR SEÑOR MORALES

by June Williams

THEY HAD COME ON THE STROKE OF MIDNIGHT, riding out of the darkness to put to the torch his crops and the out-buildings housing his tractors and threshing machines that had been shipped to him at great expense from the USA. Not content with that, they had ridden off with most of his horses, their blazing torches lighting the sky as they thundered away, yelping like coyotes. Surveying the expanse of scorched earth they had left behind them, Señor Morales cursed the revolution and all those who supported it. He vented part of his rage by knocking to the ground, and then kicking half to death, the poor peon who had had the misfortune to accompany him on his tour of inspection. Feeling slightly better, Morales then took himself back to his hacienda, where he ordered his breakfast to be brought to him.

Sitting there, sipping at his coffee which tasted like bile on his lips on that unhappy morning, Morales watched a group of his peons pass by, on their way to clear up some of the damage. It was for ignorant swine like these, he reflected bitterly, that Mexico had been brought to its knees with one revolution after another. In its name, presidents had been deposed or removed by the assassin's bullet with such rapidity that he had almost lost count of how many men had ruled Mexico for the last fifty years or so.

As if all this were not enough, the revolution had bred a true devil's spawn, rebels who were not content with killing off the old president or two, or with shouting slogans that did no one any harm. Instead, they had organised the peons into rebel bands who now roamed the land, robbing and murdering in the name of the revolution. Some of them, like Pancho Villa and Emiliano Zapata, had become so feared that even the Government's Federal troops, themselves vicious brutes to the last man, quailed at their very name and made a point of keeping out of their way. This left landowners like himself almost completely at the mercy of any band of marauders who might choose to descend on them, killing with pistol and machete anyone who opposed them. Morales sighed wearily. It was enough to make a man spit.

Heaving himself from his chair, Morales left the table and retired to his office. There a great monster of a man with a face seamed with heavy lines was waiting for him. This was Pepe Gonzales, his overseer, come for his orders for the day. Only a few months before he had been sitting in a rat-infested cell, waiting for death at the end of a rope for stealing cattle. Morales had seen him while being taken on a tour of the jail by the local governor, and had decided that this was just the man he needed to keep his peons in order. A few strings had been pulled, a few paltry bribes given, and Pepe had walked out of the jail a free man. In exchange for this favour, Morales had bought himself a man he knew would lay down his life for him if necessary.

'That raid last night,' Pepe began. 'A terrible business . . .'

Morales silenced him with a raised hand. 'I wish to talk briefly of other matters. As you know, my son arrives home this afternoon. From the moment he arrives, you will be his personal bodyguard.'

'It will be my pleasure, señor,' Pepe said. 'I will guard him as if he were my own son.'

'See that you do,' Morales said grimly. 'These are dangerous times. If anything should happen to him, you are a dead man.'

'Señor Morales,' Pepe protested. 'I assure you I will not let him out of my sight. As it is, I am concerned that he has chosen to ride from the railway station alone. You should have insisted that he be accompanied.'

Morales flushed at the implied rebuke. 'My son is a grown man. He would have greatly resented it if you had gone to meet him. Now get back to your work.'

Left alone with his thoughts again, Morales permitted himself a few moments of relaxation while he thought of his son, Juan, who was returning home after completing his education in Europe. It had been an expensive business, but he had not begrudged the money. It had not been so hard to raise it anyway, because he had worked his peons for longer hours and cut down on their food rations. Further money had been found by not carrying out the long overdue repairs on the hovels in which they lived. When you had something like a hundred men working for you, those sort of little economies made a great deal of difference to the credit side of your ledgers.

The train bringing Juan home was due to arrive at eleven o'clock. Morales assumed that he would have something to eat after buying himself a horse, and therefore estimated that his son would be with him somewhere around 3 in the afternoon. In the meantime, he had much to do.

The hours went by quickly. After a light lunch, Morales settled down to working out what the raid had cost in terms of lost crops and ruined machinery. This depressing task occupied him so fully that he lost count of the hours, until suddenly he became aware that it was now after five o'clock. He was not greatly perturbed that there was still no sign of his son. The Mexican trains were, after all, well known for their inefficiency.

By ten o'clock it was quite another matter. Now beside himself with worry, Morales paced up and down his study, his mind in a turmoil. Suddenly, to his intense relief, he heard the sound of drumming hooves. Rushing out on to the verandah, he watched the rider coming out of the darkness. To his disappointment he saw that the rider was a complete stranger. 'Señor Morales?' the rider called out.

'Yes.'

'This is for you.' The rider threw a small leather pouch at his feet and then galloped off without another word.

Stooping, Morales picked up the pouch and opened it. Inside it was a handwritten note. It read: 'Your son is in our hands. Unless you agree to pay us the sum of 50 000 pesos, he will be executed by a firing squad. You have three days in which to bring the money personally to my camp in the Silver Hills. A look-out will be waiting for you to make your appearance.'

The note was signed Miguel Lerdo. He recognised the name as belonging to a rebel leader whose exploits were already beginning to rival those of Villa and Zapata.

A wave of nausea swept over Morales as he stood there, holding the note in a hand that shook as if he had the ague. Then with bowed head he went back to his study, where he sat in silence for a long time. Finally, he summoned one of his servants. 'Bring Pepe to me,' he ordered.

When Pepe came, Morales showed him the note. Pepe read it and then placed it carefully on the desk. 'Courage, señor,' he said quietly. 'At least Lerdo has been considerate enough to tell us where he can be found. I will ride to the Federals' headquarters at once.'

'A waste of time,' Morales said. 'The Federals will not risk the life of a single man for my son. Lerdo knows this. Which is why he has been so free as to his whereabouts.'

'Then you must pay the ransom,' Pepe said.

'That, too, would be a waste of time,' Morales said harshly. 'Many people have been captured by the rebels. Not a single one of them has been returned alive, even when the ransom money has been paid.' He looked up at Pepe. 'Is there any reason to believe that Lerdo is any better than the others?'

'None,' Pepe admitted. 'Only a few days ago he hanged a landowner who had put the whip to one of his peons' back for stealing. The landowner offered him a small fortune if he would spare his life. But Lerdo would have none of it.'

'You see,' Morales said. 'They are all the same. They wish to kill anyone who has been more fortunate in life than they are. That is why I must consider my son already dead. All that is left to me now is to find some way to avenge his death.'

'That will not be easy.'

'I have already given the matter some thought,' Morales said.

'And you now have something in mind?'

Morales nodded. 'I have indeed.' Avoiding Pepe's questioning look, he stared at the ceiling. 'You would be the first to admit that you owe your life to me?'

'Yes,' Pepe said warily.

'I have a plan,' Morales said. 'It is one in which you will be the instrument of my revenge. The plan is basically a very simple one. You will go to Lerdo's camp, posing as a peon on the run from a harsh task-master, and ask to join his band. He will undoubtedly take you in. Once you have gained his confidence you will kill him.' Morales spread out his hands in an apologetic gesture. 'I know I am asking much of you. But I can hardly go myself, can I?'

'Señor,' Pepe stammered. 'You know I am prepared to give my life for you if necessary. But it will not work. They would never allow me to join them on trust. They would need proof that I am what I say I am.'

'We will give them proof,' Morales said calmly. 'I will have you flogged. The stripes on your back will be your passport into Lerdo's camp.' Seeing the look on Pepe's face, he added

His feeling of unholy joy mounted when he saw that Pepe was carrying on the saddle before him a piece of sacking wrapped round a bulky-looking object.

soothingly. 'The 20 000 pesos I am going to pay you, will help lessen the pain.' He leaned back in his chair and smiled at Pepe. 'Is there anything you wish to say?'

'Only that you strike a hard bargain.'

'That is why I am a rich man,' Morales said. 'The flogging will take place tomorrow morning.' He paused. 'There is just one other little matter. I must have proof that you have killed Lerdo. You will therefore bring me his head.'

Pepe was visibly taken aback. 'That may be difficult, señor.'

'You are a cunning man,' Morales murmured. 'You will find a way.'

The flogging was carried out at noon the next day, the excuse being that Morales had found Pepe trying to open his safe. Afterwards, Pepe was sent on his way, accompanied by the jeers of the gathered peons, who all had good cause to hate him.

Surprisingly, when Pepe staggered down the long dusty road that would lead him to the Silver Hills, he had no feelings of ill will towards his master. He knew full well that he could be going to his death, but this was of no immediate concern to him. He had committed many crimes in his life, but he still liked to think he was a man of honour. Morales had saved his life, and had now presented his bill for that service. Pepe knew that he could avoid paying it by quietly going on his way, but the idea of doing so never even entered his head.

Pepe returned a month later, riding a fine white stallion. Watching his approach, Morales knew that he would never have returned if he had not been able to carry out his mission. His feeling of unholy joy mounted when he saw that Pepe was carrying on the saddle before him a piece of sacking wrapped around a bulky looking object. Ignoring the puzzled peons crowding around him, Pepe dismounted and came to Morales, carrying the sack, a broad grin on his face. 'Senor –' he began.

'No,' Morales said, 'we will talk inside. This is a moment I wish to savour in privacy.' Leading the way into his study, he closed the door on them. 'May I assume this is a moment for celebration?'

'It is, señor,' Pepe said, grinning hugely. 'I bring you the head of Miguel Lerdo.'

'Then we will indeed celebrate,' Morales said. 'Place what you are carrying on my desk.' Opening a cabinet, he poured out two large glasses of brandy. He lifted his glass '*Saludos.*'

'*Saludos,*' Pepe said, downing his brandy in a single gulp. 'It was no easy task you gave me. I had to leave very hurriedly, I can tell you. Fortunately, I was able to get to a horse.'

'Tell me your story later.' Morales put his glass aside. 'Now let me see the head of the man who killed my son.'

'With pleasure, señor,' Pepe said. 'I warn you though, he is not a very pretty sight.'

'I'm not a squeamish man,' Morales said, 'as you well know. Unwrap your bundle.'

Slowly Pepe unwrapped the folds of the sacking, and then stood back so that Morales might better see the grimacing head of his victim.

'There, señor,' he said proudly. 'The head of Miguel Lerdo.'

Morales stared at the head, and then let forth an anguished cry. 'Juan – you have brought me the head of my son, Juan!'

Pepe's eyes bulged. 'No, señor. I assure you it is the head of Miguel Lerdo.'

'It is the head of Juan,' Morales shrieked, his voice rising to a crescendo. 'It is the head of Juan!' His eyes were now like those of a madman. 'You have betrayed me and entered into a devil's pact with Lerdo to play this fiendish trick on me.

You will pay for that with your life!' Beside himself with grief and rage, Morales pulled open the drawer of his desk and produced a pistol.

'Please,' Pepe said, backing away. 'I do not understand – ' Looking into Morales' eyes, he knew that words were useless and that his last moment had come. In the same instant, Morales placed a bullet squarely into his heart.

Afterwards, when his servants had dragged Pepe's body away, Morales sat alone at his desk, looking with horror upon the head of his son. Although still beside himself with grief, a tiny doubt had begun to nag at his mind. Would Pepe have really come back, knowing that he was carrying the head of his master's son? It seemed unlikely. How, then, could this have happened? Time and time again, he asked himself the same question, but could find no answer.

How indeed had it happened?

Miguel Lerdo was shaving himself in front of a mirror hung on a tree, when one of his men came to tell him that a peon who called himself Pepe Gonzales had stumbled into the camp, asking for sanctuary.

'Have him brought to me,' Lerdo ordered.

They brought Pepe Gonzales to him. His clothes were torn, and he was in a state of near collapse. Lerdo noted immediately that the back of his shirt was heavily stained with blood. Without a word, he ripped the shirt of Pepe's back and studied the marks of the lash on his back. 'Someone has done a good job on you, amigo. How did it happen?'

Pepe told him the story he had rehearsed with Morales. When he had finished, Lerdo nodded his head. 'And you have come to me in the hope that I will take you in?'

'Yes, señor.'

Lerdo regarded him thoughtfully. 'It's true I can always use a man like you – particularly a man who has suffered at the hands of those we wish to destroy. When you have recovered, you will ride with us. In the meantime, go and rest.'

Pepe was led away, and Lerdo returned to his shaving. Contemplating his reflection in the mirror, he thought on the strange course his life had taken. Born Juan Morales, the son of a rich landowner, he had nevertheless been convinced that his heart really belonged to the Revolution, a conviction that had become so overpowering that he had given up his studies in Europe and returned secretly to Mexico, where he had taken a new name. Soon, now, when his father arrived with the ransom money, he would learn the truth – that his own son had tricked him.

He had thought long of his father, a man he had detested from the moment he had been able to think for himself. For that reason, he had worked out his little plan, even going to the trouble of arranging that a letter should be sent to him from Europe, saying that he was coming home. The raid, which had been none of his doing, had probably helped.

Finishing his shaving, Juan Morales thought briefly of the man who had come to his camp. He would do very well, he decided. Perhaps in time he would make him one of his trusted lieutenants. A man who had suffered so much, deserved nothing less.

Which is how Señor Morales eventually came to acquire the head of his son.

THE MIDNIGHT STAGE

by Ross Trapnell

THE WILD, EXCITED BAYING OF THE HOUNDS filled the night air. Ritchie Eckhardt could tell that, in hunter's parlance, they'd 'found'.

He had heard that chilling sound twice before in the six months he'd spent in Hard Rock Pen. That howl of triumph signified the beginning of the end of freedom for some poor wretch who'd thought he could escape, but who soon discovered, as he stumbled through the tangled underbrush, staggered across vine-choked thickets, splashed knee-deep in swamp ooze, that freedom was a hopeless mirage, a teasing will o' the wisp.

Hard Rock Penitentiary was just too deep inside the Florida Everglades, too far off the beaten track.

To escape, you needed time. With time on your side you could hole up, plan your route, skirt the black swamps, and avoid the bad patches – the areas where bald cypresses stood close together, blocking the path; where thorn and scrub and mulberry were so thickly entangled you needed a machete to hack your way through. With time, you could make your home-run by easy stages.

But time for an escaper was short. Once a break-out had been discovered, and the harsh shriek of the siren had blared hoarsely across the surrounding fields, it did not take long for the mastiffs to be let loose from their pens. It took even less time to offer them something of the prisoner's to sniff. Once they caught that, cast about, and found the scent, the escaper's remaining period of freedom could be calculated in minutes rather than hours.

There were no roads to Hard Rock, save one. It was a dirt road, almost a track, which connected with the main State highway a little way away and it was the sole means of getting to and from the dreaded prison. If you were an escaper, you avoided that road like the plague. It was the only easy way out, yes. But, following on from that, it was also the easiest stretch for the guards to patrol and control. So the would-be escaper had a choice of going through oozing swamp or thick forest.

Fat choice! thought Eckhardt, as he plunged into a patch of briar that snagged his thin clothes and tore at his face. Angrily he thrust aside the spiky tendrils and stumbled on.

Above, the moon shone fitfully through ragged clouds, now bathing the forest in stark yellow light, now plunging it into a deep gloom. Eckhardt's boots thudded into thick soft moss, then splashed into water. He cursed and crouched down, narrowing his eyes to peer into the darkness.

Ahead, he could just make out a stretch of stagnant water, which seemed to extend on both sides of him. He cursed again and glanced back over his shoulder, although the darkness was now so thick that he could almost touch it. But he could hear the hounds again, barking and yelping, the sound carrying on the night wind. It faded and then rose again as the breeze tore at it. It was a hideous, horrifying sound at the best of times. At the worst of times, as now, it chilled the blood.

For the hounds were after *him*.

If they caught him, that would be bad enough. Even if he stood stock-still as they bounded towards him, there was every likelihood that two or more of the brutes would leap at him and hurl him to the ground, worrying at a leg or an arm with their teeth. That was how they automatically behaved to the cons. It was what had been thrashed into them by the guards and handlers.

But worse would follow. When hustled back to the penitentiary, he would be brutally beaten by the guards and tossed into solitary confinement for up to two or three months. After that, he would lose all privileges, such as they were. After that, too, lay the greatest danger: Shroeder . . .

It was Feeney, his cellmate, who'd muttered the information to him one night as they'd queued for food, whispering the words out of the corner of his mouth, as the thirty or so guards had gazed bleakly down from the galleries that ringed the room, carbines always to hand and ready to shoot.

'Watch Shroeder. Don't turn your back on him. He's had orders from outside. To close your mouth. Permanently. Dunno who from . . .'

Ritchie Eckhardt knew. He knew exactly who would go to the lengths of bribing someone to carry a message from the outside world to one of the most vicious killers in the pen.

His ex-partner, Herb Lomas.

The guy who'd put him in here in the first place. The skunk whom he'd discovered had been cooking the books of their export firm in Miami to the tune of around 20 000 bucks, which in 1937, so soon after the Great Depression, was one whale of a sum. The snake whom he'd threatened to expose unless the money was returned. The rat who had then murdered the firm's lawyer because Eckhardt had told him of the swindle. The unspeakable monster who had seen to it that Eckhardt was convicted of both the killing and the theft.

Eckhardt felt bile rise in the back of his throat as he thought of Herb Lomas, the man who had so cruelly betrayed his trust.

He had been given a twenty-stretch in Hard Rock, with only one slim chance of getting out legally. Leon Sikorsky, his defence attorney, was searching for an old guy named Harry

Bates, a beach-bum who had been known to sleep rough near that part of the beach down from Fort Lauderdale where Lomas had shot his victim, and who might have seen something. But Bates hadn't been found yet, had drifted off elsewhere, ridden the rails north, or maybe just died. Who knew? It was a very slim chance, anyway . . .

That was why Eckhardt had decided to make a break for it, even though all the odds were stacked against him. Whatever he did in the pen, however long he managed to keep out of Shroeder's way, the final outcome could only be death. His chances of survival were slimmer than those of finding Harry Bates. It was either escape, *or die*!

Suddenly the moon broke loose from the clouds, shedding its revealing rays over the swamplands.

And even as Eckhardt saw that the lake in front of him ended not far to the left, where cypress and giant willow clustered thickly, a yell of recognition cut through the silence.

'*There he is, boys!*'

A shot rang out, then another. Eckhardt, ducking frantically, felt the wind of their passing.

Across the swamp behind him, the guards had burst through the thickets and were now gathered on a high knoll, starkly outlined against the sky.

Eckhardt sprinted madly along the edge of the unfriendly stretch of water, bullets humming around him and zipping into the lake.

'*Let 'em loose!*'

As he plunged through a barrier of thorns, he heard the wild howling of the dogs as their handlers unclasped the straps and the fearsome animals hurled themselves across the space between them and him.

Ritchie Eckhardt knew real terror for the first time in his life. He crashed through bushes, tore through flailing vines, smashed his way into dense thickets of moss and creeper, and hurtled out the other side. Recklessly, he splashed through shallow swamp water and bounded across narrow sluggish streams, well aware that at any moment he might disturb alligators who would, in seconds, inflict far more ghastly injuries on him than a dozen of the pursuing mastiffs.

He sprinted across gloomy, reeking glades ill-lit by the moonlight filtering thinly down through the roof of branches, vines and creepers. Even when the moon sank back behind the dense clouds, he still kept on running, staggering over rotting logs and fallen branches, and blundering along seemingly endless tangles of devil's-claw vine.

The throaty yells of the dogs were not so loud now and the firing had ceased, but this did not mean he was outdistancing his pursuers. He knew too well what tricks the Everglades could play on someone who was taking no notice of direction but simply running as hard and as fast as he could. At the back of his mind was the terrifying thought that, in his mad sprint, he could actually be moving in a steady circle back to where he had come from.

A narrow corridor between densely packed cypresses suddenly revealed itself, as the moon once more sailed free of the clouds high above. He pounded along it, his breath erupting in short, throat-rasping gasps, his heart thudding like a steam-hammer.

Then at the end of the corridor, he fetched up with a groan of despair. Ahead was a glade enclosed by muscadine, overcup, and willow, all thickly curtained with tangled vines. From them hung ghost orchids, eerily, almost glowingly, white in the moonlight. To one side was a stagnant pool on which giant moon-faced water lilies floated motionless. Wild iris, liriope, myrtle and leather-fern smothered the grass in a thick carpet.

But it was what lay on the other side of the glade that had caused him to gasp – a tumbledown shack made of logs, with light streaming from its windows.

He peered at the dwelling, frowning. There was something queer about its roof. It seemed to have knobs or lumps all over it. At first he thought these were mounds of moss, built up over the years into strange shapes; but as he stared harder, he realised that they were birds, wild pigeons, clustered together wing-to-wing in a solid mass, so still that they could have been brilliantly carved statues. Except that they were alive! First one, then another, shifted on its perch, ruffling its feathers, turning its head slightly, delicately lifting a single leg.

A cold chill ran up Eckhardt's spine. He recalled an old Black handyman of his father's, Jeb Byrne, who, once in a while, used to fascinate him with tales of the old days, legends of the swamps. There was one he remembered about the wild pigeons that used to roost in the hickories and then, when someone was dying, flock densely to the roof of the dying person's house, neither preening nor strutting, but watchful and motionless in a dark and sombre mass. The pigeons from hell, they were called. When the person finally died, they would rise up into the skies as one, the beat of their wings filling the air, and disappear back into the swamps as though carrying the departed soul with them.

Remembering that was too much for Ritchie Eckhardt. Yet even as he turned to flee that accursed place, the door of the shack swung open and light splashed out on to the grass. In the doorway, silhouetted against the light, stood an old woman who lifted an arm and beckoned.

'You're late! Come quickly!' The voice was harsh, rasping.

Sweat running down his brow, Eckhardt stood as though turned to stone.

'Quickly, I say! Can you not hear the hunters?'

On the breeze came the sounds of pursuit, the baying of the hounds, the shouts of the guards. Nearer, nearer.

The old woman lifted an arm and beckoned. 'You're late! Come quickly!' The voice was harsh, rasping.

Eckhardt sprinted across the glade and pushed through the low, narrow doorway, shutting the door behind him. Already the old woman was seated on the other side of a table set in the centre of the tiny but cluttered room. A smoky oil lamp spluttered on the table near him, half-blinding him by the closeness of its flickering radiance.

'The lamp,' he muttered hoarsely. 'They'll see it.'

'Those who cannot see, will not see.'

Eckhardt half-turned his head, the better to hear, but all was now silent save for the hiss and sputter of the lamp. His hunters seemed to have passed the glade by.

The old woman rapped on the table with a hand that looked as though it were made from parchment.

'I . . . I don't understand,' mumbled Eckhardt. 'What did you mean when you said I was late? How did you know I'd be coming here? I only decided to make a break for it today.'

The old one had produced a cracked corncob pipe, which she lit, puffing smoke into the air with clear enjoyment.

'To those who seek, all is revealed. This is but one stage in your journey, a half-way house. Now you must take the midnight stage. But you must hurry! Time is short! If you miss it, the chance will not come your way again.'

'Stage?' muttered Eckhardt. 'But – where?'

'On the old road.'

'There's no road through here.' Eckhardt stared at the old woman in disbelief. 'The road to the State highway's the other side of the swamp. There *ain't* no other road!'

'Quickly! *Quickly!*'

The old woman was pulling him out of the chair, hustling him through the door, jabbing with the pipe towards the north.

'There's your path. Remember, climb aboard the midnight stage. You'll find your just reward!'

Eckhardt, not understanding, his brain a fog, staggered

into the bushes, then swung round wildly as a sound like gathering thunder beat upon his ears. The pigeons! In a dense cloud they rose into the air, starkly etched against the moon, and wheeled away over the trees with furiously beating wings.

He plunged into the undergrowth and ran as though something supernatural were chasing him.

Then, once more, he came to a shuddering halt and stood stock-still as clear voices came to him upon the breeze:

'Those damned brutes; I don't understand it. They had the scent fine, then suddenly they didn't!'

'He's gotta be around here someplace. Man cain't just vanish into thin air.'

The first speaker laughed harshly.

'He'll vanish for good once we spot him again! Two hundred bucks apiece for you and me from that city slicker says that Eckhardt's a dead man!'

The voices faded as the men moved off, and Ritchie Eckhardt shivered.

Herb Lomas not only had given the word to Shroeder, but to some of the guards, too. He wasn't to be taken alive. He was to be shot. 'Evading capture', they'd put in their report. A black cloud of despair closed in on his mind. It was hopeless. He'd never escape. Herb Lomas had won.

'In the bushes! I see him! *Fire!*'

He gave a cry of terror as carbines crashed and the dogs once more set up their mad baying. He turned and fled back through the thickets, and then uttered a gasp of shocked bewilderment as, smashing his way through a dense wall of shrubbery, he stumbled out on to a road.

A road where, surely, no road should be!

Even as this thought flashed through his mind, he heard the clatter of iron-rimmed wheels, the jingle of harness, the snorting whinney of hard-driven horses.

Round the bend ahead careered a stagecoach, its six horses galloping madly. The driver was a crouched figure plying his long whip, hunched on the box, only vaguely glimpsed.

The coach hurtled towards him and Eckhardt made a lightning-fast decision. He began running ahead of it and, as it clattered past, he leapt for the step, his fingers clutching at the glassless window-frame as he jumped aboard. Heaving at the door, he tugged it open and fell inside.

He glanced out and saw that they were now passing the dogs who had raced out of the swamp. Then the horses seemed to be galloping faster and faster, and the countryside outside was almost a blur. Yet he recognised parts of it, and realised with a tremor of dismay that the stagecoach was taking him round in a half-circle, heading back towards Hard Rock Pen itself.

Yes! There was the road, the road to the pen!

Then he stared hard through the window, the wind pummelling his face. On the road were three cars. The car in front was instantly recognisable as his lawyer's Packard. Trailing it were two cars from the county sheriff's department.

Sikorsky? Heading for the prison at this time of night? It could mean only one thing. *Freedom*!

He hammered on the side of the coach with his fist.

'Stop the stage! For God's sake, *stop!*'

But the driver lashed at the horses with his whip and the thundering beasts raced faster . . . faster . . . faster . . .

He jammed open the door, the wind tearing at him and howling as though filled with demons. He sprang out, arms flailing. He hurtled through the air and hit the ground, bouncing twice. Lights and exploding stars filled his brain. Then his senses left him . . .

'Ritchie! Can you hear me? You're gonna be okay.'

The voice filtered through the fog that filled his mind. He opened his eyes, winced with pain and groaned.

'Leon? Where . . . am I?'

Sikorsky leaned over him, his plump face beaming.

'Get this into your head before the nurse gives you something to make you sleep peacefully. We found Bates. He was there when Lomas killed Nagel, saw everything. Ran away because he was scared. But we found him and he's told everything. I've been through the firm's books, and they stink. Lomas has been arrested. We didn't know you'd made a run for it, and we were on our way to spring you when you dropped out of the sky!' He laughed uproariously. 'Where were you, Ritch? Up a tree?'

'The cabin . . .' mumbled Eckhardt.

'Oh, you must've stumbled across that old ruin in the swamps. I know this area. There was an old lady lived in the swamps, used to work for John Brown and the abolitionists. Used to hide runaway slaves for the Underground Railroad back before the Civil War.'

Eckhardt's fingers scrabbled at the sheets.

'The stage. I took . . . the midnight stage . . .'

Sikorsky turned to the nurse.

'Poor guy's rambling. Not surprising after all he's been through. I'll sue the State for half a million in compensation!' He laughed again. 'Midnight stage! Hasn't been a stage through the swamps in fifty years!'

THE SIX BILLION DOLLAR BOY

by M.S. Goodall

I'M GOING TO TELL YOU A STORY about a kid called Damion Holzenholler the Third. The fact that it's a true story is neither here nor there.

Damion's daddy, Samuel Holzenholler the Second, was a billionaire many times over. Six times over, to be exact, which was one reason why his son had earned himself nicknames like 'Superspender Mark One' and 'The Six Billion Dollar Boy'. Another reason was that young Damion, although only fifteen and a half, was never short of a buck. Come to think of it, he was never short of a hundred thousand bucks. And all in hard cash. Greenbacks everywhere. Wads so thick you needed both hands to hold them. The Beverly Hills area of Hollywood, where the Holzenhollers lived, was a pretty free-spending neighbourhood, but Damion was way up there near the top of the big spenders.

It was all his big daddy's fault. Ol' Sammy's philosophy was that the boy should learn how to handle money by himself as soon as possible. To handle it, come to appreciate it, and so to learn its true value. Of course, it didn't work with a kid like Damion.

He was too young to open his own bank account, so he had to 'learn' all about money by handling hard cash. Like I said, the kid had so many dollars on him all the time, he was like a mobile bank. And *spend*! Wow, he made those Middle-East oil sheikhs look like paupers. Once Damion had bought his way through all the normal youthful pleasures – like half a dozen new bikes on the same day, four riding ponies, a couple of motorised go-karts and a private indoor swimming pool – he began to get sulky and bored. As a cure for boredom, his lavish spending took a freaky kind of turn. For instance, he'd go to the fanciest car saleroom in town, buy a brand-new pink Chevvy, and then throw a tantrum 'cos he was too young to drive it away. He cured that by hiring a film studio stuntman to drive the car for him, and then wreck it completely in a series of daredevil stunts. Yes, little Damion got a real kick out of that. He even bought a small yacht and had an ex-Marine blow it up in San Pedro Bay.

When told of these exploits, old man Holzenholler just shrugged and turned on his philosophical look. 'Give the boy a free rein,' he said 'and sooner or later he'll learn the error of his ways. Damion must realise for himself that money cannot buy happiness. Let him do what he likes, when he likes, and he'll gradually see how idiotic it is to fling his money away.'

As time went on and Damion's spending habits became rasher and rasher, people began to wonder why he'd never once been robbed. The kid was a mobile bank. He'd even had his own miniature mansion built in the grounds of his father's estate, so how much cash he had lying stacked in there was anybody's guess. Damion used to boast: 'I'm a real tough cookie. I can look after myself. Yes, sir, I sure can.' Funny, but it was almost as though the kid was throwing out a challenge . . . as though he *wanted* a pair of hard-nosed hoods to try and take all that lovely lolly away from him.

And, of course, there came a day when a pair of hard-nosed hoods did try. I'll call them Smokey Joe and Big Al. They were losers from way back, jobless bums from the Bronx who'd drifted west looking for work, and trying to make it big with all the wrong kinds of people. They'd been run out of Vegas and ended up in LA, hoping that the sunshine state of California would shine a little sun on them.

But it was the same old hard-luck story of dead-end jobs and no future until, one day, they saw Damion Holzenholler the Third out shopping for fruit. The kid had developed a taste for fresh tangerines, and instead of buying the odd kilo from his local supermarket, he went straight to the wholesaler and bought himself a lorryload. Smokey Joe and Big Al were sweeping out a warehouse when they saw Damion handing over the cash. Wads of dollar bills. They'd never seen so much money before. They made up their minds there and then to relieve the boy of some of his burden. Not too much of it – just a million or so. They'd break into his pad and help themselves. Heck, the kid wouldn't even notice it was missing. And it wouldn't be like stealing at all; more like teaching a spoilt little brat a lesson.

Smokey Joe and Big Al made their way up to Beverly Hills that night. The Holzenholler estate was a seven-acre hill-top site, and Damion's private mini-mansion was built at the lower end in the middle of a small wood. The two men didn't even have to break in. The kid's back door was unlocked.

Dimmed wall lights led them along a hall to the main staircase. The whole house was silent. Not a clock ticking, no thin, tell-tale wires of an alarm system. They crept upstairs. The door to a master bedroom faced them across the landing. Smokey Joe bent down and peeped cautiously through the keyhole. He saw a lavishly furnished bedroom with huge pop posters decorating the wall. A circular bed occupied the middle of the room, and there, propped up on pillows with a satisfied smirk on his face, was Damion Holzenholler the Third. His fingers hovered over what appeared to be the remote control of a television set.

Outside, Smokey Joe stood up, gestured at the door, and placed a finger to his lips. Big Al nodded, understanding at once that the boy was in bed inside. They intended to burst into the room, grab him, gag him, and then search the house for money. Slowly, Smokey reached out and gripped the metal door handle. At exactly the same time, Damion's finger jabbed at a button on the box he was holding.

There was a mighty flash, a crackling roar, and Smokey Joe was sent reeling backwards across the landing. Big Al, who'd been standing close behind Smokey Joe, a hand resting lightly on his pal's shoulder, was sent hurtling back with him. Both men hit the far wall with a violent crump and passed out.

When they came to, they were sitting side by side in a pair of solid, hard-backed dining-room chairs. Their ankles had been firmly strapped and their hands and arms were tied behind them at the backs of the chairs. They were in a small, square, windowless room, empty except for a long refectory table which ran the length of the room. Smokey Joe looked at the table, blinked, then looked again. In tall stacks along the length of the table were neatly wrapped bundles of thousand dollar bills. Fifty to each bundle. Then Big Al lifted his head and saw it too. 'Woweee,' he mumbled softly, 'There must be more'n a million bucks sitting there.'

'Maybe two million,' said Smokey Joe.

'Wrong gentlemen,' said a third voice. 'You are looking at precisely *three* million US dollars. As you know, I have money to burn!'

Joe and Al glanced up. Set into the ceiling was a small circular loudspeaker. Then they saw the unwavering eye of a closed-circuit television camera, mounted at a high angle on the opposite wall. Damion was obviously enjoying himself as he observed the two men's reactions closely.

Smokey Joe scowled at the camera. 'I guess folks were right when they said it sounded as though you *wanted* somebody to try and rob you. This whole set-up is one big trap and we walked right into it.'

'Like a pair of prize suckers,' said Damion gleefully.

'What did you rig up to the door of your room?'

'An electric shock . . . with voltage big enough to knock you for six, but not quite big enough to kill you.'

'Thanks for nothing,' said Big Al angrily. 'What are you going to do now, call the cops?'

'Nothing so simple,' said the echoing loudspeaker voice. 'There's a long night ahead and I want to have some fun. Money, as you know, is nothing to me, but you two are obviously in dire need of it or you wouldn't have tried to rob me.'

'A brilliant deduction.'

'Thank you . . . so how would you like to have the three million dollars that are lying on the table in front of you? Free . . . a little present from yours truly.'

There was a silence for a minute and a half. Smokey Joe and Big Al just stared at the mountain of money.

'What,' said Smokey at last, 'do we have to do to get it?'

The loudspeaker laughed mockingly at them. 'Escape, that's all. Untie yourselves and get out of that room. I've locked the door, of course, and I have the key in my pocket, but you're intelligent guys and I figure you might be able to find a way out.'

'For three million bucks I could bust out of the state penitentiary,' said Big Al loudly.

'Okay,' said the distant Damion, 'the bet's on. Three million bucks says you'll never get out of that room.'

'Done!' yelled Al, and began to tug and strain wildly at the ropes that held him to the chair.

Smokey Joe looked at the money and frowned. Young Holzenholler had a mean, nasty streak to him. There was something basically evil about the rich little brat. Three million to watch a couple of grown men struggling to untie themselves from two dining chairs? No, there had to be something more than that. Something more *sinister*. But until he knew what it was, all Smokey Joe could do was help his pal.

'Al,' he said sharply, 'stop wasting your energy trying to bust them ropes. I've got a penknife in my jacket pocket. Bounce that chair over here and face away from me. Then try and slide your fingers into my pocket.'

With a strange crab-like motion, Big Al teetered his chair close to Smokey's. Straining his bound wrists to the very limit of the rope's tension, he wriggled his fingers blindly towards the slanting pocket of Smokey's leather jacket. It was a short, zip-up bomber jacket, and the pockets were shallow. Five minutes later, Al was easing the penknife out, fingers fumbling sweatily to open the blade. Then, with a gentle, unsteady sawing action, he attacked the ropes that bound Smokey Joe's wrist.

'Oh, very clever,' jeered Damion over the speaker. 'You'll soon be out of the chairs . . . and ready to face your *real* test of the night!'

As the fibres frayed and the ropes parted, Smokey suddenly heard a faint pattering sound in a dark corner high on the opposite wall. As he freed his legs, he saw for the first time that there was a small opening there. It was obviously the opening to a horizontal shaft that formed part of the house's air-conditioning system. At one time a grille had been fixed over the hole, but that grille had now been removed. Still watching, Smokey Joe saw a scuttling shape emerge from the darkness of the shaft, run swiftly down the wall and vanish behind the money-laden table. Then came another, and Smokey saw it more clearly this time. It was a large white rat with pink eyes. Then came another and another and another.

By the time Smokey Joe had cut Big Al free, there were twenty or thirty rats racing round the room. And still they came along the shaft. Dozens of them. They seemed to carpet the room, a moving blanket of shining white fur and snapping teeth. Al and Smokey leapt up on to the chairs, hearts pounding. Something was wrong. The rats weren't even afraid of them. They were actually trying to reach the men's feet and legs, to claw, to tear, to bite!

The truth hit Smokey Joe like a hammer. 'They're after food,' he screamed. 'These ruddy rats are starving! They'll attack anything in sight.'

There was a babyish giggle from the ceiling speaker. 'Right first time, pal,' said Damion. 'They haven't had anything to eat for nearly a week. I'll be interested to see how long you can keep off 600 starving rodents.'

'Six hundred?'

'That's right. It was another little hobby of mine that I got bored with. Most kids have one or two white rats as pets, but I lashed out and bought 200. Then they started breeding and I got bored with them . . . until I suddenly hatched my little plan of trying to get myself robbed. Don't forget, suckers . . . I'm betting you three million bucks that you never get out of that room. You keep trying and I'll keep watching!'

By now, Smokey Joe had three rats halfway up his right trouser leg. Tearing them off, he flung them violently at the wall. All three rodents fell senseless, to be buried beneath the heaving bodies of their companions. Suddenly, the money on the table meant nothing. Compared to the struggle for life, it was all so much worthless trash, money to burn.

Money to burn! In a brief second of blinding, stunning, clarity, Smokey Joe knew he'd found the way out of that room. A quick glance at the air conditioning shaft told him that the rats had stopped pouring out of it. All 600 rodents were now in the room. 'Al,' he yelled above the squeaking din from below. 'Gimme me your cigarette lighter, quick.'

Without a word, Big Al tossed it over. Taking a deep breath, Smokey Joe balanced himself on the chair and leapt

They seemed to carpet the room, a moving blanket of shining white fur and snapping teeth.

boldly on to the money-laden table. Dollar bills tumbled over and vanished into the carpet of rats below. Clearing a space for himself, Smokey ripped off a handful of wrappers and made a loose pile of a couple of hundred thousand dollar bills. Then he clicked the lighter and watched the flame flicker and grow. Money to burn! Their passport to freedom. As the bills flared brightly and the fire spread to other bundles, Smokey hurled them into the seething rodents below. Smoke rose and the air grew thick. 'For the love of Pete, what are you doing?' screamed Big Al.

Dumbly, Smokey pointed to the mouth of the air shaft. 'That's our way out,' he croaked hoarsely. 'Clear a path through the rats with burning notes, then put your chair under the opening. Haul yourself up, go in head-first, and start crawling. I'll be right behind you.'

Big Al didn't need any second telling. As the money flamed and burned and crackled around them, and the terrified rats fought to get out of the way, the two men heaved themselves one after the other into the shaft. It ended in a fixed wire grille high in the wall of Damion's bedroom. Another, smaller, shaft led off the main one, showing how the army of rats had found its way along and into the windowless money room.

The lens of his television camera was obscured by smoke, so it was several minutes before Damion realised exactly what was happening, and by then it was too late. Big Al smashed the wire grille away and dived into the bedroom after it like a human torpedo. He was on his feet and reaching for the Holzenholler brat. As his fingers closed on a pure silk dressing gown, Damion twisted free and bolted for the door. He was outside in a flash, racing along a narrow passage that led to a secondary staircase, where a pall of smoke was suddenly drifting upwards.

Big Al and Smokey Joe started to give chase and then stopped. The fire in the money-room had spread fast. Even as they peered over the top of the stairs, they saw a spout of flames erupt from a blazing door half-way down. The blast of fire caught Damion Holzenholler the Third as he tried to cross a lower landing. His silk dressing gown went up in a flash. Next second he fell, screaming, into a smoke-filled darkness from which there could be no escape.

Big Al and Joe didn't stay a second more. As they reached the main road, they looked back. Damion's mini-mansion was blazing like a torch and the wail of a fire engine could be heard in the distance. It was going to be too late.

'The kid had money to burn,' said Smokey Joe thoughtfully. 'I guess it ended up burning him.'

And that, more or less, is the whole story. Big Al died not long afterwards of a heart attack. I guess the shock of that night was just too much for him.

I suppose you're wondering why I know all this, and why I haven't told the authorities, if it's supposed to be a true story. Well, the answer's simple.

My name is Smokey Joe.

ONCE UPON A LIFETIME

by Angus Allan

JIMMY LANGDON THREW DOWN HIS PEN and leapt to his feet. The chair crashed to the floor behind him, a shower of papers fluttered from the desk, but still it went on, the 'piff-paff, piff-paff' that had nearly driven him crazy!

'*Dad*! For goodness sake, stop pacing up and down, up and down! It's more than anyone can bear!'

Professor Magnus Langdon halted in mid-stride, swayed off balance, clutched at a standard lamp, and brought it to the carpet, its shade reeling drunkenly into a corner. 'What – what's that . . .?'

Jimmy bit his lip. 'Sorry, Dad. Didn't mean to go nutty, but I *am* trying to do my homework. It's those shuffly slippers of yours. They're driving me daft!'

'Ah. I get your point,' said the Professor, stooping to pick up the lamp. 'If I'd kept my shoes on, though, there'd have been a regular clipping and clopping on the parquet floor that would have irritated your mother. One of these days, I must get a carpet for our study.'

'It'd be more to the point,' said Jimmy, collecting his scattered papers, 'if you didn't bring your work home with you. When I'm grown up, I'm going to leave the office at five, and that'll be that.'

'I always said as much myself,' replied his smiling father, one of the country's most brilliant nuclear scientists. 'The trouble is, one's work doesn't tend to finish when the clock says so.' He sat down, and amiably tossed his piff-paffing slippers into a corner. 'I'm actually a bit overwrought, old chap. How about you?'

'Just an essay, Dad,' said Jimmy. 'A composition. "Describe the imaginary visit of a time traveller back to the Stone Age." I was thinking about dinosaurs.'

'There weren't any in the Stone Age,' said the Professor. 'They'd all gone by the time people appeared on earth. There were animals, of course, mammoths and so forth . . .'

'Um. All right, then. So what's bothering *you*?'

'A discovery, my boy,' said Magnus Langdon. 'An incredible breakthrough I've made concerning a totally new energy source. It makes nuclear power pale by comparison.'

'But that's marvellous,' gasped Jimmy. 'You'll go down in history, Dad! And think of the benefit to the world!'

The scientist shook his head worriedly. 'It has,' he muttered, 'a clear and definite potential for military use. In the wrong hands, this power would create a possibility for destruction on an undreamed-of scale. The point is, can mankind be trusted to use this force wisely, or would mankind go its usual way and bring about disaster – perhaps the total extinction of the human race?'

They stared at each other for a full five minutes. He could clearly see the problem confronting his father. Does anyone else know?' the boy said at last.

His father shook his head. 'I could publish my findings at next week's conference. And you were quite right. This could make my name as important as that of Einstein. Maybe more so. Honestly, old son, I don't know what to do.'

Deep in thought, the man fetched his slippers from the corner and put them on again. Once more, there came the 'piff-paff, piff-paff' of his restless pacing . . .

Jimmy Langdon gathered his schoolbooks together and, with a sigh, made his way up to his bedroom. He did a sketchy job of his essay, swapped jeans and T-shirt for a pair of pyjamas, and went to bed. Within moments he was fast asleep, but it felt no time at all before he was abruptly awakened by a bright light that filled the room. Jimmy sat up and blinked. He saw that his window was wide open, although it had been closed before, yet curiously, he felt no fear or no alarm. He went across, peered out into the night, and found himself looking at a curious craft hovering there – a cigar-shaped vessel made of glistening white metal. There was no sound from it as it drew closer.

'I'm dreaming,' said Jimmy decisively. Rather casually, surprised that he felt less astonished than he ought, he put his clothes on again. Then he clambered over the sill and into the beckoning doorway of the strange machine.

There was no living soul inside, and there were no controls of any kind. Only a bolted-down metal chair, facing a large front window that hadn't been apparent from the exterior. He heard a voice. It was his own, inside his head, bidding him to sit down, and he obeyed.

All at once there came a sense of vibration, not in the least bit unpleasant, and the night view of his own garden outside blurred to an overall greyness. It cleared quickly, and he saw the sun and the moon chasing each other across the sky. Faster and faster, they became a dizzy whirl, and Jimmy knew that his dream had placed him in some sort of time machine. He said in quite a detached way: 'Wonder where I'll end up?'

At last the sense of motion halted, and through the window of the craft, Jimmy could see the deep black shadows of a craggy landscape sweltering beneath a high and lurid sun. There were trees, though they had an unfamiliar, almost tropical appearance. And a small animal he couldn't identify scurried across his field of vision.

'I knew it,' said Jimmy with satisfaction. 'I'm back in the

Stone Age.' He stood up, went to the door, and stepped down into the heat.

'Nothing to fear from dinosaurs at any rate,' grinned the boy. 'That is, if Dad was right.' He cupped his hands to his mouth and called: 'Any mammoths about?' Only echoes came back from the cluttered rocks.

'Don't go away now,' he said to the time machine, and set off to explore. 'If I can remember all this when I wake up,' he thought, 'I might re-write that essay . . .'

He hadn't gone fifty paces before he heard the shrill whistle. It wasn't the call of a bird, and when it was repeated, this time from a different place, and taken up again from yet another, he realised that it was a human sort of noise. Was that a figure, briefly glimpsed on a nearby skyline . . .? He paused, watchfully. 'Hope this isn't going to turn into a rotten nightmare,' he said aloud.

With a startling clatter, the flung spear bounced off the rock beside him, and as Jimmy jumped with a nervous yelp, he spun round to see the squat, bearded figure clad in animal skins snarling down at him.

'Go easy,' said the boy. 'I'm not your dinner!' Vaguely, he reckoned that, even in a dream, he ought to be frightened. But he wasn't. For long seconds, he looked the bestial figure in the eye, taking in the low forehead, the clawed, misshapen hands and the odd, almost scab-like mottling on the forearms and legs. 'You cave dwellers aren't exactly a pretty sight,' he said.

'All stranger go die!' The voice was harsh and croaking. 'No glowmund krekk about this lands!'

'I know you can't speak English,' said Jimmy. 'Not even funny English with daft words! Cave people just didn't do that!'

'Run, devil! I kill!'

'Oh well, anything's possible in a dream,' sighed the boy.

'And since it obviously is going to be a nightmare, I suppose I'm going to find myself rooted to the spot when he starts to chase me.'

In fact, Jimmy found no difficulty at all in running, and he took to his heels quickly enough when more barking, guttural voices in that artificial English came from behind and to the side of him. The boy took off down a gulley, with the spears that were flung after him rattling at his feet.

His pursuers were nimble. For all their grotesque stature, they sprang easily from rock to rock, and kept pace with Jimmy, pausing from time to time to pick up fragments of stone and hurl them after him. A couple struck him glancing blows, and he began to get just a little annoyed. 'Blow this for a joke. I want to wake up now, thank you.' But he didn't wake up, and as more and more of the Primitives (he found himself calling them that, and shortening the term to 'Prims') joined in the pursuit, Jimmy darted into the shelter of a cavernous opening in the hillside where his flight had led him. He was aware that he might be heading into a place from which there was no other exit, but some instinct told him it was a tunnel, and his instinct was right.

When once more he emerged into the sunlight, he found himself on the fringe of thick, dense jungle. For a moment, the glaring eyes of a wolf-like creature stared at him from the undergrowth, an animal that bared its fangs and raised the patchy hackles on its ragged-looking neck. The boy shouted, and the creature turned and fled. 'I suppose the Stone Age is all very well if you're a Prim,' muttered Jimmy. 'But on the whole I'd rather live in my own time, school and all.' Now he could hear the sounds of the chase coming through the tunnel behind him, and with a do-or-die shrug, he headed for the jungle. Carefully, to leave no trace behind him, he crawled under the tangle of fringing plants, and only stood up when he was deep in the humid forest. He saw the wolf-thing again,

His pursuers were nimble. For all their grotesque stature, they sprang easily from rock to rock, and kept pace with Jimmy.

only briefly before it slunk away. Yet he had time to notice that the animal's coat was sparse, and that its skin showed the same unsightly blotching as that of the Prims.

All at once, Jimmy stumbled upon the track. There were the prints of human feet there. Or were they human? They looked it, but the impressions showed that in every case there were only three toes. 'Can't recall anything about Stone-Age people not having proper feet,' the boy mused. And then, remembering it was only a dream, shrugged it off.

Very cautiously, he followed the track until it broadened out. He slipped into the shelter of some heavily and unpleasantly scented bushes as he caught a glimpse of rough wooden huts in a clearing ahead. There were Prims there – men, women and children – but they were different from the ones who had chased him. These were pallid creatures, sickly and frail, almost tiny in stature. The only similarity with the others was that ever-present skin-blotching . . .

Two of them passed close enough to him for the boy to overhear their conversation, again in that odd half-English tongue . . .

One said: 'Samuel hear the harak whistle of Jakka hunters. Best makane for pobsul attack.'

'Yun,' replied his companion. 'When Jakka hungry, munch all. One vullage last moon, suffer gably. Twelve eaten.'

'Glad I got away from them,' thought Jimmy. 'I don't fancy ending up in a cannibal cook-pot, not even in a nightmare!'

Then he flattened himself to the ground as a chorus of barking cries came from the track behind him, and his original Prims hurtled past, their spears raised! Their yells mingled with the shrieks of terror from the scurrying villagers.

'I'm off,' muttered Jimmy. 'If my dream won't let me wake up, I'm jolly well going back to the time machine and see if it'll take me somewhere else!'

There was only one snag. He retraced his steps without much difficulty, but saw from the jungle fringe that the Prims had left two of their number on guard at the entrance to the tunnel.

'I might have known,' groaned Jimmy. 'Oh well, it's going to be the long way round, along the hillside and over the top. I wish this was like the usual sort of dream, where suddenly you find yourself in a completely different situation.' He brushed the sweat from his forehead. 'I wouldn't even mind if I took one more step, and there I was, walking down the High Street in my underpants!'

No such luck. Jimmy had quite a struggle to outflank the watchful Prims and scramble up the rocky hillside out of their sight. It was toilsome work, and he paused frequently. He felt thirsty, and the novelty of his dream was wearing decidedly thin . . .

He gained the summit of the hill and cast around for the sight of his time machine. With the glaring sun right in his eyes, he couldn't spot it. Maybe it was behind those distant rocks . . .? No. He hadn't run that far . . .

Peeved, he began to plod downwards, and then, in the gulley that suddenly appeared to his left, he saw it. Not the time machine, but something much more mind-boggling. It stuck drunkenly upwards from the tumbled shale – a bronze weathercock, the four compass points eroded but recognisable. And the weathercock itself was in the shape of a long-tailed dragon. A *familiar* dragon.

'What on earth . . .? It's – it's the one from Saint John's Church, in the village!' Jimmy stopped and examined it. There could be no doubt about it. He'd never seen it this close, but it was a local landmark, one which he passed every day on his way to school.

The boy looked up, frowning. Now *this* was an odd aspect

to his dream . . .

A nagging thought came into his mind. This wasn't the Stone Age at all. The time machine had taken him, surely, into the far distant future . . .

But where was the village? What had happened to it? And who were the savage Prims and their frightened victims? Why were they and the jungle animals so curiously blotched? Possessed of only three toes? Come to that, what was *jungle* doing here . . .?

Jimmy had read plenty of science fiction, and it was only a moment before he came to the only possible conclusion. The world – *his* world – had been devastated by some ghastly apocalypse. These creatures were mutants, survivors of the disaster, or more likely, the descendants of those survivors. He shuddered at the thought.

As if to shut out the vision, he willed with all his might for the dream to end. His eyes shut tight, he clenched his fists and yelled for the nightmare to stop. He stumbled painfully against the wretched weathercock, hearing and feeling a pocket in his jeans rip against the brittle, corroded bronze.

Then he was running again, leaping rocks and boulders on his way out of the gulley as if all the Prims that lived were after him. Yes . . . and there it was again . . . the whistling. The exchange of signals! He hadn't been scared before, but now Jimmy felt horrible fear overtake him as the heights around became alive with the screaming Prims. Spears showered about him as he ducked and dodged, his breath sobbing in his throat . . .

Just when it seemed that all was lost, just when it seemed that the closest of the hunters would leap down and cut him off, Jimmy found it. The blessed, glistening cigar-shape of the time machine, its doorway so invitingly open! Although a stitch in his side almost doubled him over, he hurled himself inside and sprawled across the bolted chair, his wide eyes seeing the last spears glance from the window before rocks and trees whirled into a grey nothingness. Then the sky once more became the home of the sun and moon in their hectic chase . . .

Sunlight of a much more pleasant kind wakened Jimmy Langdon early in the morning. It came streaming through the glass of his bedroom window, and he blinked his eyes against it.

Then he sat bolt upright in bed as all the curious details of his dream came flooding back to him. *What* a dream! He puffed his cheeks and blew out, glad it was all over. Then he said: 'Whew', and a second later, 'gosh'. He got up and looked out at the old familiar garden, the roofs of the village beyond the sycamore trees. His watch, on his bedside table, told him it was six-thirty. Wide awake now, he reached for the schoolbook and tore out the sheets of his essay before he began to make his re-write. A Stone Age in the future. He hoped his teacher wouldn't think it was too far-fetched . . .

Exactly an hour later, he laid his pen aside, pulled off his pyjamas, and reached for his jeans.

'Hullo! The . . . pocket's torn . . .'

A strange shiver ran down Jimmy's spine as he turned the garment over in his hands. Something fell from the torn pocket.

It was a badly corroded piece of bronze, but it was recognisable as the letter N, the north compass point from a weathercock . . .

Jimmy sat down on his bed, his face in his hands, his brain reeling. It hadn't been a dream at all. Or, or maybe he was *still* dreaming, without knowing it. He actually pinched himself.

He remembered the binoculars that he used for bird watching. Shakily, he got them from his cupboard and aimed them towards the village. He brought the spire of Saint John's Church into focus, and caught his breath in horror as he saw that the letter N was no longer there beneath the dragon weathercock!

Very slowly, Jimmy dressed himself, and even more slowly, he set off down the landing towards his father's bedroom. He *knew* he'd been shown the future, but would he be able to convince his father that under no circumstances should he ever publish the secret of his energy discovery? For such a young boy, the sense of responsibility was truly awesome.

THE POE FANATIC

by June Williams

IT WAS IN THE LATE AUTUMN OF 1880 that I had the misfortune to meet Harold Pym. I was travelling by train from Boston to Baltimore to see my aunt when a man entered my carriage and sat down opposite me. I can see him as clearly as if it were yesterday, a slightly built man, shabbily dressed in black, with a large domed forehead and piercing black eyes that seemed to bore into my very soul.

But before I tell you more about Mr Pym and what came out of our meeting, I should perhaps tell you a little about myself. Then perhaps you will understand why I allowed myself to be drawn into a situation which any man in his right senses would have avoided at all costs.

My name is William Reynolds and I am a writer. The stories I write are mere trifles, needing little more than a vivid imagination and the ability to put words in their right order in a sentence. They are macabre stories – walking corpses and screaming skulls, ghosts and nameless horrors from beyond the grave, headless horsemen and vampires – these are my stock in trade.

Be that as it may, I take my craft seriously, and I always try to make my stories believable, however bizarre the plot may be. In this, I have always found it helps enormously to draw one's characters from life. In that lay my undoing as far as Harold Pym was concerned.

So there I was on that fateful day, sitting quietly in my seat, with no one else to disturb my thoughts, when this stranger joined me. I acknowledged his presence with the slightest of nods, and then went back to mulling over the plot of a story I was working on. Suddenly, a voice broke into my thoughts: 'Cold evening, even for this time of the year, don't you think, sir?'

I looked up and saw my companion regarding me expectantly. 'It is indeed,' I said shortly. Realising this was the opening gambit from someone wishing to pass the time with idle conversation, I reached for the *Boston Courier* at my side, intending to bury my nose in it. But there was something about the stranger's manner that made me stay my hand. There are some people that you know are tiresome bores before they even open their mouths. Others have a look that makes you wish to know more about them. I decided he was such a man. So instead of pretending to read my paper, I allowed myself to be drawn into a conversation. After we had disposed of the weather, the deplorable lack of heating in our carriage, and the railways' careless treatment in general of its passengers, my companion informed me that his name was Harold Pym and that he lived in Baltimore.

'You are in business there?' I ventured to ask.

He shook his head. 'Fortunately, I do not have to work in the common marketplace. If I had to put a name to how I occupy myself, I suppose I would call myself a dabbler with a specialised interest. And you, sir. What line of business are you in, if I may be so bold as to ask?'

I told him and was gratified to see his face light up. 'You have heard of me?' I enquired hopefully.

'I have indeed,' he said. 'Moreover, I have read some of your stories. They impressed me greatly. They are well written, and are clearly the work of someone who has a remarkable intuitive knowledge of the evil that lurks in the heart of everyone.' He continued: 'But with respect, your stories do not match those of Edgar Allan Poe, surely the greatest master of the macabre the world is ever likely to see. I am a great admirer of Poe's works. You are, of course, acquainted with his writings?'

'Of course,' I said curtly. Poe had written a great number of stories in his short lifetime, most of them with macabre themes. They were well enough done in their way, but I had found them repellent rather than entertaining. They showed the workings of a diseased mind, I thought – an opinion that seems to have been shared by the critics, who ignored him during his lifetime. It was true that thirty years after his death it had suddenly become fashionable to refer to him as the founding father of the supernatural tale. I remained unimpressed, as I had been when I had read his work as a young man.

But to have said as much to Pym would have been discourteous. Anyway, I knew it would be a waste of time. Any adverse comments from me would be seen merely as a childish display of professional jealousy from a lesser writer. So I contented myself by making some vague complimentary remarks about Poe's work.

The effect on Pym was remarkable. Leaning forward, he took one of my hands in his, and wrung it fervently. 'How rare it is to meet someone who really appreciates and understands his work.' He beamed at me. 'Dare one hope you are a disciple?'

'Possibly,' I mumbled, withdrawing my hand from his cold clasp. I could not resist adding: 'I like to think, though, that I have added something of my own to the genre.'

'Of course. Of course,' he said hastily. He leaned back in his seat and stared thoughtfully at the ceiling. I had the impression that he was trying to make up his mind about something before he spoke again. But, as it happened, he did not say another single word until we reached Baltimore. As we prepared to alight from the carriage, he placed a tentative hand on my arm. 'I hope you will not think me too bold on so short an acquaintance, but I would like to invite you to my house. I have some Poe memorabilia that I am sure would interest you greatly.'

I hesitated. To tell the truth, I had not taken greatly to Pym. I found his conduct odd, his manners questionable, and his literary tastes poor. But he was clearly an eccentric with a somewhat mysterious background and, as such, possible material for my pen. I therefore accepted his offer. 'I have to tell you, though,' I said. 'I am staying in Baltimore for only a very short time. If we are to meet, it will have to be tomorrow evening.'

'That would suit me very well,' he said. 'I live some miles outside the town, and my house is a little difficult to find. I would suggest, therefore, that we meet somewhere else first. Tell your cab driver to take you to Ayer's Ferry. Shall we say at eight?'

'I shall be there.' We shook hands briefly, and went on our respective ways.

The following evening, after a trying day with my aunt, who is a rather demanding old lady, I set off to keep my appointment with Harold Pym. It was one of those dank, foggy nights so common to Baltimore at that time of the year, and as we drove away from the house, I could not help thinking I would have been better off to have stayed there, toasting my toes before the fire, even though it would have meant having to listen to my aunt gossiping away for most of the evening.

The journey seemed to take an age, but at last we reached Ayer's Ferry, where we found Pym already waiting for us in a horse and trap. Paying off the driver, I went over and joined him. As I clambered into the trap, I noticed he had a flask in his hand. 'Whisky, to keep out the cold,' he said, noting my faint look of surprise. He took a vigorous swig from the flask and then offered it to me. 'You could probably do with some of this yourself.'

'Thank you, no,' I said stiffly. 'I never drink.'

'You are a wise man,' he said, taking another swig at the flask. 'Alcohol is a demon that can destroy a man.'

We proceeded down a long, winding country road. Pym asked me how I was enjoying Baltimore, and I told him that I liked it well enough, but that it was not my favourite city. 'I agree with you,' Pym said. 'It is not the most gracious of places in which to live.' We drove on for a few minutes and then Pym said suddenly. 'Poe died there, you know.'

'I know,' I said shortly. 'And alcohol contributed to his death.'

Pym was silent. I realised that he was probably something of a drinking man himself and that I had touched him on a raw spot, so I said nothing more until we came to a halt in front of a large Gothic-style building set well back from the road. I was surprised at its size and wondered if there was a wife and a band of servants to run it. As if reading my thoughts, Pym said: 'As I live here alone, you will find my hospitality somewhat basic.' He gave me a strange glance. 'But I don't think you will regret coming – not after you have seen what I have to show you . . .'

Saying that he was going to take me back to Baltimore himself, Pym hitched the horse and trap to a tethering post, and then let me into the house. To my surprise, there were candles everywhere in the spacious hallway, either placed in sconces on the wall or in candelabra set on a number of small tables. 'It sets the right atmosphere,' Pym said quietly, watching me, as my gaze roamed around the hallway.

'For what?' I asked blankly.

'For my museum,' Pym said. Taking a candelabrum from one of the tables, he beckoned me to follow him. 'You are about to see something no other man has ever seen.'

Above the shallow pit that had been made in the floor a giant pendulum with a vicious blade swung backwards and forwards.

Even now, after all these years, I can still remember my utter wonderment as Pym took me on a tour of his house. The whole place was truly a shrine to the works of Poe. With the aid of waxworks and stuffed animals, he had recreated scene after scene from his stories. In one set-piece, the headless body of a woman lay on the floor with a huge ape hovering menacingly over it – a scene which I recognised at once as being from *The Murders in the Rue Morgue*. That story, of course, deals with a series of horrifying murders in the Latin Quarter of Paris, which turn out to have been committed by an escaped ape. In another set-piece, a group of masked dancers stood looking towards a figure dressed from head to toe in red, a scene this time from *The Masque of the Red Death*. In the story set in France during a cholera epidemic, the figure in red was Death, who had come to claim the victims of the disease.

And so it went on from one room to another, each of them bringing to life some scene that had originated in the sick mind of its author. Here was *The Black Cat*, sitting on the head of its dead master, with its single eye glaring out at me from behind a half-bricked wall. Here, too, was Poe's *Ligeia*, trailing her funereal robes, and here, too, was *William Wilson*, running his sword through his doppelganger – his ghostly double. Finally, there was a scene from *The Pit and the Pendulum*.

'You may know the story,' Pym said at my elbow. 'A man, tried and sentenced to death by the Inquisition, is placed in a pit and tied down under a great blade that swings backwards and forwards like a pendulum above him, gradually lowering itself, inch by inch, until it reaches his body . . .'

'You needn't go on,' I said. 'I know the story.' I stared round the room hung with heavy draperies, and then at the shallow pit that had been made in the floor. Above it, as in the story, a giant pendulum with a vicious blade attached to it, swung slowly backwards and forwards over a waxwork figure. All that was missing were the rats that had so plagued the unhappy victim.

'One day, when Poe is fully appreciated,' Pym said, 'I will open this museum to the public. Until then, my doors will be closed to the world.' He sighed gustily. 'That poor man – so greatly underrated to this very day.'

Perhaps I should have kept my mouth shut and left as soon as it was decently possible. But I found it impossible to contain myself any longer. 'Not underrated, but rightly seen as the drunken literary fake he was.' I turned to face Pym. 'If I may say so, your money could have been better spent.'

Taken aback, Pym could only look at me with stricken eyes.

'I might as well be honest with you,' I said. 'I consider Poe's work little more than the self-pitying ravings of a madman.'

'Enough,' Pym said in a low voice. 'Enough!'

'If I had my way,' I went on cruelly, 'I would have his work banned . . .'

This time I had gone too far. With a strangled cry, Pym hurled away the candelabrum he had been holding and flung himself upon me with such force that I staggered back to the very edge of the pit. Knowing that I was fighting for my very life, I struck blow after blow upon his body. None of them seemed to have any effect.

To make matters worse, I suddenly became aware that I was now faced with an additional hazard to my life. The candelabrum that Pym had flung aside had set light to the draperies, which were now blazing like some gigantic torch. It was this, more than anything else, that gave me the strength to free myself from Pym's maniacal grasp. Knocking him to the ground with a forceful blow that must have knocked him out, I fled from the chamber.

I cannot tell you for how long I stumbled through the seemingly endless corridors, pursued by billowing clouds of smoke which turned into flames as the fire raced from one waxwork to another. Finally I was standing, outside the house. Looking back I saw that the whole upper part of the building was enveloped in flames. If Pym had not recovered from my blow in time to reach the lower floors, he was surely now dead.

Sobbing hysterically. I ran towards the tethered pony and trap. Unhitching them, I flung myself into the trap. The pony was as anxious as I was to get away from the scene, and we went off at a fine old lick. Half an hour later, I was back in the city.

You may be surprised to learn that I did not report any of the terrible affair to the police. Instead, I left the pony and trap in a quiet alleyway and then took the first train I could out of Baltimore. I did this for what seemed to me a very good reason: as I had been indirectly responsible for Pym's death, I could well be caught up in the machinery of the law while it was decided whether or not I had anything to answer for. I have no idea what my aunt thought of my hasty and unannounced flight. I eventually wrote to her in a deliberately rambling way, pleading that I had had a brainstorm. All I know is that when she died, she did not leave me a single cent.

There is one last thing I have to tell you. Recently, I had occasion to refer to a volume of Poe's works, and in it was a picture of the author. I was immediately struck by Pym's remarkable resemblance to him. Was it possible, I now ask myself, that Pym was the unhappy spirit of Poe himself, forever seeking the recognition that had been denied him in his lifetime?

That thought will haunt me to the end of my days.

DEADLY SHOT

by John Sanders

HAMMOND READ WITH SURPRISE, THEN PLEASURE, the telegram thrust into his hand by the page boy at the Speke Hotel. Surprise because he had got beyond believing that anyone would employ him again; pleasure because more than anything he needed a job. But there it was, in the pidgin language of telegrams:

HAMMOND SPEKE HOTEL KAMPALA COME URGENTEST STOP HAVE PROBLEM FOR SOLUTION BY MARKSMAN STOP STACEY KAABONG MISSION KAABONG KARAMOJA

Mechanically, Hammond rose from the old leather sofa in the foyer, downing his beer and twisting the telegram into his pocket all in the same motion. No one cared to wait in dangerous Kampala. Everyone thought only of leaving this steaming city of crumbling streets, closed-down hotels, and half-wrecked buses, trucks and cars.

It took him twenty minutes to pack and another fifteen to wrap up his prize Winchester rifle in oilskins; another five to check out and ten more to start up his dusty hired Skoda. The shadows of the sticky evening were creeping into the city as he bumped down the north road. The first groups of Mufata Mingi – the armed bands of robbers who wore military uniforms and ruled the city's nights with terror – were already spilling from the darkened edges of the side streets along with the mad dogs. It was good to be leaving Kampala even if he couldn't yet be leaving Uganda.

Hammond had come to East Africa as a United Nations Supplies Overseeing Officer, filled with idealistic notions about helping the Third World. The Ugandan dictatorship which took over a few months after his arrival was a death blow to all that youthful idealism. Hammond had watched with rage, then indifference, the government's horrifying slaughter of Asians and tribal rivals, had watched the once-merry, ragged people mown down with panga knives by government soldiers drunk on banana beer.

Cut off from all aid from UN headquarters in Geneva and with no more supplies to oversee, he had spent his days at target shooting, a sport he had since developed to perfection. Thus, while Hammond waited by day for the political climate to change, and avoided the Mufata Mingi by night, he had filled in the idle hours by becoming something of a minor legend amongst the English-speaking community as a crack shot – a marksman second to none in the country.

In these last few months, Hammond had been providing impromptu shooting exhibitions to wide-eyed, pot-bellied Ugandans, rather like some nineteenth-century Wild West marshal. At least, he said to cynical friends in the dwindling white population, it took their minds off their empty stomachs for half an hour or so.

As Kampala slipped behind him and the road bumped and yawed into the distance, Hammond considered the telegram. He had never heard of Stacey, but judged him to be one of those unsung missionary heroes who never gave up, supplying help in the midst of war and famine as in peace. He had never been to the Karamoja cattle country, but he had heard the Kampala whites describe it with a shudder. It was a place, therefore, where the only whites were likely to be missionaries.

What was more intriguing was the 'problem for solution by marksman'. What could a religious mission possibly want with a marksman? To entertain the starving villagers? That seemed hardly worth a long journey. No one had actually employed Hammond as a marksman before. This was, he thought with wry amusement, the first time he had been summoned as a gun for hire . . .

At midnight, six hours after leaving Kampala, he pulled the Skoda in at a lay-by on the bush road, calculating that he had travelled half-way to his destination. He filled the petrol tank from the jerricans he was carrying, set up his primus and steamed a portion of green beans and a bit of meat.

A couple of banana trucks had pulled into the lay-by for the night. Hammond caught sight of one of the drivers sleeping curled up on the front seats. The nearly full moon, pinned like a medal on the black sky, was the only silent witness to a night shrill with the many sounds of unseen jungle life.

The moon had gone and the sun was up when Hammond drove into the dust bowl that was the Kaabong Mission. A swarm of naked children crowded the Skoda as he switched off the engine outside the wooden mission house. At once the door opened and a short, bespectacled white man came bouncing down the two wooden steps. Hammond noted his dog collar and his pink-hued skin. The clergyman held out his hand. 'Welcome to the Kaabong Mission,' he said with a pronounced Scottish accent. 'I'm Gordon Stacey, minister in charge. It's good of you to come all this way. They'll have some breakfast ready for you in half a jiffy.'

'I could do with that,' Hammond said. The meat and steamed beans were already far away in memory.

'We can provide you with a bath of sorts. Come along in and I'll tell you what it's all about.'

Inside the mission hut the Reverend Stacey gave clipped orders, at which barefoot black servants set a scrubbed table with a plate of maize cakes and jug of banana beer. Hammond was surprised to see a tall, black man, dressed in a leopard skin and with brilliant blue hair, already seated at the table.

Stacey grinned apologetically. 'This is Mbo, the local *nganga*, or witch doctor,' he explained. 'He's quite harmless. He isn't exactly converted yet to the teachings of our Lord, but we're working on it. I thought you might like to talk to him after I've explained our problem.'

Mbo looked across the scrubbed table at Hammond and showed his upper teeth. His bottom lip was pierced with a brilliant ivory ring which had extended the pink flesh grotesquely.

'Does he always go about looking like that?' Hammond said with a slight shudder. Stacey looked amused. 'The ivory ring identifies his rank of nganga,' he said. 'All Karamojang warriors wear a ring in their lower lip. It is their sign of masculinity. The warriors' rings are made of hair. Only the nganga is allowed to have an ivory ring. All the Karamojang warriors dye their hair, you know.' He spread his hands and sighed. 'This is not an easy country in which to spread the Lord's word, Mr Hammond.'

Hammond bit into a maize cake and eyed the witch doctor warily. 'How does he come into it?' he asked.

'He is actually the new nganga,' Stacey explained. 'He has been in the job, so to speak, for only a couple of weeks. The last nganga died a month ago, and that's when our troubles began. The problem is this, Mr Hammond. When a Karamojang warrior dies, the natives believe that his spirit enters the body of a wild animal. So they wrap up the body in banana tree leaves and carry it as far as they can from the village to a burying place. They reason that the warrior will try to get back to his village by urging the wild animal which he has entered to go in that direction. But, of course, the villagers don't want to have their huts surrounded by wild animals. That's why they take their dead warriors as far away as possible, hoping they will not be able to find their way back as animals.'

Hammond nodded in understanding and sympathy, for he was thinking of the problem that a missionary like Stacey must have when describing the Christian idea of heaven to Karamojang warriors.

'In the case of the last nganga, however, the burial party did not quite act according to custom,' Stacey went on. 'They were only a short distance outside Kaabong when they were surprised by a band of Mufata Mingi. They dropped the body and fled. When they went back next day, the nganga's body had disappeared. Of course, you and I as Christians would assume that it was taken either by the Mufata Mingi, or by some animal. The people however, assumed that it had already entered the body of a wild animal, and I'm afraid that what happened next has made them believe it even more.'

Mbo grinned across the table at Hammond, his white teeth and ivory lip-ring sparkling in a shaft of sunlight through the open window.

'During the next three weeks, a hyena was seen to be lurking around the edge of the village. The night after it was first spotted, a child disappeared from the village. The hyena has been sighted at night half a dozen times since then, and two other children disappeared on two of those sightings. Very sadly, remains which could belong only to those children were found next morning – remains which indicate that in each case they were taken by a wild animal. The villagers, naturally, say the hyena is guilty.'

Hammond's brow furrowed. 'You're not telling me that

the warriors can't kill a hyena, are you?' he asked.

'They dare not. For they believe that the dead nganga is inside the hyena and is trying to get back to his village. Whoever kills the hyena, they believe, will himself die at the next full moon. They are poor, superstitious wretches, Mr Hammond, but we must always remember that they are all God's children.'

'I see.' Hammond chose another maize cake slowly while he considered the case. It was hard to believe this sort of mumbo-jumbo still existed in the twentieth century, even in this poor corner of Africa. He looked up suddenly from selecting a maize cake and saw the gleaming upper teeth of Mbo. The witch doctor's eyes were riveted on him and his quick, nervous fingers touching the ivory ring in his lower lip betrayed his anxiety.

'*Muzungu* kill nganga hyena?'

'A muzunga is a white man,' Stacey interpreted. 'He wants you to say that you'll do the job.'

'I suppose if the hyena dies it sort of makes sure of his promotion,' Hammond said, and then thought at once that his remark might be unfair to the new nganga. He shrugged and pushed away the plate of maize cakes. 'I'll need half a dozen beaters, some of the younger and fitter members of your congregation.'

'I'm afraid the local people will give you no help at all. No question of it. They are absolutely terrified, Mr Hammond, absolutely terrified.'

Hammond thought deeply. He could kill the hyena without beaters, but it would take longer, days perhaps, to find the animal. 'You'll have to provide me with a carcass as bait,' he said. 'I'll get some sleep now and start tonight.'

The short African twilight was beginning as Hammond slit the carcass of a cow with a borrowed panga knife. He chose a spot in the bush just north of Kaabong village and pegged out the carrion at wide intervals, forming a long crescent that crossed several well-used animal paths to a water hole. Divided into eight pieces, the carcass covered quite a distance. It was long enough to catch an inquisitive beast's attention, and not too long for surveillance. When Hammond pegged down the last bit of meat, the red sun slipped beyond the distant mountains. Suddenly it was night.

Hammond didn't feel better for his day-long sleep. He was conscious of a sore dryness in his throat and an enduring headache. He slipped a pill on to his tongue and swallowed it with a draught of warm water from his flask. Under one arm he cradled the loaded Winchester. With his free hand he felt his forehead gingerly. He was sweating, more than the heat and the last half hour's exertion should cause. 'Hang it,' he thought, 'I must be getting a fever.'

There was nothing to do then but wait and wait.

For the first part of the night, Hammond sat behind the cover of a clump of bush, downwind from the water, nursing the Winchester and listening attentively to the shrill chatter of the nocturnal wild life. Occasionally, the noise was heightened by sudden alarm signals, squawks and shrieks of warning that rose above the never-ending background din; but nothing untoward happened. At midnight Hammond began to doze. The soreness in his throat seemed to be worsening and his skin was hot and sticky to the touch. He began to want more than anything to be away from this place, to be in a city surrounded by the familiar sights and sounds of people. Soon he was asleep.

At one-thirty he shook himself awake, cursing his foolishness. The moon, high in the sky, lit the jungle scene, still noisy with chatter. Hammond strained to listen, as if making up for the time lost in sleep. A bead of sweat dropped from his forehead on to the butt of the Winchester. Still there seemed nothing wrong in the pulsating jungle.

Hammond relaxed. Relief flooded through his limbs. He had failed temporarily in his duty but nothing was lost by it. Then, conscious that he might not stay awake, he stood up, stretched, and padded stealthily up and down behind bush cover, careful always to remain downwind of the water hole. He had to stay alert. A dull ache had settled on his neck, and his head was beginning to beat out a rhythm of pain. Chewing on a maize cake, he thought longingly of the relative comfort of the Speke Hotel in Kampala. At three o'clock a vein of dawn touched the sky's horizon. Hammond contemplated giving up the dreary night's watch. He would come back when he was well, when he could stay awake.

Then he saw the hyena.

It stood stock still, a dark silhouette against the moon, only a short distance away. It looked straight into the eyes of its hunter. Hammond felt the hairs on his back prickling with alarm. The soundless suddenness of its appearance had taken him completely by surprise, freezing his hands in their relaxed position on the unpointed rifle. He felt his temples throbbing with the growing fever. It took him something like a minute to regain his composure, a minute in which the silhouetted beast before him remained absolutely motionless.

As Hammond raised the rifle slowly to the aiming position, rivers of warm sweat ran down his forehead, blurring his vision. Still the dark silhouette remained motionless. He steadied the Winchester, faltered, steadied again. A wave of nausea welled up from his stomach as he squeezed the trigger.

The single shot set the bush screaming. As if in slow motion, the animal fell. It was a clean and simple kill.

Shaking with fever, Hammond walked over to inspect his work. The dead hyena's eyes were still open, and as he turned its still-warm jaws, they glinted yellow in the moonlight. Hammond's right hand was still on the beast's muzzle when he felt something that caused his blood to run cold. Half in disbelief, half in terror, he scraped away at the hairs on the hyena's lower jaw. Then he saw it. Fixed in the lower lip of the dead beast was a white ivory ring.

Hammond didn't need a second glance to recognise it. It was identical to the ivory ring in the lower lip of the nganga Mbo. It was a witch doctor's lip ring, the mark of a nganga's rank.

The marksman stepped back in panic from the dead hyena. Seized with sudden blind terror, he began to run through the bush, causing a new uproar from the unseen creatures of the night. Only when he was panting with exhaustion did he pull himself up and slump, gasping for breath, to the ground. A startled lizard, coloured like a rainbow, observed him, quivering, from a gum tree.

Hammond was angry with himself then. 'I've imagined it all,' he said hysterically, aloud. 'I've got jungle fever. I'll have to rest up here.'

The Reverend Gordon Stacey was sitting on the steps of his wooden mission house as Hammond came down the jungle path into the wide clearing that was Kaabong village. The Winchester on the marksman's shoulder was framed in the first light behind him.

'I heard the shot,' Stacey said. 'You got him?' Hammond nodded.

'This is a good day. The Lord has been merciful to us.' Stacey peered at Hammond as he came closer. 'I say, are you all right? You look a bit feverish. You'd better rest up.'

Two days later, the marksman shook hands with Stacey in the clearing of the Kaabong mission, then revved up the engine of the battered Skoda. The fever had left him as suddenly as it had come. Now, refreshed and alert again, he was almost looking forward to the sights and sounds of

Seized with sudden blind terror, he began to run through the bush, causing a new uproar from the unseen creatures of the night.

Kampala.

There was no alternative to the road south. Ahead of him lay the same route, the same monotonous twelve hours he had driven in the reverse direction from Kamapala to Kaabong.

Night had already begun when he reached the bush lay-by half-way along the Kampala road, the place where he had cooked his meal four nights earlier. A solitary banana truck had pulled in ahead of him, and the driver and his mate were taking a nap in the cabin. Hammond pulled up behind them, turned off the engine, reached for his primus and the bag of dried green beans, and opened the car door.

Before him the roadside jungle clearing was sharply illuminated, almost, it seemed at first glance, as if it were already daylight. Surprised, Hammond looked up at the sky. He had just sufficient time to notice the full moon.

With shrieks and whoops and cries that came of fear and hate and the lust to kill, half a dozen Mufata Mingi came out of the jungle. They sprayed the sleeping banana truck with their automatic rifles and turned it into an instant ball of fire. They cut a swathe across the roadside lay-by, shooting at everything and nothing. Hammond died instantly, riddled with bullets, still clutching his primus and his bag of dried green beans.

The moon, full and round, shone brightly over the scene.

SECRET DEVIL'S SPIRE
by M.S. Goodall

ASIAN AIRWAYS FLIGHT NUMBER 417 from Bangkok to Rome ran into trouble an hour after leaving Calcutta. Warned of hurricane-force winds sweeping inland from the Bay of Bengal, the pilot had changed course slightly to try and avoid them. He was heading north-west along the Himalayan foothills when a violent electrical storm came up at 30 000 feet. Black clouds suddenly split open as an eye-blinding bolt of lightning hit the wide-bodied jet slightly aft of the main cabin.

'*Flame-out*!' The dreaded word broke like a scream from the flight engineer's throat. With no power in any of the four engines, the plane was buffeted off course like some giant, wounded bird. The captain was a true professional. He knew he was as good as dead, but he still fought for control. The aircraft broke cloud cover, and just for a moment, the crew saw a majestic, endless vista of snowbound peaks. Then they were down. The 'plane's belly ground into hard-packed ice on the edge of a glacier, bounced twice as the wings sheared off, and then slammed with shocking force into the eastern col of a knife-like Himalayan peak. There were 180 passengers and crew aboard the stricken aircraft. Not one of them survived.

On the slopes of the same mountain, in the tiny Nepalese village of Dehra Pur, men, women, and children looked up and shook their heads. They had seen the blackness of the looming storm, and had heard the droning of the engines so suddenly and savagely silenced. They knew what to expect next, and were watching with calm, expressionless faces as the tiny silver dart above them burst out of the clouds and plunged to its doom on the snow-covered slopes. They knew their mountain well, and they feared it. In their own village dialect, it was called Mak Ang Phupta. In the language of the Europeans who had so often tried to climb it, it was called The Devil's Spire. Many had died on its blizzard-swept slopes. Now more had met their death. The villagers shook their heads once more and turned away. There was nothing they could do. Better that the mountain be left in peace to bury its own dead.

One man of the village continued to look upward, however. His name was Sherpa Parba Yam and he was eighteen years of age. For as long as he could remember, the rugged grandeur of Mak Ang Phupta had had an uncanny influence on his life. His earliest memories were of roaming the high slopes in the brief calm of summer. Every year, as he grew older, Parba was drawn back to the mountain. It was his proud boast that he had been higher on the rock band of The Devil's Spire than any of the other villagers. He was a natural climber. He knew the mountain's moods, he knew its dangers, and he respected them.

Parba's mother often said that the boy had inherited his love of climbing from his dead father, Sherpa Pasang Yam. Pasang had died before Parba was born, and it was the mountain that had claimed his life, too, like so many others. Parba had heard the story many times. Nearly twenty years before, his father had gone with a European expedition as guide and head porter in an attempt to scale the dreaded north-east ridge of Mak Ang Phupta. He had last been seen going strongly for the summit with the English leader of the expedition. But neither man had returned, and their bodies had never been found. Parba often wondered whether his father had had the satisfaction of standing on the summit of The Devil's Spire before he died. 'One day,' thought Parba with a final upward glance at his beloved mountain, '*I* shall force the north-east ridge and stand on that summit.'

Three weeks later, while Parba was tending his mother's goats on the high pastures, he saw the village headman toiling up the stony track towards him. The old man was out of breath and hot from his long climb. 'Come,' he said, gesturing weakly with his hand. 'Round up your goats and return to the village. A stranger has come amongst us. He wants to speak to you.'

'Someone from another village?' asked Parba, puzzled.

The headman shook his head. 'No, this traveller is a foreigner. A European. A determined man who waves much money in the air. He says it is his wish to climb Mak Ang Phupta, The Devil's Spire. But not to the summit . . .'

'Then where?'

'To the top of the north-east ridge. To the place where the aeroplane crashed.'

Franco Spinetti was thirty-five, an Italian-American who had been born in New York and then moved back to Rome with his parents at the age of twenty. He was a small, sallow, shifty-eyed man with a quick brain and a certain questionable business expertise that had been swiftly learned on the streets of the major cities of Europe and America. It had cost him a lot of money to come to Nepal, and he intended to get it back with interest.

He sat on a low stone wall in the middle of the village and looked around. The face of poverty stared back at him. A huddle of huts, scrawny chickens, even scrawnier looking goats, the stink of dung, and the staring, silent peasants who stood in a group and watched his every move with a mixture of awe and amazement. Spinetti kicked irritably at a stone. 'This trip had better be worth it,' he thought sourly. 'No way I'm going to risk my life for nothing.'

A muted murmur from the villagers made him turn his head and stand up. The headman was coming towards him with a stony-faced, stocky youth at his side. 'This is the one I was telling you about,' he said quietly. 'This is Sherpa Parba Yam.'

Spinetti looked the boy up and down. 'Bit on the young side, isn't he? I'm looking for a guide with experience. Someone who knows that mountain like the back of his hand.'

'Parba Yam is such a person,' said the headman stiffly. 'He has been roaming the high peaks for as long as anyone can remember. He is young, yes, but also strong, and he climbs with the speed and swiftness of a mountain goat.'

'Do you know the north-east ridge?' asked Spinetti bluntly, speaking directly to Parba for the first time.

The boy nodded. 'I know it well,' he said, 'although I have never forced the crest of the ridge and climbed to the summit of The Devil's Spire.'

'I'm not interested in the summit. I just want to reach the 'plane that crashed three weeks ago.' Spinetti dug into a pocket of his fur-lined anorak and withdrew a fistful of notes. He waved them rudely under Parba's nose. 'These are for you,' he said, 'if you can get me to the wreckage and back again in one piece.'

Parba stared, fascinated, at the thick wad of money. There was enough there to keep himself and his mother, probably even the entire village, in food, grain and skins for at least five years. It was a fortune. More riches than the Nepalese boy had ever dreamed of. He reached out with a trembling hand and touched the money. Then he withdrew his fingers and frowned. Something was wrong.

'Why,' he asked quietly, 'do you want to reach the wrecked aircraft?'

Spinetti's dark eyes flickered nervously for a moment. 'Because I'm a businessman,' he said harshly. 'One of the guys who died on that 'plane was a partner of mine. We had a big computer deal going between Bangkok and Rome. My partner was carrying plans, secret industrial designs for a new electronic set-up that stood to make us millions in profit. That kind of money I can't afford to lose. Which is why I want those plans.'

Parba Yam frowned and looked deep into the foreigner's eyes. He understood very little of twentieth-century business or technology, but he did understand people. And this particular one he didn't like. But if all he had to do was guide the ferret-faced stranger up his beloved mountain, why should he turn down the chance of being handsomely paid for it as well? He nodded tersely. 'If you can provide the necessary equipment, then I will take you.'

'I ordered some gear in the city before I came up here,' said Spinetti. 'A yak-load of it should arrive here tomorrow.'

'The Devil's Spire is a mountain of many moods,' said Parba quietly. 'Have you ever climbed before?'

'Sure. Nothing as high as this, but I did some rock climbing back in the States when I was a kid.' Spinetti waved a hand confidently in the air. 'If you lead, and blaze with a trail of fixed ropes, I can make it across the snowfields.'

'Very well. If the weather holds, we'll leave the day after the equipment arrives.'

The weather did hold, and they left in the cold, crisp air of a pre-dawn morning. When the sun finally broke through a layer of thin, persistent cloud, the climbers huddled on a narrow ledge directly below the brooding bulge of the rock band. Off to their left, a near-vertical slope of frozen snow stretched towards the mouth of a gully. Ridged and glistening in the sunlight, the snowfield had an innocent beauty that belied its dangers.

Spinetti wanted to force the pace. Tightening a crampon, the little Italian jumped to his feet. 'We push straight up, yes? Scale the rock band on fixed ropes and reach the base of the north-east ridge before noon.'

'Too dangerous,' said Parba flatly. 'We'll traverse the snowfield and pick up the ridge route via the west gully.'

'But my way will save four, maybe five hours,' said Spinetti angrily. 'If we traverse the snowfield and waste time, the weather might break.'

'I am leading,' said the young Sherpa quietly, 'and we go where I say.' Without another word, Parba Yam moved out on to the slope of the snowfield. Spinetti was a short distance behind, the rope dangling slackly between them. Cramponed boots taking the strain, Parba dug his axe into the snow and hammered a long ice piton into a crack. He clipped into it and, taking rope tension from the Italian, worked his way from one small spur to the next. He was being thrown dangerously off balance by the weight of his rucksack and the thick coil of spare rope. At the entrance to the gully, the Sherpa rested. Burying a snow anchor, he fastened the rope and shouted across at Spinetti to join him. Slowly and carefully, the Italian began to follow.

By two in the afternoon they were on the north-east ridge and the crashed aeroplane lay visible above them. The broken fuselage was half buried in fresh snow, and the severed tailplane was jammed between two pinnacles of rock. The wreckage lay on a small, smooth plateau at the base of the summit spire itself. 'Hurry,' said Spinetti harshly, as Parba hauled him panting up a treacherous curve of ice-covered rock. 'Time is running out. I must get to that 'plane.'

Even behind the tinted goggles, Parba could see the strange expression in his companion's eyes. He had seen that kind of expression before, down in his own village. It was when someone had been haggling with his mother over the price of a goat. That look was of avarice and greed, a deep, never-ending lust for money. Puzzled, the boy turned to lead the final stretch. Spinetti gave him an impatient push on the shoulder. 'Come on, get moving. The last bit to the plateau is easy.'

Silently, Parba pointed with the shaft of ice axe to a slight dip in the hard snow ahead of them. 'Crevasse,' he said bluntly, 'spanned only by frozen snow. If that bridge gives way while we're crossing it, we could fall for ever and be dead before we even hit the bottom. We'll move one at a time and work our way over on our hands and knees. *Slowly*.'

It took them half an hour, with the hard-packed snow groaning and creaking beneath the weight of their bodies. Then they were at the 'plane, and Spinetti was tearing off his spare gear and his rucksack, dropping his axe in a frenzy of excitement. 'You stay here,' he yelled. 'It'll be a mess of dead bodies inside that fuselage and I don't want to scare you. As soon as I find my dead partner and those plans, I'll be back out again.' Next moment he had gone, squeezing his way through a jagged gap in the metal into the silent blackness beyond.

Parba Yam took his equipment off as well, and sat down to rest. They hadn't carried oxygen gear with them on the climb in order to save weight, and anyway, at the height they'd climbed to it hadn't been absolutely essential. But time was passing, and the Sherpa was eager to get started down again. He glanced at his watch. Spinetti had been inside the 'plane for twenty minutes and a towering mass of storm clouds was beginning to pile up behind the summit spire. If the weather broke, a fast descent could well become impossible. Parba stood up and walked to the broken fuselage. He didn't like the sight of death any better than anyone else, but driving snow had covered many of the twisted bodies. It had given them a peaceful, shroud-draped appearance, as though they were waiting in silent rows for a priest who would never come.

Spinetti was crouching in the middle section of the fuselage, shoulders hunched, head bent low over a torn leather briefcase. In his left hand he held a large velvet bag which had a drawstring neck pulled wide open. In his right hand, the Italian held a heap of small, irregularly shaped, glittering objects, and he was dropping them one by one into the velvet bag in a steady, sparkling stream. There were dozens of them. Perhaps hundreds. Parba had only seen pictures of such objects before, in the tiny school in the city where he had gone for a few brief months as a child. Pictures in a book. But he remembered the European name for them.

'*Diamonds*,' he said out loud, as he approached Spinetti unseen from behind and peered over the Italian's shoulder. The little man spun round as though he'd been shot, jerked the drawstring tight, stuffed the bag in his pocket and leapt to his feet. And that was when Sherpa Parba Yam saw murder in his companion's eyes.

'What a pity you saw those stones,' said Spinetti in a soft, hate-filled voice. 'We were getting on so well together, and you had to go and spoil it all.'

'You lied about those industrial plans,' said Parba quietly. 'There weren't any.'

'Of course there weren't. My partner and I were into a neat little diamond-smuggling racket between Bangkok and Rome. The hefty profit I mentioned was true enough, but it would have come from this sackful of stolen gems and not any electronic trash.' Spinetti made sure the diamonds were safe in his pocket and took a step forward. 'The authorities are also on their way up here to find the 'plane and bury the dead. I'm just twenty-four hours ahead of them. If you'd kept your nose out of my business, we could have gone back down

The Italian held a heap of small, glittering objects and was dropping them one by one into the velvet bag in a steady stream.

to the village and you wouldn't have been any the wiser. But now you're a witness, kid . . . and now I have to kill you!'

As Spinetti made a sudden, violent leap forward, hands outstretched and clawing for Parba's throat, the boy ducked, turned, and ran. A desperate leap took him through the jagged rent in the fuselage and into thigh-deep snow outside. But the Italian was still at his heels. Parba knew that it would be useless to plead for his life or to suggest that Spinetti could not descend the mountain without him, because with a series of fixed ropes it would be easy, even for an inexperienced climber. The Sherpa boy knew his only hope lay in flight.

In those desperate minutes, both of them had forgotten about the snow bridge across the crevasse. They were halfway across when it gave way beneath them, soundlessly and completely. As Parba and Spinetti fell together, wind-blasted snow particles drove deep into their nostrils, mouths, chests, and lungs. It was like breathing white smoke, and there was no escape from it. They fell for what seemed like ages and then stopped abruptly, their bodies cushioned painlessly by drifts of deep soft snow. Unbelievably, they had landed on a wide ice ledge jutting out from the side of the crevasse. They were alive and unhurt, separated by only a short span of powder-dry spindrift.

Spinetti cleared a space for his body and got to his feet. He began to laugh, nervously, almost crazily. The wall in front of him was smooth and shiny, almost blue-black in colour. A rampart of extremely solid ice. 'Some equipment . . . a hammer, pitons, even an ice axe, that's what we need.' Spinetti's shrill voice reverberated eerily in the now silent air around them. 'Cut foot and hand holds in the ice wall and we'd be able to climb out of here. But what did we do? We left all our blasted gear up by the 'plane. We're *trapped*!' The Italian lashed a fist uselessly into the glistening ice wall and sobbed with fury. The look of murder had gone from his eyes now, and fear had taken its place. He glanced along at Parba Yam, but the Sherpa boy seemed lost in a world of his own. He was staring straight ahead, gloved hands pressed flat against the blue-black ice, staring at something the like of which he had never seen before and which he hoped he would never see again.

It was the body of a man entombed in ice.

The corpse was of a man in his late thirties, a Sherpa in full climbing gear with a wooden-hafted ice axe still clutched firmly in his right hand. Every single particle of flesh, clothes, and equipment was perfectly preserved. The man seemed to be floating in mid-air, as though suspended in life rather than death. The strong, relaxed face with a small cleft in the chin was separated from Parba Yam's by only a thin wall of ice. The boy had seen a face like that many, many times in his lifetime. It was fixed in a small wooden frame which stood on a carved table beside his mother's bed. It was a photograph of a man who had gone to climb a mountain and had never come back.

Sherpa Parba Yam was meeting his long-dead father for the first time.

That was when Spinetti saw the body, too, and suddenly he was laughing again, but this time from sheer disbelief and a surge of new-found hope. 'The ice axe,' he screamed. 'Chip it out of the ice. Get it out of the dead man's hand we'll be able to cut steps for ourselves. Climb out of the crevasse. It's like a free gift from beyond the grave. We'll be saved!'

Parba could see the sense of it. He had a small skinning knife in one of his pockets. Taking it out, he began to pick and chip slowly, patiently, at the gleaming wall of ice. It took him two and a half hours to reach his father's body. As he forced the ice axe free, he passed it back over his shoulder to Spinetti without a word, because in that solemn moment, the Sherpa boy had seen something else. It was a small diary sticking rigidly out of the top pocket of his father's climbing jacket. With trembling hands, Parba chipped it free. He was trying desperately to thaw the long-frozen pages when Franco Spinetti hit him hard on the back of the head with the haft of the ice axe.

Parba came round half an hour later. He was lying in deep snow on the edge of the ledge, and a blizzard was blowing. There was no sign of Spinetti. Roughly cut steps in the sheer ice wall told the story. The Italian had hacked holds for himself with the axe. By now, he was probably near the top of the crevasse, heading for the west gully and the line of fixed ropes that would lead him to safety. It would be impossible for Parba to follow. Even if he climbed out of the crevasse using the foot and hand holds made by Spinetti, he would lose all sense of direction in bad weather. Without equipment as well, he was done for.

So Parba propped himself against the wall of ice and prepared to die. Above and behind him was his father's ice tomb. Soon there would be a second corpse, father and son, both claimed by Mak Ang Phupta, The Devil's Spire. Parba shrugged. If fate had decreed such a course, then so be it. Idly, he stared at the half-frozen pages of his father's diary. It told the story of how he and the Englishman had forced the north-east ridge and climbed to the summit of The Devil's Spire. Parba felt a warm flush of pride and pleasure. So his father had done it after all. He had succeeded in conquering the mountain that was to claim his life.

Parba turned the pages. The final entries told of a descent in bad weather that had turned into disaster. The edge of the west gully route proved to be a death trap when the wind blew. Massive ice falls and avalanches. That was where the Englishman had slipped and died. Suddenly Parba gasped and re-read the paragraph again. The edge of the west gully

. . . bad weather. *That was the route Spinetti had taken*!

Even as he jerked his head upward to stare into the drifting whiteness, the boy heard a faint, distant shout that turned into a long, high-pitched scream of death. Franco Spinetti and his stolen diamonds had gone for ever. As if in a dream, Parba turned his attention back to the final lines of his father's journal, which said he was too weak to follow a sunken ledge that ran all the way through a deep crevasse below the plateau of the summit spire. This ledge he knew for a fact led to the shelter of a rock cave, and safety on the leeward side of the north-east ridge.

With tears in his eyes, Parba Yam looked for the last time at his father's icy grave. The ledge he had written about was the one Parba now stood on. To reach safety, all he had to do was follow it. As the tears trickled and froze on his cheeks, Parba turned left and stumbled through the drifting snow. From his frozen wall of death, Sherpa Pasang Yam had reached across the years and given his only son the gift of life.

HAPPINESS IS THE HAUNTING
by Angus Allan

AN EMBATTLED ENGLAND GROANED under the strains and stresses of civil war as Roundhead battled Cavalier. Peaceful meadows became bloody battlefields, and the shires rang with the clash of steel on steel and stank with the reek of burning homesteads. It was an unhappy age, and one in which it was utterly impossible to be neutral. You were either this, or that. And if you picked the wrong side, so much the worse for you.

Well, young Jonas Duval, scarcely into his teens, happened to pick the wrong side. He was a brash sort of lad, an orphan, apprenticed to the blacksmith in the village of Marnham-in-the-Hedges. The moment he had seen the troop of Royalist cavalry pass through, he had been enraptured by the colourful, plumed hats, the ruffled lace, the swashbuckling merriment of the Cavalier army. Without further ado, he'd taken old Monument, the nag in the paddock, and had ridden up to the Manor House. The very name of the squire, Deliverance Mold, proclaimed him as a follower of Cromwell's puritan cause, but Mold was away. Jonas had, with great bravado, pinched sword and buckler, and ransacked an upstairs wardrobe for the squire's discarded finery. Such grand clothing, reasoned Jonas, was only going to waste. Deliverance Mold certainly had no further use for lace and feathers, for this sort of dress was unsuitable for a parliamentary 'crophead'.

So it was that Jonas Duval rode out, in a hat far too big for him, boots that slid about on feet unaccustomed to them and with a sword he could hardly wield, to follow the king's standard.

We can draw a curtain over the brief and unfortunate ambush that took place within mere hours of the lad's reckless decision. It's sufficient to say that Monument was able to return to his paddock in relative peace, having lost his young master to a Roundhead bullet somewhere in Wenslow Woods.

Thus, Jonas Duval became a ghost.

'You have,' said the ancient skeleton who welcomed Jonas into the League of Spectres, Midlands Branch, 'joined an honourable company.'

'I have?' said Jonas, looking about him at the cloudy room which was not a room, and at the dimly seen ranks of new phantoms waiting for orders. 'Is this Heaven?'

'Certainly not,' snapped the skeleton, making disapproving noises with his clacking jaws that Jonas found quite fascinating. '*You* can't go there, because you've done wrong. You not only stole a horse, but you also stole that ridiculous outfit.' He added: 'You could have taken something that fitted.'

Jonas felt cheeky. 'I got more than *you* did, bare-bones. And what did *you* do to keep you here in The League of Spectres?'

'Never you mind, young shaver. And watch your manners. I'm older than King Canute, I am, and if you want to get on while you're here, you'd better keep that lip of yours under control. Report to Ghoul-post number ten – on the double!'

Naturally buoyant, Jonas decided to make the best of it. He did as he was told, and came under the guidance of Harald-the-Heavy, a Saxon who'd done some rather shady horse trading in the days of the Viking invasion. A ghost given to great oaths and pretended fury, much like a modern-day sergeant-major, Harald was nonetheless a kindly instructor, and, with a liking for Jonas, steered him through the first difficult bits – removing his head and carrying it under his arm, for instance. And rattling chains. The trouble was, Jonas was forever dropping his head – other student spooks would play football with it – and as for the chains, he was hopeless. 'By Wotan,' Harald would rave, 'Clank 'em, boy! *Clank* 'em! You're supposed to be making a horrible sound, not tinkling away like a merry wind-chime!'

It was supposed to take a month to turn out a skilful ghost, one who could go out haunting and, so to speak, keep up the good traditions of the service. But more than a century passed, and Jonas *still* hadn't made the grade. He hadn't aged, for ghosts don't age, but Harald-the-Heavy claimed that he himself had got much older. 'Of all the long-suffering wraiths in the business,' he sighed, 'I'm the unluckiest. Why, oh, why did I have to get you?'

'I didn't do too badly on my last exam,' grumbled Jonas. 'I admit I went to the wrong place . . .'

'The wrong place! You materialised in a white sheet, ran screaming down a corridor waving your arms around to try and frighten the people standing along the walls! And what was it? A museum. They weren't people at all, they were suits of blooming armour!'

'I'll try and do better next time,' said Jonas, hopefully.

It was while the world brought in the year 1900 that Harald-the-Heavy finally gave up. He knew he would have to stay in the Ghost-Training establishment longer by falsifying Jonas's release papers, but he did it, and sent the useless spook down to flounder about on his own.

Just as could be expected, Jonas made the mistake of going back to the village of Marnham-in-the-Hedges. It was called Marnham now, and had become a Victorian-built suburb of a large industrial town, which threw him a bit. He clanked some chains in a busy factory, but nobody noticed because of the noise. He cavorted wildly in the old church during service, but not a soul saw him. He even took to trying to appear as flitting lights on the lonely road by the canal, in the small hours of the morning, but that was no good. He perked up once, when he heard a bargeman ask his wife: 'Hullo, what's that over on the towpath, Maude?' Then he was brought down as the woman replied: 'It's about time you left the beer bottle alone, you old fool.'

Jonas hovered unhappily under the gibbet on Rushmere Common. He was tired out. He'd been dangling there for a good three hours, and though he'd been passed by four sets of late-night travellers, a packman, and a couple of caravans of gypsies, not one of them had seen him. 'I'm a proper failure,' he said. 'I'm never going to be able to haunt anything! I wear a shroud, my Cavalier clobber,' (he'd listened to local chat and was well up with twentieth century talk) 'and I've even learned to bay like a blooming werewolf. I wish I were dead.' Then he giggled. 'No, that's silly. I *am* dead!'

'The trouble is,' said a sepulchral voice close to his ear, 'you're trying too hard.' Jonas looked round, and clapped his eyes on a cloaked figure with spindly legs, a bald head, and a rather neat beard. 'It's Will Shakespeare, isn't it?'

'Alas no,' said the ghost. 'Will has gone above. I am the wretch who attempted to steal his manuscripts and publish them as my own. Thus I am haunting, as you are – or as you are *attempting* – until my debt is paid. My name is Francis Swift.'

'Can you help me out?' asked Jonas, hopefully.

'Aye, laddie. Come, let us transcend time together, and I will endeavour to smooth thy unhappy course . . .' Theatrically, Francis took hold of the boy's hand and sped him forward to the 1980s . . .

Together, they drifted over a housing estate. Jonas spent a good ten minutes marvelling at it before his companion set him down on a balcony. 'Now, my boy. I have myself haunted this place, quite successfully, I flatter myself, on numerous occasions. I met my end on this spot, you see, having taken a draught of hemlock upon the occasion of the mocking of my greatest play. They threw eggs.'

'Nasty,' said Jonas, sympathetically.

'Smelly,' corrected his ghostly companion. 'The point is, a youth resides here. His name is Terry Wilkinson, a curious and new-fangled name, is it not? I had the greatest trouble being seen, for ages. And I mean, *ages*. Yet he was able to discern me. I go now to pastures new, but zounds, I offer him to you.'

'Zounds!' said Jonas, brightly. 'It's a jolly long time since I've heard that word. But thanks, all the same. Maybe my luck will change.'

Francis Swift departed as rapidly as his name suggested, and Jonas drifted through the wall of the nearest flat. His spirits, if you'll pardon the pun, perked up as a dog, lying in its basket, lifted its head and snarled at him, baring its teeth. 'Ah, Fido,' said Jonas. 'I know that animals are supposed to detect us more readily than humans, but do you know, you're the very first who has ever sensed my presence!' He adjusted his hat (he'd re-assumed his Cavalier costume) to a rakish angle. Several times, as it kept slipping from one side of his head to the other. The dog lowered its head and went back to sleep.

'Oh well, press on . . .'

Jonas found Terry Wilkinson in his bedroom, studiously disobeying his parents' orders by sitting up and reading comics with the aid of a torch. Jonas came through the wall and spread his hands, dramatically. 'Er . . . whooooooo!' he said. Was there some hope? Terry glanced briefly up from his

Jonas came through the wall and spread his hands, dramatically. 'Er . . . whooooooo!' he said.

magazine.

'Hyahhhheeeeeee!' wailed Jonas, fluttering round the bed.

Terry put down the comic and folded his arms. 'Hey. Are you a ghost?'

Jonas could hardly contain his delight! 'Can . . . can you *see* me . . ?'

'Of course I can see you,' said Terry. 'You've got a sort of lopsided nose, a neck full of soppy-looking lace, and a hat that's about to fall off any minute. You look like that old highwayman, Claude Duval, gone wrong.'

'Claude Duval,' said Jonas, hugging himself. 'I never thought I might be related to *him*! I'll have to ask Harald-the-Heavy, if I ever see him again!'

'You're a bit chatty for a spook,' said Terry, frowning. 'But not half as daft as that Francis Swift wotsit who's been around here. All poems and posing, he is.' He added: 'My dad and mum don't believe in him. They think I'm daft.'

'Oh, no, no, *no*! You're not daft,' said Jonas. 'Believe me, you're the most wonderful thing that's happened to me in, let's see, three centuries! I say, can I go and scare the daylights out of your parents?'

'Feel free.'

Rejoicing in what he considered to be his suddenly discovered power, Jonas Duval whipped into the next bedroom and capered around Terry's sleeping parents. He pulled out all the stops. He screamed, made the atmosphere like ice, caused their bedside light to flash on and off, opened and slammed the door a couple of times, but they slept like logs. Not a sausage. Disgruntled, he returned to Terry.

'No go?' said Terry.

'Hopeless,' agreed Jonas, parking himself on the bed. 'Oh. One thing strikes me. Why aren't you gibbering in fear?'

'You've got to be joking,' said Terry. 'Ghosts can't hurt anybody. Go on, try and pinch me. Here . . .' He held out his arm.

'You're right,' sighed Jonas. 'Can't, of course. But some of us can do poltergeist bits. Flinging stuff around and so forth. Not me, though I can slam windows and things,' he added defiantly.

'Don't bother, Jonas old son,' said Terry.

'How do you know my name?' said Jonas, baffled.

Terry frowned. 'I dunno. Sort of . . . came to me. Here, maybe you and I are gonna be pals. We are,' he considered, 'about the same age?'

'Give or take a few hundred years or so.'

'I'm not scared of you,' said Terry at length, 'because I *like* the idea of ghosts. I had an aunt, bit of a weirdo, used to tell fortunes. She said to me once "Terry, you've got the second sight." Well, I believe it. I've seen spooks in old castles my mum and dad have taken me to, and they don't bother me one bit.'

'That worries me,' said Jonas. 'We're supposed to make people jump out of their skins. All our training goes into trying to turn people's hair white . . .' He reached forward and touched Terry's head, not that Terry could feel it. 'Yours is sort of coppery coloured.'

'Call me carrots and that's the end of a beautiful friendship,' warned young Wilkinson. 'I had to bop a bloke at school for that, yesterday.' He pondered for a moment. 'I suppose you wouldn't like to come to school with me . . ?'

'Why not? I haven't got any other pressing engagement for the next millennium or so. I went to what they called "dame school" myself, for a couple of years before they apprenticed me to a blacksmith. Can't say I liked it. She kept strapping me on the hand when I got my addition wrong.'

'Okay,' said Terry. 'Now be a good ghost, and turn in while I get some kip. I think we'll have fun, mate, you and me . . .'

While Terry slept, Jonas Duval sped back to his home of centuries before. He scared the wits out of the old nag, Monument, by rousing him at midnight, and when the manor window flew open and Deliverance Mold looked out to see what all the clatter was about, threw a panic into the squire by turning himself into a Jack-o-Lantern that covered the shrubbery with flickering, eerie flames. 'Gahhh, you old hogshead,' whooped Jonas. 'Just wait till you take your nightcap off tomorrow!' (Deliverance Mold did, in fact, go white overnight – and served him right, for he was a miserable old devil.)

The skeleton at the gates of the League of Spectres, Midlands Branch, greeted Jonas cordially. 'Yes, I remember you,' he clacked. 'The duffer. The dummy.'

'Not any more,' said Jonas. 'I made it at last! In 1984, if you please, and a young feller my own age!'

'So I see from my records,' said the skeleton. 'But don't be so hasty. You haven't actually *terrified* him.'

'Oh, no. He's nice,' said Jonas. 'I don't want to give him fits or anything.'

Harald-the-Heavy waddled up. 'Dear, dear me. Just as foolish as you always were, Duval. The whole point is, that you *must* frighten people if you're going to be a successful ghost. I've noticed that twentieth-century boy myself. An imp. A lad of rare mischief. Well, he attracts spectres, but he's no conquest. You did attempt to petrify his parents . . ?'

'Ye-ess . . .'

'To no avail?'

'To no avail.'

'Sorry, old son. You haven't made it yet, and that's the truth.'

Livid, Jonas Duval whirled his way back through time and space to Terry Wilkinson's bedroom. He had no trouble rousing the youngster from sleep. A few groans and a series of heavy footfalls did the trick. And Jonas passed on what Harald-the-Heavy had said.

Terry spread his hands. 'Don't worry, chum,' he said. 'All right, you can't scare *me*, but that doesn't matter. You wait, cock, things'll work out . . .'

But Terry was over-optimistic. At breakfast next day, he told his long-suffering mother and father that he'd got a new ghoul-friend, and they told *him* not to be such an idiot. Jonas did his best to curdle their eggs, mush their cornflakes, make the kettle keep boiling after it had been turned off, and even set his own skull down on the table in place of the jam pot. No good. Nothing. Terry saw it, but they didn't. On the way to school, Jonas spirited up a ghostly penny-farthing cycle and rode it alongside Terry's racer. Not a single motorist took any notice, not even when faced with an apparent head-on collision. Terry began to lose faith in his phantom friend. Worse, a whole flock of interested ghosts, filling the sky above Jonas, urging him on and giving him every encouragement, were beginning to get disappointed. Count Dracula himself, giving Jonas the power to turn himself into a vampire bat, was disgusted when all Jonas did was to try and bite a traffic warden. 'He may as vell try to get blood out of zee stone,' complained the Count.

School was no better. Was Jonas able to throw panic into the form master and drive him from the classroom in time to stop him giving Terry a hundred lines for talking (to nobody visible)? Unhappily, no. Did he, when the class sneak opened his desk, fly out with waving arms and slobbering mouth, screeching in spine-chilling fury? Well, yes, he did. But the class sneak didn't see him.

'I'm sorry, chum,' said Terry, when school was over. 'I'm going back to Francis Swift, poems and all. He can haunt, and that's the beginning and end of it. *You* can't.'

'Don't be like that, Tel . . .' (Jonas had heard Terry's

schoolmates use the short form). 'Just give me another chance! I've got to be a good ghost, I've *got* to!'

'Nahhh. Leave it out,' said Terry. 'Tell you what, you can come and haunt me any time you like. For practice, see? But you'd better go back to college or whatever you call it, an' take another course. Have another go at, what was his name? – Harald-the-Hairy?'

'Heavy,' said Jonas, dismally. 'I don't think he'll want to know.'

He didn't. Which is why Jonas Duval still stalks the earth, looking for someone to haunt. Are you as receptive as Terry Wilkinson? Maybe a little more so? Do you long to be frightened, even by someone not very good at frightening? Go on, snuggle down in bed tonight and keep your eyes open for a hesitant spook in an ill-fitting Cavalier hat. If it's Jonas, do him a favour, eh? Give a little scream. You'll do a feeble phantom something of a good turn!

IS ANYBODY THERE?

by Christopher Bendel

I HEARD THIS STORY under the most unlikely conditions – covered in dust and crouching under what was left of the reception desk in the wrecked foyer of the Miramoir Hotel in Beirut, while M-60 machine-guns and mortars and grenade-launchers and automatic rifles created an infernal racket outside.

I forget who was shelling us, and we probably couldn't have figured it out anyway. Besides, they weren't actually shelling us directly; we just happened to be in the middle. It didn't make much difference. We were pinned down, and that was that.

Some bright spark suggested that we all rush out the back of the building and make our way together to the British Embassy. But as the rear of the hotel was being mortared as well, this did not seem like a wise move.

So we stayed. There was plenty to eat and drink and Flores, the Spanish manager of the Miramoir, was a matey soul who quite liked journalists. At that time, 1979, this was unusual. International Press Cards did not cut much ice with most of the combatants and factions who seemed to have turned the once-lovely city of Beirut into a private battle-ground for settling old scores.

There were over half a dozen of us sitting, sprawling or crouching behind the reception desk: Jonathan Mirsky, an American who had covered most of the hotspots since Vietnam in 1966; Harry Barlev, who looked like a college professor, but was in fact a security guard on the Israeli airline, El-Al; George Slingsby, a veteran journalist, who was coming up for retirement and wasn't keen on this dangerous assignment; Joey Brown, a stocky little Cockney and my photographer; a short fat bloke in his late thirties called Lowder who was something boring in the British Embassy consular department, and one or two others whose names and faces didn't register in my memory.

It might be thought that the ruins of a glass, wood and aluminium reception desk did not offer much in the way of protection against anything that might be thrown at us from outside, but actually we reckoned we were in the safest billet in the entire hotel. This was because Flores had had the foresight, during the Civil War of the mid-1970s, to reinforce the front of the desk with a long sheet of pierced steel planking. Where he'd got it from no one knew or cared (it had probably fallen off the back of an army lorry), but it kept us pretty safe from a frontal assault. It's true that the wings of the desk were shattered and the top was a mess, but it would have needed a direct hit from a heavy bomb before we cashed our chips in.

It was after a particularly vicious and noisy bombardment had ended that there suddenly occurred one of those uncanny silences you often get slap-bang in the middle of a furious battle. Like the eye of a hurricane. It was as though everyone outside had suddenly been transported up to Mars. You could have heard a pin drop.

As it turned out, what did drop right in the middle of that eerie silence wasn't a pin but a piece of glass.

It was probably one of the few pieces left in the swing doors that let out on to the main street. Possibly a vibration dislodged it, or a stray gust of wind. Anyhow, it crashed to the tiled floor out of our sight and we all jumped and laughed nervously and glanced at each other in mild embarrassment.

Jokingly, Joey said, 'Is . . . is anybody there?' – and Lowder, the fat consular chap, shot him an odd look and said, 'Good Lord, that takes me back.'

Up till then this bloke Lowder had been a bit of a pain in the neck. I forget exactly why he was there in the first place: something to do with passports, maybe. Round about that time, some West Beirut racketeer had been doing a lucrative little line in forged travel warrants for the PLO. Lowder may have been at the Miramoir in connection with that. Not that it matters.

No one seemed eager to take him up on what he'd just said, so to save slight awkwardness I said, 'What, the glass tinkling?'

He shook his head, frowning.

'No. It was the words your photographer used. Those exact words were once used by a friend of mine. I hadn't thought about them in twenty-five years.'

'I should think people have been saying "Is anybody there?" at least fifty times a day all over the world for the past five hundred years,' said George Slingsby acidly.

He popped an indigestion tablet into his mouth and glared round. He had terrible heart-burn problems, due entirely to his ceaseless worrying about whether he was going to make it to retirement in one piece. (Matter of fact, he actually retired last year, and I hear is now selling second-hand books somewhere up in the Yorkshire Dales.)

'No, you don't understand,' said Lowder. 'It was . . . very strange. You know, eerie. *Weird*.'

'Sounds good,' said Mirsky, something of a sucker for the supernatural.

Harry Barlev broke out another bottle and passed it round. We all swigged it straight from the neck. It seemed to me that during the next ten minutes or so we were going to be needing all the help we could get. Lowder spoke.

This all happened in the last week of my last term at prep school in the late 1950s. In the autumn I was going on to a minor public school, and having passed all the exams and so on, there wasn't much for me to do. The school itself was situated in the heart of the Worcestershire countryside, a marvellous place for a youngster to ramble around. Apart from lots of interesting woods and coppices, there was a prehistoric circle of standing stones a couple of miles away, a Civil War battlefield within easy distance, Ludlow Castle not twenty minutes' drive in a car, and, actually in the grounds of the school itself, a wild and tangled spinney with a deep pool at its centre in which, it was said, a boy had drowned under mysterious circumstances a hundred years before.

There was also Quarry House.

Quarry House was a large and imposing Victorian dwelling set off from the main road down a long driveway lined with beech trees. At this time it had been empty for at least five years (as long as I had been at the school) and was fast falling into disrepair.

Why it had been empty for so long no one knew exactly, although there was a local tradition that it was haunted. One version of events was that there had been an appalling tragedy there some time in the 1890s – a farm labourer had gone berserk with a mattock. Another story told of the mass disappearance of an entire family (large even by Victorian standards) one wild and stormy night. Yet another version had it that a mysterious disease had struck the neighbourhood, concentrating on Quarry House and wiping out its occupants.

Whatever the truth of the matter, it was said that whoever had vanished or been slaughtered or struck down by the plague continued to haunt the place, which was why no one cared to buy it. There was certainly an odd smell about the house, though this was no doubt due to old and faulty drains.

Quarry House definitely played on the minds of generations of small boys who lived and had their scholastic being not half a mile away. It was a good place for a dare – although frankly, on our half-days of Wednesday and Saturday afternoon, especially during the spring and summer, it was chaos. There was so much activity amongst the shrubberies and overgrown gardens and even inside the empty shell itself, by boys aged between eight and thirteen, that the place looked like Piccadilly Circus during the rush-hour.

Anyhow, one day a boy called Farrer – a hefty lad who tended to throw his weight about – dared me and a particular friend of mine called Watson to go there one night, and the suggestion was seized upon with great glee by all and sundry.

Although not by us. It was not something I particularly wanted to do. Watson, the youngest son of a mildly eccentric Church of England vicar who tended to explode with the words "Damn, blast, devil's curses!" when roused, had no great eagerness for the adventure either. Nevertheless, when dared – and especially when dared by a young brute like Farrer – it was difficult, not to say impossible, to refuse.

Consequently I worked out a plan with Watson whereby we would both go sick the night before we were due to visit Quarry House. The date fixed by Farrer for the visit was two days before the end of term.

Then we heard the astonishing (to our minds, anyhow) news that Quarry House had been sold at last, and the new people were going to be moving in shortly. It appeared that they were going to live in the most habitable part of the house while renovating the rest by stages themselves.

To Watson and myself this was pretty grim. The news had broken on a Friday, and Farrer demanded that we should go that very night. When we hedged, he accused us of rank cowardice. The fact that his accusation was perfectly justified did not help matters, and finally we agreed to do it. We had to bring something back from the house to prove that we had actually been inside – some largish, but at the same time easily movable, object. Someone remembered that in one of the larger downstairs rooms – probably, in its time, a dining-room or the Victorian equivalent of the lounge – there were a number of wall-brackets, most likely candle-holders, fixed to the panelling. The screws or nails holding some of these to the wall were now in the last stages of decay, and it would be simple to wrench a bracket off and bring it back to the dormitory.

Because it was July, the nights were short. So although we senior boys went to bed at eight o'clock, it wasn't until well after eleven that it was dark enough to be able to make an exit through a downstairs window without the risk of being seen.

It was extremely hot that night. Indeed, it had been hot all that week, and as darkness fell the weather turned positively sultry. Despite my misgivings about the whole affair, I can recall being suddenly grateful, in an odd sort of way, that we could escape from the close atmosphere of the dormitory and out into the night. Grateful, that is, until disaster struck. It began to rain.

That, in fact, is a spectacularly mild description of what actually occurred. It *bucketed* down!

I've had postings to Jakarta, Bangkok and New Delhi, so I know what the Monsoon is like. Yet even allowing for the fact that all this happened a quarter of century ago and one's memory as a child tends to exaggerate and over-dramatise across the years, I truly believe that that night's downpour was not far behind the Monsoon in its naked power and sheer elemental fury. Not only did it rain as though stair-rods were dropping from the skies, but it thundered as well – great ripping explosive crashes that actually hurt the ear-drums. And the lightning! No horror film special effects department could ever have hoped to create those jagged flares of eyeball-searing light!

Of course, if the storm had been at its height when we started out, I would have refused point-blank to go – and hang Farrer! But it was merely spotting with rain when we climbed out of the tuck-room window and set off down the slope, past the cricket pitch, and into one of the coppices that lay beside the road.

We were over half-way to Quarry House when the real storm started, and we sprinted towards it to get to shelter of any sort. We were both wearing only our normal day clothes, so it was not long before we were soaked to the skin and feeling as miserable as drowned rats.

We pelted down the driveway and plunged through the shrubbery at the rear of the old house. The odd thing was that, although all that lightning ought to have shown us a scene that should have frightened us half to death – the old haunted house, the terrifying storm: you know the kind of thing I mean – neither of us took a blind bit of notice. All we were concerned about was getting out of that terrible pounding rain and into shelter.

There was a loose window at the rear, near to what I suppose would have been the servants' quarters in the old days, and we wrenched it open and tumbled over the sill. Inside, almost immediately, Watson stiffened, turned to me, and whispered, "I can smell cooking!"

It was true. Lingering in the air was not the smell of damp and decay that normally pervaded the old house, but a quite distinct aroma of cooked meat.

The explanation struck me almost as soon as I'd identified the smell for what it was. The newcomers had moved in already, that very day. The house was no longer unoccupied. We were trespassing.

I was just about to say all this to Watson when we heard a scuffling sound from somewhere fairly near. The room we were in was an ante-room to the main kitchen area. I knew from when I had been there before that there was a door to the right, and it was from there that the noise emanated. Watson, by now in a fit of terror, was clutching my arm so tightly that it hurt.

"Is . . . is anybody there?" he quavered.

Instantly the door banged open and light from a flickering candle held by a plump woman in black flooded into the room. The situation was even clearer to me now than before. These people had moved in so hurriedly, the local electricity authority hadn't even had time to switch them on at the mains.

The woman stared at us with a dumbfounded expression on her face. Already I was trying to work out what I was going to say to the Headmaster during the now inevitable interview in his study in the morning, and its doubtless extremely painful sequel. Not unnaturally, a good excuse refused to form itself in my mind.

"Who are you and what are you doing here?" said the woman angrily.

As she said this, a tall bearded man appeared behind her, also carrying a candle and also looking extremely cross.

There was only one thing for it. By now I was drenched to the skin and fed up to the back teeth with the entire business. I decided to tell them everything.

Astonishingly, as I explained what we were up to the tall man burst out laughing. He slapped his knee with his free hand and generally acted as though I'd just told him the funniest story that had ever been invented. He kept saying, "Boys will be boys, eh, Clara? Boys will be boys!"

To cut a long story short, they took us into one of the downstairs rooms, bundled us up in blankets, sat us both down on a large and very comfortable old sofa, and gave us cups of hot chocolate. By this time I was very tired, and the

'Who are you and what are you doing here?' said the woman angrily. A tall bearded man appeared behind her.

scene in the room began to take on the foggy-edged aspect of a dream. The flickering light of the candles hurt the eyes, and the deep shadows beyond seemed to shift and surge like the sea. At one point I do remember the man – whose name, he told us, was Mr Robert Sampson – picking up one of the candles, blowing out the flame, and handing the candlestick to me. It was very heavy.

"That's to prove you've been here," he said jovially. "Now mind you bring it back."

I suppose we were there for an hour or more, all told, and we finally left when the downpour outside stopped. We were almost asleep on our feet by then, but I recall turning, as we went up the driveway, and waving to them as they stood in the front doorway, framed in the candle-light of the hall.

Lowder stopped talking. Just like that. He stared at the dusty floor as though he had become paralysed.

'Is that it?' I said. 'That's got to be the most boring story I've ever heard in my life! Where's the punchline?'

He looked up and gave me a lop-sided, apologetic smile.

'Oh, the punchline,' he said slowly. 'Yes. Well, we went back next day and the removal vans were there.'

'So? You said these Sampson people moved in early.'

'Ah. But these people weren't called Sampson. They were called Warrender, and they didn't know anything about any candlestick. In fact, they didn't know what on earth we were talking about. They'd just arrived, that very morning, with the removal vans. There was no big sofa downstairs, and no way anyone could have made hot chocolate anywhere in that house at all. There was just a lot of dust.'

Slingsby winced and stuffed another indigestion tablet into his mouth. Barlev took a long pull at the bottle. Mirsky stared at Lowder as though the fat man had suddenly grown two heads.

'So what you're saying is. . . ?'

'What I'm saying is that I made enquiries much later and discovered that a family called Sampson had indeed lived at Quarry House, and I found an old photograph of Mr Sampson. He was the same man, all right.' Lowder paused and rubbed his chin. 'It was a very old photograph indeed. Taken in 1885, in fact.'

'1885,' muttered Mirsky.

'I've still got the candlestick. Watson didn't want anything to do with it. It was solid silver.' He gave me another apologetic smile. 'That was why it was so heavy, of course . . .'

Just then the high-powered hardware opened up again outside, and I reached for the bottle. I felt I needed it more than ever, because what really bothered me was that Lowder was the kind of bloke who didn't have an iota of imagination in his noddle.

Which meant, one had to assume, his story was true . . .

GHOSTLY WARNING

by Beverley Watts

THERE WAS NOTHING THAT UNUSUAL about the graveyard at the seaside village of Brideswood. Just the usual rows of tombstones and grassy banks – a few wooden benches for visitors to rest their feet, and the odd bunch of flowers, some shrivelled and dead, most drooping unhappily.

No one tended the wild roses that tumbled over the boundary fence, but they bloomed beautifully anyway, small, pink and delicate. In the field on the other side of the fence lay another small graveyard, an unofficial one for the beloved pets of the Brideswood villagers. There, on the south side were the last remains of Mrs Pritchard's pet cat, Fluffy, and further along, with a magnificent headstone, lay General Garrard's parrot, Jim Lad, who had screeched his last squawk some three years back.

The atmosphere was quiet and peaceful. Sometimes young courting couples sneaked into the graveyard at night to be alone, cuddling together in the moonlight, unaware of all those lost souls floating in the breezes.

On this sunny July day, though, the air was tense and tortured. A funeral was taking place and there were many people surrounding the coffin, all weeping and all dressed in plainest black. Three figures especially watched closely as the small wooden cask, covered in red and white flowers, was lowered into the grave. The wreaths were beautiful, the largest in the shape of a heart with a simple message attached, 'Goodbye, our beloved daughter, Anne-

Marie Gregson – love as always, Mummy, Daddy, Kathy and Ambrose.'

The tragedy had happened three days earlier. Anne-Marie, just fourteen and full of life, had been run down by a car. There was nothing her sister Kathryn, who had been with her on the fateful day, could have done to save her. They'd been walking their dog, Ambrose, when he'd suddenly dashed across the road to give chase to a cat. Anne-Marie had run after him, straight under the wheels of a speeding motorist, and death was instantaneous. The wing of the car had also clipped Ambrose, and he'd broken his leg, but the vet said it would mend in time.

Slowly, Anne-Marie's coffin was covered in earth and the vicar read the service in his dreary, deep-toned voice. Bees buzzed and birds called, but their natural sounds of happiness were drowned by the sobs of Anne-Marie's closest relations and friends. She'd been such a sunny girl, bubbly and with an infectious sense of humour. How she had loved Ambrose, too . . .

The little West Highland White was the family's dog really, but he'd always made an extra fuss of Anne-Marie. She carried his photograph in her satchel and always took him for long walks each night. It was only because he'd pulled away so suddenly that she'd lost her grasp on his lead the day of the accident. Her only thought was for his safety, not for herself.

No one blamed the dog for her death. He couldn't have known what he was doing. The whole family loved him as much as ever. They would have taken him with them to the funeral if he'd been well enough, but Mr Brown, the vet, had kept him at his surgery for observation. His leg had been set in plaster, and Ambrose still seemed stunned and not his usual self.

After the funeral was over, the mourners filled the waiting

black cars and drove slowly home to the Gregson's house in the centre of the village, a picture-book whitewashed cottage with a thatched roof. They all sat in the garden for a while amongst the hollyhocks and snapdragons, eating cucumber sandwiches without appetite and remembering the cheeky and endearing things Anne-Marie had done as a child.

There was a time she'd dressed puppy Ambrose in one of her doll's dresses and hats to have his photograph taken, and another occasion when she'd fed him all the chicken her mother had put aside for Sunday tea. Somehow, by talking about Anne-Marie, it didn't seem that she'd really gone, that her warm and energetic little figure was not really lifeless and still in the ground.

Later in the afternoon, as the guests left in small groups, Kathy Gregson lay on her bed and wept harder than she ever had in her life. She'd never see Anne-Marie again, and neither would Ambrose. How they'd both miss her! She held her pillow close to her face and sobbed alone in the room she and Anne-Marie had shared. Next to her was her sister's twin bed with its pretty patchwork cover, and at the end, Ambrose's basket with its colourful blanket which Anne-Marie had knitted from odd balls of wool. Night fell, and Kathy drifted off to sleep, her cheeks still wet with tears.

Next day, Mr Brown called very early in the morning. He reported that Ambrose didn't seem to be pulling through after the accident. He and his son, Simon, had sat up all night with the dog, attending to his every need, but his condition continued to get worse. His leg was fine, but he wouldn't eat.

Kathy went back to Mr Brown's surgery with the vet and tried to help poor Ambrose. When she called his name, though, he did not as usual jump up and cover her face with affectionate licks. He lay on his side on the floor, eyes glazed and ears still.

'Please get well, Ambrose,' Kathy whispered, stroking his

head, but the little dog could hardly summon up the energy to give a short wag of his tail. She begged Mr Brown to let her take Ambrose home, but he said that the best place for him was in expert hands. Instead, she visited Ambrose every morning, and she and Simon tried to tempt him to eat with tasty little chunks of meat, his favourite dog biscuits and even his passion, choc drops. Nothing worked.

Less than a week later, Kathy arrived at the vet's to be met by a pale and tired Simon. 'I'm very sorry, Kathy,' he said. 'Ambrose died in the night. He seemed to have given up the will to live. Would you like him to be cremated? It's the best way.'

Kathy didn't have to think twice about her answer, though she could hardly accept his chilling words. 'No,' she answered steadily, even though her lower lip was quivering. 'I want Ambrose to be buried at the pet's graveyard. I'll tell Mum and Dad.'

Mr and Mrs Gregson didn't try to argue with their daughter. Of course, Ambrose could be buried if that's what she wished. So they collected his little white body in the car and drove to the field behind the church. There, they found a place a little way from the foot of Anne-Marie's grave, just over the tumbledown fence, and Mr Gregson buried Ambrose so that the dog could lie undisturbed, in peaceful sleep for ever.

Kathy insisted that he be wrapped in his special blanket for burial, and placed a small wooden cross in the ground. On it she'd painted a few words in wobbly letters. 'Ambrose, age nine, friend of Anne-Marie.' Then she sadly scattered a couple of flowers on to the spot and bravely walked away. She'd never see Ambrose again, never feel his wet nose or shake his muddy paw, but at least he was with Anne-Marie. He could be happy . . .

Gradually the Gregsons tried to begin a normal life again.

It was difficult for all of them, but no one could change the past. What had happened had happened, and it was final.

The local newspaper was the first to report the strange happenings at Brideswood Village graveyard. Nearby villagers had heard peculiar noises in the middle of the night – a weird, chilling howl unlike any human sound they'd ever heard. One night, the village butcher and his fiancée had been sitting together under the stars on one of the wooden benches, when a frightening sight appeared through the trees. A quick, silvery apparition had dashed past their legs and disappeared behind the church.

A group of local boys had waited with a net the following night to try and catch the mystery ghoul, but all had stayed silent until nearly dawn. Then, long after the last owl had hooted, a distant high-pitched whine pierced the air and the boys had fled, scattering in all directions and running for their lives.

It wasn't long before a reporter turned up at the Gregson's door. All the villagers were being interviewed and were invited to give their views on the alarming goings-on. Some thought it was just a youngster's prank, others the sound of a lonely woman, perhaps mad, crying for her lost love. Mr Gregson said he had no comment to make. If people would just forget about it, whatever it was would go away. But he was wrong.

Kathy Gregson sat doing her homework while the reporter chatted and drank tea. She guessed who was causing all the trouble. It was simple, though she couldn't explain it, and wouldn't have dared to say what she thought. Instead, she finished her French composition, tidied up her books and said goodnight. She was sleepy, she explained, and felt like going to bed.

After drinking her cup of cocoa and turning out her light,

however, Kathy carefully dressed again, took her father's torch from the cupboard, and tip-toed quietly downstairs. A floorboard creaked, but no one stirred, so she let herself out of the front door and was away into the night.

It was scary walking through the darkened village. If she bumped into anyone, the village policeman or any adult, they would wonder why she was out alone and send her back. The moon was full, and kept peeping out from behind the clouds, so Kathy kept to the shadows and winced every time the gravel on the road crunched under her foot.

The spider's web that caught her face at the graveyard gate made her heart jump, but what was there to be scared of? A few silken threads could harm nobody. With the torch, Kathy found Anne-Marie's grave and sat on the nearest bench. There were no courting couples tonight, only a few chirping crickets and a solitary toad with a curious nature.

The minutes ticked by. Kathy looked at her watch and saw it was nearly ten o'clock. How long could she wait, she wondered? The day had been very warm, but the night was cold and she pulled the belt on her coat tighter. For twenty minutes Kathy stared into the distance, the mist swirling up from the nearby sea and lying low across the horizon.

Then, like a wailing baby, the noise began . . . and started to get nearer. Kathy wasn't frightened, however, and instead of running away like everybody else, she stayed where she was. Out of the mist and dusky shadows a silvery white figure appeared, close to the ground and with four very short legs. 'Ambrose!' she hissed softly. 'It's all right, boy, it's me, Kathy. Come on, boy, come on.'

The ghostly dog padded over on silent paws. He nuzzled his face against her hand, and his nose was like the touch of snow but softer even than snowflakes. For a little while, he stayed perfectly still, then he trotted over to Anne-Marie's grave and sat on the bottom edge. Head tilted to the sky, and

'Ambrose!' she hissed softly. 'It's all right, boy, it's me, Kathy. Come on, boy, come on.'

ears pinned back tightly, he wailed his doggy cry. 'Anne-Marie,' he seemed to be sobbing, 'I'm so sorry, Anne-Marie.'

Kathy watched hypnotised, not knowing what to do. Poor Ambrose blamed himself for Anne-Marie's death. Would he never be able to rest in peace? The dog's wail grew softer and softer until it faded completely, then the silent spectre turned and was there no more. Kathy switched her torch back on and made her way home. Luckily, her parents hadn't noticed her absence and she quietly climbed back into bed. Poor Ambrose, poor Anne-Marie . . . what could she do?

Months later, the people of the village had grown bored with the tales of things that went bump in the night. The groans and snuffles in the graveyard were ignored, or rather tolerated, and the stories of sightings became part of the local folklore. Nobody went amongst the tombs after dark any longer, but otherwise life went on the same.

Kathy, now an only child and lonely, invited lots of friends to stay with her at the house at weekends, and her parents encouraged her to go out to discos and parties where she would meet people. They all missed Anne-Marie, wondered if she would have liked this new dress of Kathy's or the new curtains in the bedroom, but they knew they couldn't bring her back.

Nearly a year after Anne-Marie's death, Kathy was invited to a friend's birthday party at a cliff-top bungalow. It was to be a fancy dress affair and Kathy decided to go as Titania, the fairy queen, from *A Midsummer's Night's Dream*. It was Midsummer's Night, after all.

The evening was light and scented, and everyone danced in the garden until very, very late. Then lamps were lit and hot potatoes brought from the oven for all the hungry guests.

One of the boys there was Simon Brown, the vet's son,

dressed as Prince Charming. After they'd eaten, he suggested that he and Kathy go for a walk together along the cliff edge. The moon was fairly bright and they knew their way.

The path wound away from the house, upwards and winding. Kathy felt happy and contented, but strangely afraid. Then, up ahead, not far in front of them, a small glowing figure appeared in their way. The four short legs and pointed ears could only belong to dear Ambrose, and he was determined to block the path, howling strangely and pawing the ground.

'What on earth is that?' Simon exclaimed. 'Let's take a closer look!'

Kathy held back. 'No,' she begged anxiously, 'it's Ambrose. He's trying to warn us; something must be wrong.'

'Don't be daft,' Simon laughed. 'You chicken or something? Come on!' But Kathy wouldn't budge, and she finally persuaded him to retrace their steps and to rejoin the party.

The following morning, the postman, as usual, brought the news along with the post. 'Terrible landslide last night,' he mumbled. 'Whole part of the cliff-top slid into the sea. Very dangerous. It's a wonder no one was killed. Hasn't happened in years. They're going to fence it off now.'

Kathy shivered as she heard his words. She knew Ambrose had been warning her of danger. He'd saved her life, as he would have saved Anne-Marie's if he could. Maybe now he could rest his face on his little paws and sleep peacefully. She breathed a long sigh of relief and felt thankful for her lucky escape.

The wailing in the graveyard was never heard after that night. Ambrose slept contentedly at the feet of his mistress, and courting couples again whispered in the moonlight on the graveyard benches where they hugged. One couple was there quite often, and felt it was their special place. Their names were Kathy Gregson and Simon Brown . . .

VOODOO

by John Sanders

As soon as the Creole messenger came up to me and introduced himself, I was uneasy about him. He was a short, swarthy character, a Haitian of mixed blood, and his quaint French reminded me of Molière.

'I have the honour to be your servant, sir,' he said, bowing absurdly. 'My name is Cambonne and my duty is to take you to my master, M'sieur Donnison.' But his mind wasn't on his laboured introduction. He looked around him all the time, taking in the bustling harbour scene in all its detail, shiftily, uneasily, like a man with a bad conscience.

We were on the Upper Quay of Port au Prince, capital of the mysterious, poverty-stricken island of Haiti. I had decided, for all sorts of reasons, to break ship here on my round-the-world adventure.

First of all, I had a letter of introduction to Donnison, a friend of my father's, who had invited me to spend a week on his up-country rice plantation. Second, I was fascinated by all that I had read about sinister Haiti and its voodoo cult. Thirdly, the patois they spoke interested me because I was going up to Keele next term to do modern languages. Fourthly – but what more reasons could anyone want?

I soon saw that people don't come to Haiti for the sight-seeing. The nervous Cambonne threaded me through a jostling crowd which at first sight appeared to be wholly composed of beggars hideously deformed by terrible diseases. Exhausted women slumped in the heat, silently holding out their limp and dying infants to all who passed, and ragged children balanced overflowing water cans on their thin shoulders.

'We have much typhoid and malaria here,' Cambonne threw over his shoulder, as if that explained everything. Quickly he settled me in a dust-covered jeep, and then drove out of town as if we were being pursued by an army. Beyond the harbour, I caught a glimpse of European suits parading insanely in the withering heat, and barefoot youths straining, half-naked and glistening with sweat, to pull impossible cartloads of charcoal fuel from the waterfront. Then Port au Prince disappeared and we were heading north.

As soon as the last house was behind us, Cambonne did an extraordinary thing. He opened the glove compartment and took out a packet of what looked like salt. With not so much as a glance in my direction, he opened the top of the packet with his teeth and threw its contents over his shoulder and out of the vehicle. I watched the substance spray into the air before the half-empty packet hit the dried mud road.

'What was that for?' I asked. But Cambonne set his teeth. He clearly wasn't going to answer questions.

What I remember most about the rest of the journey is studying a map – Donnison's plantation was in a village in the rice-producing Artibonite river valley. I also recall the ceaseless, anxious head-turning of Cambonne as he bumped recklessly along, and my wonder that Donnison, who had been at school with my father, had chosen to settle in this awful place. . . .

'Actually, it's a very friendly and attractive country,' Donnison said. My host was speaking after a pleasant supper in his plantation bungalow, where I had been welcomed and settled in as if I were a long-lost relative rather than a round-the-world freeloader. Donnison was a big, no-nonsense man, a throwback to colonial times. 'You know, these people have courage,' he went on. 'When the French, the Spanish and the British were very powerful, in the early nineteenth century, they defied them all and proclaimed their own republic on this island. Look at that view.' He pointed out at the garden, fringed with palm trees and heavy with magnolia blossoms. 'You won't see a view like that in Bethnal Green.'

Bennett, his partner, who had joined us for supper, smiled wanly. 'It's also a squalid, undemocratic country, Jim,' he said. 'After a rainstorm in Port au Prince you don't quickly forget the rats and the smell of sewers.'

'Tell me about the voodoo,' I said.

'It's interesting stuff,' Donnison said cheerfully. 'The idea behind voodoo tradition is that the dead live amongst us in different forms. First there are the *viens-viens*, who are mere ghosts. Then there are the *lutins*, who are infants who die before baptism. These are really reckoned to be quite cheerful spirits. Finally there are the *zombies*. These are flesh-and-blood monsters doomed to wander the earth until the final triumph of good over evil.

'Voodoo believers on Haiti will tell you that certain of their sorcerers can use special charms or spells to make someone appear to be dead, and then to bring them back from the grave after they are buried. These are the zombies, – the "undead".

'These zombies, or resurrected persons, are then kept apart in different parts of Haiti to work on the land. The voodoo sorcerers know of a special antidote that restores life, but doesn't restore the mind. That's why zombies look like what they are supposed to be, the living dead. Gaunt, with cold, glazed eyes and totally stupid. And, of course, being mindless, they are totally unaware of their misfortune.'

Suddenly I remembered how Cambonne had thrown salt, and mentioned it. Donnison's brow furrowed crossly. I saw

Bennett glance inquiringly towards him in the ensuing silence. The oil lamp in the room began to gutter and the light fell, leaving Donnison half in shadow. When he spoke again, he was clearly uneasy.

'I was hoping that business would come to nothing,' he said heavily. 'Cambonne believes the voodoo sorcerers want to kill him. Lately we have been hearing their drums pounding a rhythm in the lower valleys of the mountains. There have been all sorts of signs. Last week a half-crazed old woman working on the plantation bit the head off a live chicken in front of Cambonne.'

'In short, Cambonne thinks they will kill him and turn him into a zombie,' Bennett said slowly. 'Don't ask why. No non-native understands how they choose their victims.'

'And the salt?'

'The voodoo sorcerer is first supposed to use a potion to put the prey into a trance. The only antidote to this is salt.'

There was another long silence while the oil lamp spluttered again and finally went out, leaving the room lit only by the moonlight through the open windows.

'It's very difficult to understand these people's fears,' Donnison suddenly said. 'I've heard that when victims are put into a trance, they actually make for the cemetery because they know they're already a walking corpse. Then comes resurrection as a zombie and banishment to work in a gang on the land. They say that if you actually come across these shambling, silent figures raised from the dead, with their downcast eyes, you'll be struck blind.'

Despite myself, I felt my flesh creep slightly and wished that the oil lamp was still alight.

Next morning I had forgotten all about the mumbo-jumbo of voodoo as Bennett and Duhamel, the Haitian manager, showed me around the rice plantation. Donnison and

Bennett employed around a hundred workers in their paddy fields, most of whom, like the majority of Haitians, were black. It seemed that the plantation was something of a show-piece on the island, and the partners enjoyed what little government favour there was to enjoy.

'We pay all our workers much better than the average wage, which is unbelievably low,' Bennett said.

'There isn't much they can buy with their money, though. They live on fish and mangoes and relief from abroad, such as flour and oil. The rice we grow is collected by the government agency, and I can tell you not much of it goes to the people.'

I learned a good deal about rice growing that week, and I was almost sorry when the time came to go. Donnison, Bennett and I were having supper on my last night at the plantation when there was a knock at the door. A servant showed in Duhamel, the manager, and the man's eyes were staring with fright.

'The voodoo drums, m'sieur,' he blurted out. 'They say they are coming to get Marcel Cambonne tonight.'

Donnison stiffened. I saw him adopt his colonial, no-nonsense stance like a suit of armour.

'We won't have any of that rubbish, Duhamel,' he said. 'You are not to put fright into the workers.'

'But m'sieur, they mean death and they're *coming* . . .' The man was beginning to gibber, and Donnison's impatience was visibly mounting. I listened, silent and amused, to their arguing, until Donnison said, with great exasperation: 'Bring Cambonne to the bungalow. Give him the *chambre d'amis*. He is not to leave the room tonight.'

Duhamel left like a flash to carry out the order.

An hour later, supper over and coffee simmering in the pot, we were sitting on the verandah when around twenty men appeared soundlessly from the shadows of the palm trees at the end of the garden. They moved unhurriedly into the centre of the lawn. Although there was no apparent threat at all in their movements I began to feel distinctly anxious. Donnison broke off in mid-conversation and watched them without moving. When they were all together on the lawn, one of them stepped forward and addressed us.

'Cambonne is with you in house, M'sieur Donnison. Send him out. We want him.'

I saw the old colonial instinct bridling again in my host.

'You clear off!' he rasped. 'You're trespassing. Get off my property or I'll put some buckshot up your backside!'

'We want Cambonne. If you no send him, we fetch him.'

'Cambonne does not want to see you. I don't want any trouble, but I warn you. If you try to break in, we are armed and we won't hesitate to shoot.'

'We take Cambonne or we burn house. You give up Cambonne or you all die. We make lots of fire.'

The situation seemed suddenly very critical. I glanced around me. The bungalow was lightly built, with a thatch of attap, or palm leaves, and would scarcely last a minute if a torch were put to it. We were heavily outnumbered, and I had never used a gun in my life. I was prepared to offer some compromising advice when Donnison revealed that he was made of sterner stuff.

'You take one more step forward and I'll shoot to kill you,' he said with slow deliberation.

There was silence from the shadows on the lawn, a silence in which I heard the rhythmic pumping of my heart. Then:

'All right. We clear off. But we come back, pretty soon.'

At that the shadows seemed to melt away in the darkness.

Donnison turned to Bennett and myself, and for the first time betrayed unease. 'We'll have to get out of here quickly,' he said. 'They'll come back for certain, and if we're still here they'll burn this place over our heads. We couldn't hold out against them.'

‘Where can we go?’ Bennett asked.

‘The caves in the Artibonite mountains.’ Donnison turned to me to explain.

‘They’re a mile from here, and I know them well. We could hold out against an army there if necessary.’ He rang the bell on the table and a servant, clearly terrified for his life, rushed out. ‘Get Monsieur Duhamel,’ he said.

While Bennett unlocked a gun cabinet on the lounge wall, Donnison explained his plan. ‘I’ll send Duhamel with a note to the police at Macon, telling them exactly where we are. Duhamel’s an athlete, you know, very fleet-footed. If he takes the forest path, he may not be seen, and even if he is seen, he can outrun any man I know. We’ll have to take Cambonne with us. We’ll all be safe in the caves until the police arrive.’ He grinned suddenly. ‘I’m sorry this has come to disturb your last night,’ he said.

I followed him back into the dining room, which was suddenly alive with bustling servants in a state of panic. Donnison gave orders sharply in Creole, then went to the gun cabinet. As two servants cleared the supper table, they left the last item on the tablecloth – the salt cellar. Instinctively, as if it were the most natural thing in the world to do, I picked it up and put it in my pocket. I could not tell you to this day what went through my mind at that moment.

With astonishing rapidity, what was a quiet supper was transferred to a war party. I found it difficult to take it very seriously until I saw Cambonne. Brought from the *chambre d’amis* by Bennett, the man was quivering with fright. He could scarcely stand, and when he lifted his head, his eyes were staring white like those of a man in another world.

When Donnison thrust a rifle in my hands, I began to realise that all this was for real. Somehow we got Cambonne into the jeep, and Donnison drove across the plantation towards the mountains without a care for our comfort. He certainly knew the terrain. He drove unerringly to a flat area and, in the jeep's headlights, revealed a fissure in the granite wall, wide enough to take only one man. Bennett went in and lit an oil lamp. As the light flickered upwards I saw that the fissure opened up into a wide cave. This was about the size and height of a living room and reasonably dry.

Donnison dragged Cambonne through the fissure and laid him out on the cave floor. The man was unable to stand and was whimpering and crying like a terrified child.

'You'll be all right here, Cambonne,' Donnison said roughly. 'Now stop that racket. The police will be here soon.' He turned to us. 'We should have brought a deck of cards,' he said. 'We may have to wait all night.'

But he was wrong. Scarcely had I taken in my new surroundings when I heard the sound of muffled drums. It needed only seconds to realise that they were coming rapidly nearer. 'It looks as if they've rumbled us,' Donnison said. He seemed annoyed rather than worried. He looked grimly at Bennett. 'Duhamel should be at Macon by now,' he said.

'Cambonne seems to be in a coma,' Bennett said anxiously. 'I think he's unconscious.' I looked across at Cambonne, crumpled in an untidy heap on the granite. The mulatto servant was silent, though his eyes were open and his face was soaked with sweat.

'Give me your rifle,' Donnison said matter-of-factly. 'I'll put six rounds in the magazine for you.'

The pursuers had no intention of keeping us waiting. Soon the persistent drumming stopped, and within minutes the voice we knew so well was coming down through the fissure into the cave. 'You send out Cambonne now, M'sieur Donnison, and you have no more trouble. You no send him and this time you all die.'

Donnison raised his rifle carefully to his shoulder and aimed it down the narrow fissure. 'Stand clear!' he shouted.

Donnison drove across the plantation towards the mountains without a care for our comfort. He drove unerringly.

'In three seconds I will fire.'

The explosion that followed from the rifle was deafening in that closed cave. The noise rebounded endlessly off the walls as the bullet whistled down the fissure. Evidently our voodoo chief had stood aside, for we heard no cry of pain from the black night beyond the fissure.

For moments more we still heard nothing. Then I saw something that made my blood freeze.

A thin wisp of smoke was coming down the fissure, a wisp which curled, then hung in the air, then drifted slowly into the cave, a wisp of smoke which was no ordinary smoke, it had a sharp and acrid smell that made my eyes sting and my stomach retch. I saw Donnison whip a handkerchief from his pocket and cover his mouth and heard him exclaim, 'They're trying to smoke us out. . . !'

I honestly do not know exactly what happened next. I remember my eyes stung until I could see only silhouetted forms, and my mouth dried out until my tongue felt like a football. I clutched my throat and fell backwards. All sorts of scrambling sounds were going on around me. At one moment it seemed as if the cave was full of people, but that may have been only an impression because I must have been almost unconscious. I was choking on the smoke and convinced that I was about to die.

When I came to I was lying on a slab of granite outside the cave. It seemed as if a thousand years had passed. Absolute stillness reigned; there wasn't sight or sound of anyone. It was still dark and my head ached horribly. I called out to Donnison and the only response was the dull echo of my own voice. I felt my arms and legs cautiously and, finding that I was still in one piece, I got up. It was as if someone had cleaved my head with an axe; my eyes swam with the pain.

I crawled back through the fissure into the cave. It was still lit by the dying light of the oil lamp, but there was no sign of anyone. The acrid smell of the smoke that had dazed me hung on the motionless air. I got out quickly and looked around the rocky landscape, trying to clear my head, trying to think straight. Still no sight or sound of any creature. It was just as if I had been picked up and dropped all alone on that barren patch of rock.

In my befuddled state I concluded that Donnison, Bennett and Cambonne must have left the cave and returned to the plantation bungalow. I set off to follow them. But the bungalow was in darkness as I approached, and inside there wasn't so much as a servant. I dunked my aching head in a bowl of cold water, cleaned myself up and considered the position. I decided to follow Duhamel to the police at Macon in one of the vans I found.

Twenty minutes later I walked into the bare, unfriendly police station. The desk officer rubbed sleep from his eyes as he listened wearily to my recital. When I had finished he said nonchalantly, 'We had a call to go to the Artibonite caves. The report came in half an hour ago. There was no one there, but there was a strong smell of marijuana at the place you mention.'

Marijuana! So that was what they'd used to smoke us out. That was the drug they used to put their victims in a trance.

'Turn out your pockets!' the officer commanded. I protested in vain. As I emptied the contents of my jacket on the table, my hand closed around Donnison's salt cellar. As I looked at it, the thought that flashed through my mind seemed too fantastic to contemplate.

The officer's eyes gleamed, thinking that the marijuana was in the salt cellar. I persuaded him to taste it and, mystified, he gave it back. After that, the policeman was totally disinterested. Plenty of people disappear in Haiti every night, he grumbled, and why was I disturbing his work with a fanciful tale. I left, confused, got back into the van, and set off back to the plantation. There wasn't much more I could do that night.

I was close to the bungalow when I saw the crumpled figure at the side of the road. I stopped, got out, and knew at once that it was Duhamel. His face was a sight I will never forget. Where his eyes had been were two large, white opaque discs. He was completely blind. I got him to hospital and stayed on in Haiti to visit him and do what I could. He gradually was able to tell me what had happened.

After Donnison had given him the note for the police, he had set off through the forest for Macon. At the police station, no one showed much interest. They did agree to make a routine check on the cave that night and, unable to get them to do more, Duhamel decided to go to the caves himself to see if he could assist us. He must have arrived at the very moment when we were smoked out. What he saw he could tell me only over the course of several weeks, for each sentence held a memory that caused him to go into fits of terror.

Concealed behind some trees, Duhamel saw the four of us stagger, choking, out of the fissure into the arms of the voodooists. They roped us together, then made a brushwood fire. One of them produced a cooking-pot into which went some human bones, a dead toad, a sand crab and various liquids. Then came a ritual dance and some incantations, at the end of which the ropes binding us were cut.

I dropped to the ground. Donnison, Bennett and Cambonne began to run. The voodoo sorcerers followed them at a short distance, and Duhamel carefully followed them.

The three victims did not stop until they reached the Artibonite cemetery. There, like men possessed, they began to dig feverishly into the graveyard with their bare hands. Watched by the voodooists, they dug non-stop until each had fashioned a shallow grave. Then they got into their graves and lay there motionless. Within the next few minutes, according to Duhamel, all three turned into carrion before his eyes.

The sorcerers lit another fire, cooked some more ingredients, and made more incantations. Then (remember, I have only Duhamel's account of this), the three lifeless figures in the graves returned slowly to human form. They got to their feet and began to shamble silently, with downcast eyes, behind the priests, who led them away from the cemetery and into the countryside.

'They are the undead. They have become zombies,' Duhamel said, with such belief that it was impossible to argue. They must have been walking like this for a couple of hours when Duhamel, following in the shadows, saw a line of other shambling creatures. 'All wretches, all like the three with cold, staring eyes, all raised from the dead,' said Duhamel. They were tilling a field. Donnison, Bennett and Cambonne joined them and began to work silently and mechanically alongside them. Overcome with horror, Duhamel cried out. He remembered several of the voodoo priests turning towards him. After that, all was darkness. The hospitals doctors told me when I left Haiti that he would never see again.

A thousand times I have asked myself: if Donnison and Bennett, as well as Cambonne, were turned into zombies, why wasn't I? There is no answer that makes sense. But I still carry Donnison's salt cellar wherever I go.

HORROR HOUSE

by J.H. Teed

SHRILL, JANGLING LAUGHTER and weird whooping shrieks of terror rose and fell in a hideous conflict. The sound of a mighty organ, whose crashing discords and raucous sounds were such that the instrument could only have been played by a madman, blared brassily across the night.

Della Reece shuddered as she gazed at the huge wooden door that sagged open, revealing a glimpse of the shadowy interior of the sinister old house, and then told herself angrily not to be such a dummy. *Nothing* could harm her in Horror House. Positively the worst that could happen would be a few cobwebs in her dress. And synthetic cobwebs at that.

The straw-hatted barker, in his booth below the platform that led to the wide doorway, was yelling once more through his megaphone.

'*Step up! Step up!* The terror tour of a lifetime! Scream your heart out as vampire bats swoop down at you! Howl with fright at the bony clutch of grinning skeletons! Wail with woe as the masked executioner comes to get you with his axe! Yes indeed, it's all here! For just a few dimes you get the world-famous Coney Island's biggest, most heart-stopping *fear-feast!*'

Della Reece giggled. 'Wail with woe!' The guy needed a new scriptwriter. How about: 'Shudder with shock' or 'faint with fright' or 'pant with panic'?

Or how about: 'Gawp with goose-bumps'? Yeah, how *about* it!

She glanced around and saw the full brash craziness of New York's Coney Island at its height – the chattering crowds of relaxed pleasure seekers; the bawling barkers advertising their wares; the bagel and hot-dog stands; the gaudy booths with their equally gaudy occupants like the Snake Lady, Croc-Man, the Siamese Twins, the Dog With Two Heads, the Camel-Lion; the huge Ferris Wheels outlined against the hot dark sky; the sweeping searchlights picking out the intricate network of scaffolding supporting the careering Roller-Coaster.

And the noise! An outlandish mix of sounds beat against her ears – a score of different popular tunes clashing noisily as they boomed from a score of whirling carousels; the spitting crack of air rifles; shouts and cries and shrieks, and eruptions of roared laughter; the thunder of petrol-driven engines; the old-fashioned blare of fairground organs beating out a dozen well-known marches. It was crazy, but it was fun!

'And how about *you*, little lady! For just a few, a *very* few, silver coins, you *too* can experience a trip to make your spine *tingle*, your eyeballs *twitch*, your . . .'

'Okay, okay!' Della laughed as she dived into her purse and offered the grinning barker a note. What had she got to lose? It was the weekend, she'd always wanted to experience the zany old-fashioned nonsense of Coney Island, and you couldn't get more zany or old-fashioned or nonsensical than Horror House!

As she climbed the wooden steps to the platform, the barker turned and yelled to the crowd: 'Here's a lady who's *really* keen! She's so keen she gives me ten bucks and forgets about the change! That's how it hits 'em, folks! They can't wait to get their nerves shredded . . . they can't wait to get their hearts stopped . . . they can't wait to climb aboard and experience the full frantic fright-frenzy of *Horror House!*'

Grinning with embarrassment, Della turned back to the

booth, noting as she did so a slight stir amongst the laughing customers around the platform.

A youngish man, head turned in a glance over his shoulder, was pushing through the crowd. Behind him two hard-faced men in raincoats were also shouldering their way forward, as though following him.

'Here y'are, little lady, your change!'

Della grabbed the notes and coins and dived into the shadowy interior of the building. Steps led down to a wide artifical stream on which bobbed a number of two-seater boats with short-handled paddles. The lighting, from painted bulbs high in the vaulted roof, was dim. Ahead was the mouth of a tunnel, its curved edge festooned with cobwebs.

Della stepped into the first boat and was about to push herself off when there was an angry yell and a crash from outside. Then the thud of running feet.

A man jumped down the steps two at a time. It was the young man Della had spotted outside, and she felt a sudden pang of fear as she saw that he was holding a gun.

She tried to shove the boat away from the tiny pier with the paddle, but he was too quick. Without a moment's hesitation, he jumped into the boat next to her.

'Push off!' he snapped. 'Push the boat off, fast!'

She gripped the paddle with her right hand, resentment rather than fear now welling up inside her.

'Now look. I don't know who you are, but . . .'

He laughed harshly.

'The name's Phil Mason, and I'm going to be a very *dead* Phil Mason unless you either move this blasted boat or give me the paddle!'

As he said this, someone else appeared in the entrance high above them. Della recognised one of the men in a raincoat, and saw that he, too, was holding a gun.

'Don't be a fool, Mason! You can't escape! We've got you

bottled up! Give in and tell us what you know. We can do a deal . . .'

The man called Mason laughed again, and the sound, echoing eerily round the vaulted chamber, held no trace of humour in it.

'Here's the only deal you'll get from me, punk . . . a deal in lead!'

He raised the gun and fired. There was a vicious crack and the man above dived out of sight as the bullet bounced off an iron railing inches from him.

Mason sat down in the boat abruptly turned the gun on Della.

'*Now* will you move it! I don't have time to argue!'

She shoved furiously at the pier with the blade of the paddle and the boat rocked out into the middle of the stream. As she dug the paddle into the water she suddenly realised she was still clutching a fistful of dollar notes, change from the ten-dollar bill, crumpled in her left hand. Angrily, she let them go to get a better grip on the smooth-handled oar, and they fluttered to the boards.

Mason, with a muttered oath, leaned down and grabbed at the notes. He stared at them intently, smiled coldly, then thrust them into his jacket pocket.

'So that's what you are,' Della sneered. 'Just a crummy small-time thief! Do anything for a few bucks!'

'Just keep this boat on the move and quit gabbing,' he snarled. 'We're in this together now, whether you like it or not.'

Della tightened her lips. She wondered if she could somehow lift the paddle high enough to land a smashing blow on the man's head, but then realised that he was too close, the boat too narrow. Maybe at some stage later on she could elbow him over the side, but that would have to wait until the right opportunity came up. At the moment he was too wary, too watchful.

She wondered who the two men in raincoats were, and then it hit her that they'd have to be the police. She realised that Mason must be a bigger fish than she'd at first figured. They were offering him a deal. That meant he must be a member of some gang the cops were trying to bust, and if he told them all he knew about the gang, the District Attorney would be able to get him a lighter sentence – or even get him off. It was done all the time – plea-bargaining, they called it.

One thing was very clear: there was no escape for Phil Mason from Horror House!

The stream ran round the interior of the large building in a full circle, and there were no landing stages or other exits. The boat finally had to come round to the entrance again, and this time there would be a reception committee waiting. Mason didn't have a chance.

Unless . . .

Della Reece's mouth went suddenly dry as the full, terrifying understanding of the situation came home to her.

He *did* have a chance. He had *her*!

She was his hostage. The police would be powerless to do a thing. All he had to do was jam the gun to her head and walk out, a free man. She was his guarantee of safety, and a cast-iron guarantee at that.

'*Keep paddling!*'

Mason's harsh voice slashed through her thoughts like a knife.

Automatically she dug the paddle into the water and heaved – and then screamed aloud as glowing, grinning skulls suddenly popped out of the tunnel wall on her left and shrieks of ghastly, nerve-shattering laughter echoed and re-echoed around the confined space.

'Don't panic!' snapped Mason. 'You know what this place is . . . hokum, one hundred per cent. Just keep us moving.'

Della paddled the boat along the tunnel.

At intervals, there were wide bays in the walls on each side of the stream, where life-like full-size figures sat, stood or lay in horrid and gaudy poses. Just before each bay, the boat passed through an invisible beam which sent an electronic impulse to each display, triggering the figures into dreadful mobility.

An axe-murderer slammed down his fearsome weapon into his victim, accompanied by terrifyingly life-like yells of agony; a cackling hangman tugged at a lever, sending his hooded victim crashing through the trapdoor of a scaffold; a cloaked Count Dracula sprang with grisly glee through an open window, and with extended talons, clutched at a shrinking girl; human figures with animal heads lumbered into a devilish dance around a wailing wretch tied to a stake.

Bats swooped, hissing ferociously, through the gloomy air, their leathery wings flapping furiously; clacking skeletons jumped and danced; disembodied hands tore at one's hair; shrilling rats scampered up the slimy walls; bells tolled and peals of hideous laughter echoed deafeningly, madly.

But nothing, thought Della, was as real as the gun that every now and again was jabbed into her ribs, or as terrifying as the harsh voice that urged her on through this madhouse carnival of phoney horrors.

Ahead, through the murk, she caught a glint of steel high above. Suddenly a huge curved blade swung down from the shadows to just above their heads in front of them, then whooshed upwards again.

Rather like Poe's famous story, 'The Pit and the Pendulum', she thought, which featured an astonishing and cruel instrument of torture used by the Spanish Inquisition centuries ago. The victim would be tied to a block facing upwards, and a massive, razor-sharp blade would hurtle down over and over, missing each time, but sweeping closer and closer until it cut through the helpless body.

Again the blade in front zoomed down and up, but, of course, it did not drop any lower than before. This was Horror House, in the centre of New York's Coney Island, not a real and sinister dungeon where real tortures took place.

Once more the blade whirled down – and this time she frowned in puzzlement, because it truly did seem that the fearsome object was lower than it had been before. But, of course, that was stupid. It couldn't . . .

'*Down!*'

Mason grabbed her shoulder and heaved her violently to one side. The little boat rocked madly, and Della screamed as she saw that the swooping blade was now only chest-high and sweeping non-stop towards them.

It swished between the two of them in the boat, missing them by a hair's breadth, and Mason shoved her even further into the bottom of the boat as the blade reached the end of its swing up to zoom back down. Again it missed them by millimetres, and Della felt the wind of its hurtling movement on the back of her neck.

Mason dived for the paddle which she had dropped and swept the boat forward. Della looked back and saw the sharp blade actually slicing through the water with a tearing hiss, exactly where they'd been only seconds before.

'Close,' muttered Mason, 'but not close enough. Here!'

He handed back the paddle and Della took it with hands that trembled. The blade had been real, not wood or cardboard. The mechanism that worked it must have been damaged or faulty.

Without thinking, she said angrily, 'We ought to sue them!'

Mason laughed thinly, and she realised how ridiculous her words must have sounded. She wasn't even sure if she was ever going to get back to her apartment on West 72nd Street

Again it missed them by millimetres, and Della felt the wind of its hurtling movement on the back of her neck.

alive, and here she was talking about suing a crummy outfit who skimped on safety measures!

She bent her back and plunged the paddle into the water. The boat swept round a bend. A little way on, there was another sinister tableau in a bay in the wall, rather larger than the ones already shown.

Here at last was the executioner!

A concealed greenish spotlight shone down on his hapless victim, strapped to a block with his hands tied behind his back. The executioner himself was only half glimpsed, just beyond the shadows – a grim figure, standing stiffly with arms folded across the upturned handle of a mighty double-bladed axe and gazing down through a half-mask, with a cleverly painted expression of hideous and evil glee on what could be seen of his devilish face.

Della paddled the boat towards the tableau. Very soon they would pass through the invisible beam that would activate it. Presumably the axeman would suddenly lift his axe and whack it down at the neck of the unfortunate on the block. There would be more horrible, echoing laughter, more fiendish shrieks.

The executioner was certainly life-like, she thought. Even more so than the other figures. Why, it must be the weird green light playing tricks, of course, but she could have sworn that the figure's chest was rising and falling, as though the model were actually breathing.

She gasped.

It *was* breathing.

It was moving!

Della screamed and pointed as the executioner, with a wild laugh, suddenly sprang towards the edge of the bay and smashed the axe down at the boat.

There was a grating crash, the boat lurched, and suddenly Della was struggling in the water. She found that the stream was only waist-deep, but it was more than enough to slow her down as she tried to escape that madly swinging axe.

She heard Mason give a cry and saw him topple to one side as the flat of the blade smacked against his shoulder. His gun fell into the boat, clattering on the boards.

The executioner gave a crazed yell and turned towards her, springing down into the water and raising the axe high above his shoulders. She could see his gaping mouth, the glaring eyes behind the mask.

Her right hand scrabbled for the gun, clutched at it. She gripped it and swung round, squeezing blindly at the trigger, almost deafened by the thunderous crash of shot after shot.

Then she slid down into the water in a dead faint . . .

There were lights all around her, blinding her. She groaned, put a hand to her face.

'You're all right, lady. Don't you worry now. Everything's going to be fine.'

The thick, re-assuring brogue of a New York Irish cop.

She was lying on the platform outside the Horror House. There were police all around her, grim-faced men with guns.

She said: 'The crazy guy with the axe . . .'

'He's lucky to be alive, lady,' the cop grinned, 'the amount of lead you pumped into him! But he'll survive – in the penitentiary!'

'And the other crook – Mason. . . ?'

Someone laughed. She looked round. Mason stood behind her, smiling. There was a large tear in his jacket where the axe had snagged.

'*You*! But I thought *you* were one of them!'

'Uh-uh!' Mason squatted down. 'I'm a cop, too. Undercover. The guys who operated Horror House were counterfeiters. I penetrated the gang, but they found out who I was and chased me. They wanted me to do a deal, tell 'em how much I'd found out. But I knew they'd kill me anyhow. Once we were in the boat, they tried to finish us using that blade, which they could drop using remote control. The guy who took the executioner's place rushed there in case we escaped the blade. He dressed up like that to take us by surprise – and he almost succeeded.'

'So that was why you took my money . . .'

'Sure. It was fake. They could pass a heck of a lot through the ticket booth, in small-note change.'

'But . . . I don't have a cent left now!' wailed Della.

'Don't worry,' grinned Mason. 'I'll take you home. Getting right down to it, it's the least I can do!'

BANANA REVENGE

by M.S. Goodall

CLIVE BARRINGTON WAS ONE OF THOSE PEOPLE commonly referred to as a whizz-kid. Ex-public school and university, he combined good looks with a strong determination to further his career. Only thirty-two, he had already made his mark as a go-ahead research and development executive with the multi-national oil corporation for which he worked. His position gave him offices in London and the Middle East, plus a private villa in Algiers.

It was in Algiers that Barrington first met and employed Mustapha Abd el Gaffer, a fifteen-year-old Arab boy from a decaying village on the edge of the desert.

Mustapha's life was opposite to Clive Barrington's. He couldn't even read and write, he was desperately poor, the eldest of five brothers and two sisters. The boy had come to the city to find work. He found it as Barrington's servant, cook, cleaner, valet and general dogsbody. The pay was very little and the conditions of employment almost like slavery. Barrington, like so many international executives, was an out-and-out snob. It wasn't that he meant to be cruel. It was simply that by outlook and upbringing he had been taught to regard himself as a superior being, a born leader. Servants like Mustapha, therefore, were below consideration. They were there, they existed, they were more robots than actual people: obedient beings ready to perform any function demanded by their masters.

It was a dangerously old-fashioned way to think and

behave, as the many revolutions throughout the centuries have shown. As an intelligent man, Barrington should have realised that; yet strangely he did not. Perhaps, deep down, he had the arrogance to see himself as a new kind of colonial ruler, one with a technological empire to build. And so he continued to treat young Mustapha with scorn, disdain and indifference. For his part, the Arab boy tried hard to ignore the constant insults. He needed the money, his family needed the money, and so he slaved on.

Until the night of the banana dessert.

Barrington had decided to entertain some friends of his from the international set in Algiers. He invited two other English oilmen, a French archaeologist and a couple of ageing German diplomats for dinner on the elegant terrace of his villa, which overlooked the slow-lapping waters of the Mediterranean.

Mustapha, of course, had been expected not only to buy, prepare and cook the food, but to serve it as well. For a fifteen-year-old boy, it was almost impossible, but with careful planning and hard work, Mustapha achieved the impossible. The meal went well; some of the guests even said how good the meal was during the conversation round the candlelit table. The Europeans seemed happy, and Mustapha began to relax.

Then came the sweet course. Barrington had insisted on fresh raspberries, whipped cream and bananas, a dish which, he said, had been an especial favourite of his while a schoolboy in England. Mustapha carried the six dessert bowls out to the terrace on a silver tray, and placed them one by one in front of the guests. Then he gave the merest suggestion of a bow and turned to leave.

'Mustapha!' Barrington's voice cut the air with a sudden, high-pitched fury.

'Yes, sir?'

'Come and look at this banana.' As the boy leant closer, Barrington prodded the fruit with his dessert fork. 'Well? What can you see?'

'A tiny speck of brown,' said Mustapha quietly. 'The merest fleck. Most of the bananas I buy in the market are like that. It is nothing, sir . . . nothing at all.'

'*Nothing*?' Barrington's voice rose again, and in a fit of childish rage, he stabbed the banana again and again with his dessert fork. 'This banana is past its best. It is more than past its best. It is *rotten*, do you hear? *Rotten*! The fruit I expect to be served in this house must be of the best quality and fresh. Especially the bananas. They must be firm, evenly curved and white. *White*, do you understand? Not speckled with brown rot. Now take this rubbish away and dish up some more. For my guests as well as myself.'

'*No*!' Mustapha felt the word explode from his lips like a spurt of acid. He had risen at dawn and had worked for sixteen hours without a break. This nonsense about the banana was too much. He'd had enough. It was time to fight back. A stream of Arab profanities broke from his throat as he stood his ground and released all the pent-up emotions of the past weeks and months. Through a haze of anger and tears he saw Clive Barrington get to his feet.

Reaching for his banana dessert, the Englishman slid the bowl on to the palm of his left hand. With his right, he grabbed Mustapha's jacket and jerked the boy forward. Then slowly, deliberately, he rammed the full mixture of raspberries, cream and crushed bananas into the servant's face.

For a full minute there was silence in the room. Mustapha stood perfectly still, pulped fruit and cream dripping slowly, comically, off the end of his nose, cheeks and chin. Barrington giggled. A nervous sound at first, it suddenly grew into the roaring guffaws of a full-blooded belly-laugh. One by one the other Europeans followed suit. They pounded the table with their fists and tears of malicious joy flowed from their eyes.

'Ha, ha, ha, well done, Clive. That's put the little blighter in his place.'

'Not before time.'

'Deserved everything he got, answering back like that.'

'Maybe it's time you got married, Clive. A wife would be a far better investment than some cheeky-tongued Arab. Make a better servant, too, what? Ha, ha, ha.'

As the jabber of voices ebbed and flowed round the table, Mustapha wiped his face and found himself talking again. But this time it was as though the words that flowed from his mouth were not his words, but someone else's. Deeper, richer, older. Much older. Poisonous words of hate from an age long dead and times long gone. 'A curse on you, Barrington! A foul curse on you and what is left of your life!' The strangeness of Mustapha's voice made the others stop and listen. The boy's eyes were glowing, the fingers of his right hand were almost like claws as he stretched his arm and pointed at Barrington's sneering face.

'A curse, I say! As you stand there laughing, I promise you this . . . one day soon you will *die* laughing! Those are the words of Mustapha Abd el Gaffer. Heed them.'

'You little swine, get out. Pack your miserable belongings and go back to the desert where you belong. You're fired.' Whirling the boy round with ease, Barrington sent him reeling across the terrace, through the lounge and towards the front door. Mustapha left the house quietly and for ever, but there was a strange smile on his lips that Clive Barrington should have noticed. He did not.

Four months went by. In London, the sudden death of a senior executive gave Barrington the chance he had been waiting for: instant promotion to Controller of Middle-East

Affairs. This meant he would be in the corporation's London headquarters all the time. The work was hard, but the rewards high. Barrington thrived on the cut and thrust of business affairs. He was in his office at seven-thirty every morning, and was often still there at eight or nine at night. He was also thinking about getting married. He had met a young woman recently, the daughter of an earl. She would undoubtedly make an excellent partner, and perhaps help to advance his blossoming career even further. Life, thought Barrington smugly, was very sweet indeed.

Then came the spine-chilling events of the night of 24th June.

Barrington had been working especially late. It was ten-fifteen when he finished dictating his last letter, locked his private office, and strode firmly towards the high-speed lifts on the twenty-eighth floor of the company's tower block. He was wearing a dark pinstripe suit and carrying nothing except a small, tightly rolled folding umbrella of the telescopic sort. It had been raining most of the afternoon, and Barrington didn't want to get wet while he was waiting for a taxi. Since his promotion, the corporation had provided him with a chauffeur-driven car, but because of his irregular working hours, he usually allowed the man to go home at seven-thirty.

Barrington pressed the call button for the lift and waited. There were three high-speed lifts side by side on the landing, none of which was being used at this late hour. Lift number one arrived with a faint hiss, and the doors slid open. Barrington stepped inside and, as the doors closed again, he pressed the ground floor button. The lift moved smoothly downwards for three seconds and then stopped. Barrington frowned and pressed the ground floor button again. Harder this time. The lift jerked and stuck. He stabbed at every button on the board, but nothing happened. A wave of annoyance swept over the oil executive. It was late, he'd been working very hard, he was hungry, and now the lift had jammed. It was just too much.

A single, recessed neon lighting strip in the roof of the lift provided plenty of light as Barrington began to put the emergency procedure into operation. Instead of an alarm button, there was a tiny alcove set into one wall of the lift to the right of the closed doors. Inside this alcove, behind a close-fitting aluminium door, was an emergency telephone. All he had to do was open this door, lift the telephone and speak to the night security staff on the ground floor. If the lift had indeed broken down, an engineer would be sent for immediately either to repair the fault or winch the lift down by hand to the next floor. No need for even the slightest panic. Barrington knew he should be down and out of the building within half an hour at the latest.

Swiftly he opened the small door panel and lifted the telephone receiver. There was a faint crackling sound but no immediate reply. As he waited, Barrington suddenly noticed a rather squashed-looking cardboard box jammed into the alcove behind the base of the telephone. It was an old shoebox, its lid held firmly on by two strong elastic bands. Barrington lifted the box and shook it. Various small objects made a curious rattling noise inside. Thinking it must have been left by a member of the cleaning staff, he bent and placed the unopened box on the floor of the lift, close to where he had propped his rolled umbrella against the wall.

'Hello.' The voice at the other end of the emergency 'phone had a deep, husky sound to it.

'About time! Look, this is Clive Barrington, and I'm stuck in this darn lift somewhere between the twenty-eighth and twenty-fifth floors. Do something about it, will you? Sharpish.'

'I am sorry, Mr Barrington, but you will receive no more

help from anyone. Not tonight, not ever.' Once again, that deep, husky tone to the voice. It was foreign, that was it. Someone speaking English with a foreign accent. Once again, it came softly over the line. 'Goodbye, Mr Barrington . . . *and remember the words of a boy called Mustapha Abd el Gaffer.*'

Barrington stared in cold-eyed disbelief at the useless receiver still clutched tightly in his hand. Mustapha Abd el-whatever . . . yes, he remembered the brat, all right. The foul-mouthed little Algerian servant he'd been forced to put in his place all those months ago. So what was going on? Could a fifteen-year-old boy, a penniless desert waif, have somehow found his way to London and managed to trap a highly respected business executive in the high-speed lift of an office tower block? Of course not! The snivelling wretch probably had relations in England. Some of these Algerians were like the Chinese, with family tentacles everywhere. This was some kind of planned revenge, a plot designed to scare the living daylights out of him. What had the boy's words been? 'A curse . . . as you stand there laughing, I promise one day soon you will *die* laughing.'

Barrington gave a contemptuous snort and slammed the receiver down. A curse indeed! This wasn't the Middle Ages, it was nearly the twenty-first century. If the family or relations of some dirty Algerian child thought they could scare Clive Barrington in a jammed lift, they could think again. All he had to do was sit it out. Even if he had to stay all night in this steel box, the fact that the lift was out of order was bound to be reported by day staff when they came on duty. Then he'd be freed, and then he would make it his business to teach a certain Mustapha whatever-it-was a very severe lesson.

He sat down and stretched his legs out in front of him. His left elbow brushed against the cardboard box which he'd placed on the floor of the lift only a few moments before. Idly, he pulled off the two elastic bands holding the lid and peered inside, shaking the box gently as he did so. Just for a split second he glimpsed a mass of dark, scuttling creatures slithering across the bottom of the tilted box. Instinctively, he tossed it away from him, and before his startled brain could register what the creatures were . . . *the light in the lift went out.*

The sudden darkness hit him with the force of a physical blow. Velvet night seemed to press closer and closer, enveloping him, stifling him, strangling him. Barrington held his breath and listened, his body pressed tightly into the unyielding steel at his back. There was not a sound. Not a single sound. And yet in that split second, that tiny flash of consciousness before the light went out, Barrington had recognised and identified the scampering creatures in that cardboard box. They were desert scorpions. Roughly a dozen of them. Big ones. The biggest he'd ever seen. Probably from Egypt, because that was where the big ones usually came from.

There in the darkness, for the first time in his life, Clive Barrington knew the meaning of real fear.

Gradually, as the seconds ticked by and nothing happened, the fear was replaced with anger. This night of terror had been carefully planned, brilliantly carried out. The rigging of the emergency telephone, the placing of the cardboard box, the lift light being extinguished at the precise second when Barrington opened the lid . . . everything pointed to a cruel and callous revenge. But those North African villains hadn't got him yet! He'd show them! By gad, he would!

Calmly and coolly, Barrington began to think. How much did he know about desert scorpions? Not much, it was true. They could move fast and they had a terrible sting, but how *deadly* were they? That was the question. As far as he could remember from odd snippets of information he had read, very few adults had actually died as a result of poisoning by a scorpion. So far, so good. But he realised that he was in a confined space and that there were a dozen, not *one*, scorpion. If three or four of the brutes got to him, there was every chance that he might die from their bites before help arrived.

Then Barrington remembered his rolled umbrella. It was still where he had left it, propped against the wall at his side. Telescoped as it was in its case, the brolly made a short, fairly heavy and useful cosh. If, as he reasoned, the scorpions had been tippied out of the opened box when he threw it away in his moment of panic, they would have scuttled for the nearest cover available. Since the lift was carpetless and almost exactly square, this meant they could only be cowering motionless along the angles of the floor and walls, or in the corners. If, Barrington reasoned, he moved very slowly on his hands and knees along each side of the square, probing ahead of him with a hand protected by a handkerchief, he should be able to locate the dreaded insects one by one and then despatch them quickly – beat them to death, in fact – with his rolled umbrella. In the deep darkness there would be risks, many risks, but the oilman knew he would have to take such risks if he were to live this night through.

Seconds later, he started his nightmarish task. Left hand firmly and thickly bandaged in a large linen handkerchief, brolly clenched tightly in his right, Barrington set off on a slow, crawling lap of the silent steel box. It suddenly seemed as huge as the gladiator's arena in ancient Rome. Fight or die! I will fight, thought Barrington.

Suddenly the bound fingers of his left hand touched something firm and strangely resilient. It wobbled sideways, then seemed to move towards him.

'Haaarrh.'

Despite himself, Barrington screamed like a hunted beast.

He brought his poised umbrella down with all the force and fury of a cave dweller wielding a club. Contact! One scorpion squashed! Then there was another under his groping fingers. Again and again he slashed and struck with the rolled umbrella that had become his only means of survival. Another, another, another. The floor of the lift seemed to be alive with leaping, resilient shapes. Within minutes, the oilman was sure that he was winning. Time, in that blackest spot on earth, meant nothing whatsoever. Had one hour gone by . . . two . . . twelve? Barrington neither knew nor cared. All that mattered was the dead scorpion count. Nine . . . ten . . . eleven. . . ! Then he had it! The twelfth and last scorpion! Under his bandaged hand, under the tip of his slashing umbrella. Wriggling, vibrating, wobbling, once again, strangely resilient. But dead, surely. Oh, most certainly dead. Nothing could withstand the furious blows of the oilman's attack.

Then, like a flutter of air on his face, a silken, moth-like touch against his cheek, Barrington felt something else. It was the rim of the discarded cardboard box. Even as he reached inside, he knew that there was another, a thirteenth scorpion to deal with. In the sudden shock, the frightening revelation, he dropped his precious umbrella and rolled sideways. At that precise moment, the lift jerked downwards and stopped again. Then the doors slid open and light poured in. Blinded, twitching, sweating with fear and relief, Barrington saw, from his curled up position on the floor, the welcome sight of a pair of highly polished black shoes and neatly pressed trousers – the lower extremities of the oil corporation's lift maintenance man.

'Scorpions,' said Clive Barrington hoarsely, as he was helped into the passage on the twenty-fourth floor. 'Some kind of plot against me . . . North African origins. Did . . . did I get them all?'

In the sudden shock, he dropped his precious umbrella and rolled sideways. The lift jerked downwards and stopped again.

The lift engineer shook his head in disbelief. 'It's four o'clock in the morning, Mr Barrington. I had an anonymous call about an hour ago to say that lift number one had broken down and needed fixing. I got here as soon as I could, winched her down and . . . and found *you*!'

'Never mind that,' rasped Barrington. 'The scorpions . . . did I get them all?'

'These things?' The engineer reached into the lift and picked up a handful of large, strangely squashed but still resilient creatures with raised tails and spread-out feet. 'These *look* like scorpions all right, Mr Barrington, but they're toys. *Rubber toys.* Like them spider things you can buy in shops.'

Barrington picked one up and turned it over. Sure enough, the deadly stinging creature from the desert was made of hard, flexible rubber. They all were. The whole thing had been a trick, a deadly practical joke. Brilliantly timed, but still a joke. As the light in the lift had gone out, all his startled brain had registered had been the mass of scuttling creatures flooding out of the cardboard box. His imagination had done the rest. Mustapha and the curse! Hah! It had been meant to literally scare him to death, and by heavens it had come dangerously close! All at once, Barrington began to laugh and laugh and laugh. He was still laughing as he headed for the main staircase that would lead him to the ground floor and the fresh air of the early dawn. 'Mr Barrington, sir,' said the lift engineer anxiously. 'Shouldn't you wait . . . where are you going. . . ?'

'To see the police,' said the oilman triumphantly, as he swept fast round the first bend in the staircase. 'Certain people wanted to see me dead tonight, and I intend to laugh right in their faces. To laugh and laugh and *laugh*! I've beaten them, don't you see? Beaten them at their own game!' Barrington was still laughing as he whirled himself one-handed on to the next flight of stairs and rushed downwards, ever downwards.

What he failed to see was a small, dark-faced man who threw something neatly, almost daintily, from a storeroom door on the twenty-second landing on to the top tread of the next staircase. It was a very slippery and very rotten banana skin. Clive Barrington was still laughing when he slipped on it and bounced on his head the rest of the way to his death on the stone flags below.

That same night in Algiers, a fifteen-year-old under-cook in a small tourists' hotel received a private telephone call. When it was over, he nodded quietly and began to prepare his next order. It was a dessert consisting of fresh raspberries, whipped cream and bananas. That night, the young cook peeled his bananas with extra care, and made absolutely sure that not a single skin landed on the floor. 'After all,' he thought to himself, 'if someone slipped on one of those he could die laughing.'

THAT SUMMER, FAR AWAY

by Angus Allan

It was his eleventh birthday, but there was nothing for Keith McGuire to be excited about. His parents, long since separated, cared so little for him that he knew nothing of the whereabouts of either of them, and there was certainly no prospect of a party. His Aunt Lena, who had brought him up in tight-lipped, forbidding severity in her spotless, never-to-be-dirtied house, would never have allowed such a thing. She had given him a present, it's true, and he looked down at the knitted gloves on his hands, grateful at least for their warmth on this bitter November day. But if only he'd had a card, just one card. That would have made things a little better.

Keith dragged his feet listlessly through the dry, dead leaves that littered the pavement. A slight, pale-faced boy, unexceptional at sports, mediocre at his lessons, he'd told nobody at school of his birthday. He knew it would have been a grave mistake, for like many a lonely youngster, shy and sensitive, he'd have only brought on more of the bullying that he never seemed able to escape. Even his teachers appeared to be totally indifferent to his misery, refusing the kind words of comfort or encouragement that would have made such a difference to his gloomy existence. He had read somewhere that some people were born to be losers, and he accepted the fact that he was just such an unfortunate . . .

And then Keith saw her. The girl. He reckoned she was about his own age, and she beckoned to him from the green-painted doorway in the tall, ivy-covered wall across the road.

'Come on! Don't just stand there!' She was unbelievably pretty. Keith knew that, and flushed at the thought. He faltered, hesitating, and looked about him. 'Who, me . . ?' He put a nervous finger to his breast.

'Of *course*, you!' called the girl, and laughed. It was not the mocking, scornful laughter that Keith was so used to hearing, but an infectious ripple that brought a smile to his face. There was no traffic, and so he tentatively crossed and drew nearer. Even though his eyes were steadfastly fixed upon the girl, whose long golden hair fell across the shoulders of her white dress, something in the back of his mind wondered why he had never noticed the mellow brick wall and its green door before. Surely he must have passed it a hundred times . . .

She reached out for his hand. Abruptly, he tore Aunt Lena's gloves from his fingers and thrust them in his pocket. 'What do you want?' he said, flushing again.

'Someone to play with,' she smiled. 'My name's Jenny. What's yours?'

'Keith,' he faltered. 'Er, I'm not very good at games . . .'

She laughed again, and led him, unprotesting, through the door. As it closed behind them, Keith halted in utter amazement, for a vast and spacious garden stretched away from him, glorious with flower beds, each a riot of colour, and dotted with leafy trees, their branches stirred by a soft and gentle breeze. He was conscious of the glitter of a sun-spangled lake, far away, and beyond it, a white, colonnaded house. Here, a busily playing fountain, and there, the smooth marble of statuary . . .

'But, this is *November* . . .' He turned, bewildered, to Jenny, and she gripped his hand tightly. 'What nonsense,' she said . . .

Keith took away his hand with difficulty, perhaps because he didn't want to, and shrugged off his overcoat. 'Pop it on that,' said Jenny, pointing to a stern-looking statue of a Greek discus thrower, and they both giggled at the sight of it hanging from the figure's athletic, outflung arm.

'Do you live here?' asked Keith. 'I mean, I haven't seen you around at all. Why don't you go to school?'

'Oh, don't talk about *school*,' said Jenny. 'Tell you what . . . can you race me? Over to that copse?' Then she was off, her slippered feet flying over the springy grass, and Keith took to his heels in pursuit. A happiness that he'd never known was already beginning to swell inside him. For a moment, he thought she'd beaten him, but her merry face, glancing back at him, spurred him, and he flung one arm around her shoulder long before they reached the trees.

'I've got an idea,' said Jenny. 'Suppose we build a hide!'

Ignorant of anything save his aunt's strictly formal square of garden, Keith was at a loss. 'How d'you mean?'

'Well, there's a thicket of willow just behind the lake. And lots of fallen branches. We might even make a tree-house!'

The term 'love' is not used by grown-ups in connection with eleven-year-olds, for grown-ups so easily forget their own childhood. But there is no doubt whatsoever that Keith McGuire had fallen hook, line, and sinker for his beautiful young companion in that magic garden. The sun – and he had completely forgotten that it was supposed to be a grey November day – was scarcely more brilliant than the shining beauty of Jenny's eyes. He had never, never in his dreary life known such happiness, that special happiness which comes from having a very close friend. The term is absurd to a 'thinking' adult, but Keith would gladly have laid down his life for the wonderful Jenny.

They were unable to build their tree-house. Such a project takes more than mere enthusiasm. Then Jenny, careless of her pretty clothes, climbed an oak tree and got herself stuck in the lowermost fork of the branches. Keith found an amazing new strength, scrambled up, and saved her. He might have been overcome with embarrassment at her grateful peck on the cheek when he had lowered her to the ground, but the moment was soon past as they picked ripe berries from a thick tangle of brambles, and watched a pair of brilliantly coloured jays swoop across the green lawns.

Now, a squirrel chattered angrily at them, poised on the trunk of a lofty sycamore, and Keith stood up. 'I should've been home ages ago,' he said worriedly. He would have looked at his watch, but he had none. 'My aunt's going to wonder what's happened to me.'

Jenny reached for his hand again. Her eyes were pleading. 'Don't go,' she whispered. 'Stay here – for ever.'

'Don't be daft!' Now it was Keith's turn to laugh. 'How can I?'

'Anything's possible if you want it enough,' said Jenny.

'For you, maybe. Living in a place like this. Anyway, I can just imagine what your dad and mum would say . . .'

The girl made no reply. She simply shrugged her shoulders softly and gently and led Keith back to the green door. She helped him into his overcoat, and stood by, pulling up the latch. 'You'll come again . . ?'

'I'd like that,' said Keith. 'I'd like that a lot.'

He stepped out on to the pavement, and began to walk away. He turned a couple of times to wave goodbye to Jenny, and then she'd gone. He must have covered a good distance before he realised it was bitterly, naggingly cold. With a staggering shiver, he tugged out his gloves and put them on . . .

Aunt Lena was as furious as he expected. 'You wicked child! I've had your kipper waiting this past hour,' she raved. 'Don't blame me if it's all dried up and nasty. Just where have you been?'

'I'm sorry, Auntie,' said Keith. 'I didn't mean to be late. I

'You have been such a long time coming back,' she said, taking his hand.

was passing this place, and Jenny wanted me to play. She lives in a big house somewhere down Borrowdale Hill, and there's this fantastic garden, all summery . . .'

Aunt Lena sighed. 'I don't know, I'm sure. I've tried to bring you up properly, and you still fill your head with all sorts of ridiculous daydreams. You've got too much imagination, my lad. That's what's wrong with you.'

'I didn't imagine it, Auntie,' whispered Keith. But now, in the spick-and-span kitchen, he wasn't so sure. Had it been a daydream? Just a figment of his inner longings? He spilled tea on the tablecloth, and endured the usual lecture before he was packed off to bed, with what his aunt called an 'improving' book.

Keith was late for school the next morning. Luckily, one of his aunt's neighbours, on his way to town, was able to give him a lift in his car. Keith looked for the mellow wall and the green door on the journey, but, oddly, was quite unable to find it . . .

Months had passed. It was spring, but the time of year had brought nothing of any pleasure to Keith's schooldays. He had had a particularly bad day, when a gang of boys from an upper form had set on him, mocking the darns in his trousers. They wore sturdy jeans, but Aunt Lena was not one for what she called 'uncouth modern clothing' . . . Keith had a cut over one eye, a sore lip, and a graze on his knee, but all his sorrows were forgotten as, with a thrill of joy, he saw Jenny beckoning to him from the green door. 'You have been such a long time coming back,' she said, taking his hand. 'Where on earth have you been all this time?'

'Crumbs, you sound like my aunt,' smiled Keith, his sorrows melting away. 'If you want the truth, I haven't been able to find this place.'

'It's always here,' said Jenny. 'If you want it.' She led him inside, and Keith was somewhat startled to see that it was just as he remembered it. Springtime? No, it was surely high summer again, with all the trees in full leaf, and the hot sun beating down. 'I'm *not* imagining all this, am I?' he said. Jenny kissed him lightly. 'You silly. Come on. We're going to build a raft and sail it on the lake.'

Anyone watching would have smiled at their efforts to take pieces of wood from an old boathouse by the water and lash them together with lengths of bindweed creeper. But nobody was watching, and the rickety craft took the water. When Jenny looked in danger of falling in, Keith pulled her back to land with nothing more serious than wet shoes and socks.

'I wish you would stay here, Keith. You're unhappy outside. I know you are.' She touched his cheek softly, and he bit his lip.

'I'd like to. Really I would. Maybe when I'm grown up . . .'

Jenny sat down, spreading her dress on the green grass. 'By the time you're grown up,' she said, 'it'll be no good.' She shook her head, sadly. 'People grow up and forget what it was like to be young.'

Keith stared at her. Suddenly, it seemed as though Jenny herself was grown up, to say such a thing. He felt vaguely disturbed . . .

'Were you born here?' he said suddenly, wanting to change the subject. 'Are your people sort of lord and lady, or something. . . ?'

'Of course they're not,' said Jenny. 'My people, as you call them, are just the kindest folk in the world. They'll look after you, I promise. They'll be delighted to see you. Like me, Keith. You'll learn everything if you stay with me. Everything that matters . . .'

Keith felt suddenly afraid. There was a dog barking in the distance. Two crows flew low across them, screaming their raucous cries. Abruptly, he jumped to his feet and ran for the green door. Behind him he heard the girl's voice, loud yet gentle . . . 'Oh, no, Keith! Come back! Come *back*!'

Yet again, Keith faced the wrath of his Aunt Lena. She was furious that her schedule had been put out, livid that her carefully timed tea had been delayed. And once more, his tale of the white-clad Jenny in the summer garden was treated with scorn and disbelief by his last remaining relative.

'I know what you've been doing,' snapped Aunt Lena. 'Wandering around indulging in stupid daydreams, while you should have been coming home here to eat your supper and do your homework. No good will ever come to you, Keith McGuire! All your teachers say you're nothing but a fumble-brain, and I'm sure they're right!'

That night, Keith cried himself to sleep.

In the months that followed, Keith spent a good deal of time visiting Jenny's garden. It was a hot summer, and the bullying he received at school did not stop after the end of term. Foolishly, he had admitted the existence of his garden to others, and with the callous indifference of their age, they taunted and mocked him for it. They 'proved' to him that the place didn't exist. They challenged him to show them this 'magic' place. And he couldn't. Although he knew it had to be there, it never was whenever he tried to show anyone else. A row of shops? A line of houses? He simply couldn't find it unless he was alone . . .

But when he was alone . . . Ah, how different then. Jenny would be waiting, the beautiful figure in the white dress, waiting outside the green door in the old, mellow wall. She would crook her finger, and he would go running, calling her name. His heart would swell within his breast, and the very touch of her fingers would drive away all the misery of his tortured life . . .

One day he said to Jenny, 'I'm twelve today. It's my birthday!' It was the 15th November.

She drew him inside the summer garden, and shyly gave him something wrapped up in tissue paper. 'I know,' she said. 'A happy, happy birthday, Keith.'

Laughing, he unwrapped the package. It was a simple enough present, a small pebble shot with streaks of what looked like gold. Gingerly, he leaned forward and kissed Jenny on the cheek – the first time he had done anything so bold.

'Sorry,' he said, abashed.

'Sorry?' She hugged him. 'What did your aunt give you?'

'This,' he said, hanging it over the arm of the statue of the Greek athlete. It was a knitted scarf.

'Poor Keith,' said Jenny. 'This time, *this* time, won't you please make up your mind to stay here with me. . . ?'

Keith kept silent. Later, as they ran through the garden chasing butterflies and splashing their feet through the shallows of the tinkling stream that fed the lake, the boy knew that he wouldn't leave.

The feeling of happiness was so wonderful. Why, if all this paradise was offered, shouldn't he accept? Was there any point in returning to his aunt's harshness? To the taunts of his schoolmates? To the uncaring discipline of his teachers?

Breathless, they stretched out under the shade of a willow. Ducks paddled eagerly in the water, and they tossed them scraps of bread from a bag Jenny had brought with her. Swallows and swifts soared in the upper air, and somewhere, far off, a kindly voice was calling . . .

'Your mother. . . ?' Keith turned his head towards the girl.

'I call her that,' said Jenny.

'I'm here for keeps,' said Keith. He held her hand tightly

and turned his face to the grass, sinking gently into a deep, deep sleep . . .

Aunt Lena was not pleased. She had felt she must put on her best clothes to leave the house, and she had not wanted to dress up. In fact, the desk sergeant at the local police station couldn't have cared less if she'd been in rags. A 'missing person's report' was the same, whoever it came from.

'Yes, madam. This photograph is all we need,' he said. 'You say his name's Keith McGuire, and he's twelve.'

'Twelve today,' said Aunt Lena. 'I had actually baked a cake for him, but he's a disgraceful child. No sense of gratitude or responsibility at all. He should have been home from school hours ago . . .'

'Does he often go astray?'

'Once in a while. He has a make-believe garden, with some girl he calls Jenny. On Borrowdale Hill. I think he actually goes to spend time by himself; but, of course, I'm anxious because he's never been away quite this late.'

The sergeant sighed. 'Kids are always a nuisance,' he said. 'But I've got Constable Jenkins free at the moment. Like him to run you down Borrowdale Hill?'

'I don't want to be a bother, but, thank you,' said Aunt Lena.

The police Panda car moved slowly down the road, flanked by bare trees. Aunt Lena prodded the driver and pointed to a long wooden hoarding, masking off a building site.

'He used to say it was about here, Constable Jenkins,' she said.

Jenkins pulled up and they both got out. 'Hasn't been a house here for fifty years,' said the policeman, 'let alone a garden.'

But there was a green, slatted, rough-cut door in the

fencing, and the constable opened it. He hauled it wide, peered through, then stepped back to offer Aunt Lena a look. 'See for yourself,' he said.

There was nothing but a dismal expanse of wasteland, perhaps once marked for building development, but long since forgotten. Scattered with litter thrown over from the road, festooned with the brown, dead weeds of the vanished summer, there was nothing to suggest a paradise of any sort. 'This was certainly the place,' said Keith's aunt. 'Hah. I never cease to marvel at that boy's absurd imagination.' She called: 'Keith! Keith, come here at once!'

There was no reply. And though she and Constable Jenkins searched the entire area, there was no trace at all of the boy. Nor would there ever be a trace of him, for his wretched loneliness had come to an end on that grey November day. He had received that rare, precious and totally magical gift of being able to step into the *other* world – the one that runs alongside our own, yet remains almost entirely virtually unknown. Somewhere, he still runs hand in hand with his beloved Jenny, dwelling for ever in the beautiful summer garden . . .